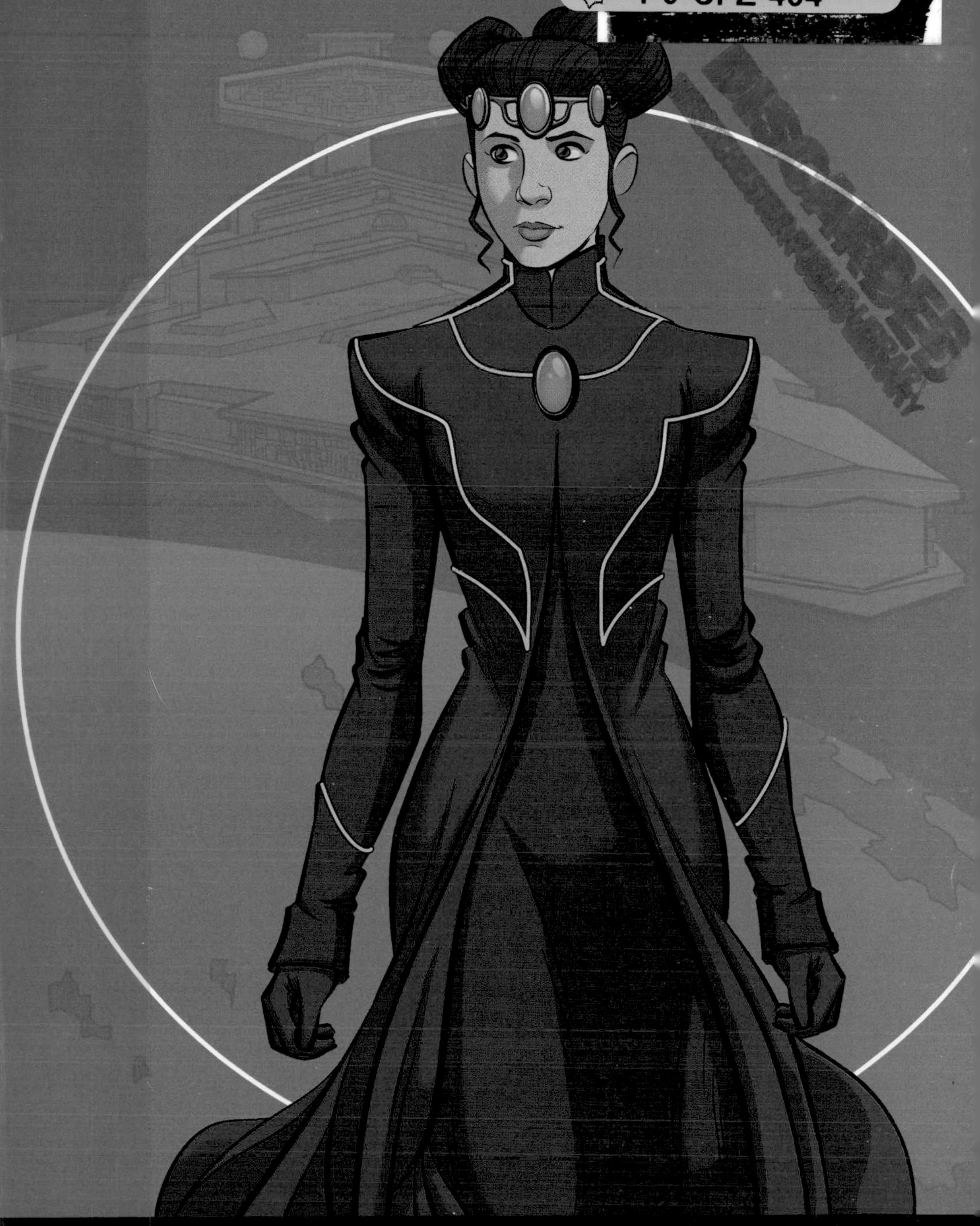

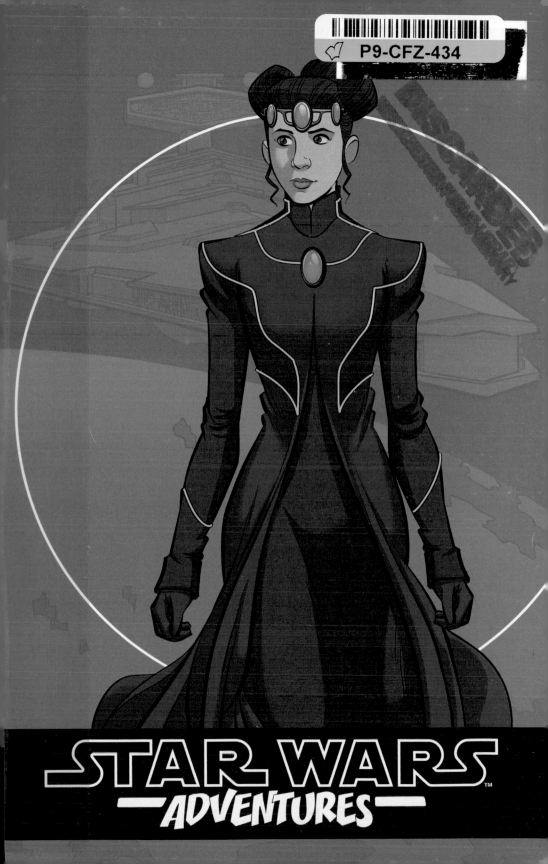

STAR WARS™ ADVENTURES

Facebook: **facebook.com/idwpublishing**
Twitter: **@idwpublishing**
YouTube: **youtube.com/idwpublishing**
Tumblr: **tumblr.idwpublishing.com**
Instagram: **instagram.com/idwpublishing**

ISBN: 978-1-68405-169-4   21 20 19 18   1 2 3 4

COVER ARTIST
NATHAN GRENO

SERIES ASSISTANT EDITOR
PETER ADRIAN BEHRAVESH

SERIES EDITORS
BOBBY CURNOW
and DENTON J. TIPTON

COLLECTION EDITORS
JUSTIN EISINGER
and ALONZO SIMON

COLLECTION DESIGNER
CLYDE GRAPA

PUBLISHER
GREG GOLDSTEIN

Greg Goldstein, President & Publisher
Robbie Robbins, EVP & Sr. Art Director
Chris Ryall, Chief Creative Officer & Editor-in-Chief
Matthew Ruzicka, CPA, Chief Financial Officer
David Hedgecock, Associate Publisher
Laurie Windrow, Senior Vice President of Sales & Marketing
Lorelei Bunjes, VP of Digital Services
Eric Moss, Sr. Director, Licensing & Business Development
Ted Adams, Founder & CEO of IDW Media Holdings

Lucasfilm Credits:
Frank Parisi, Senior Editor
Michael Siglain, Creative Director
James Waugh and Matt Martin, Story Group

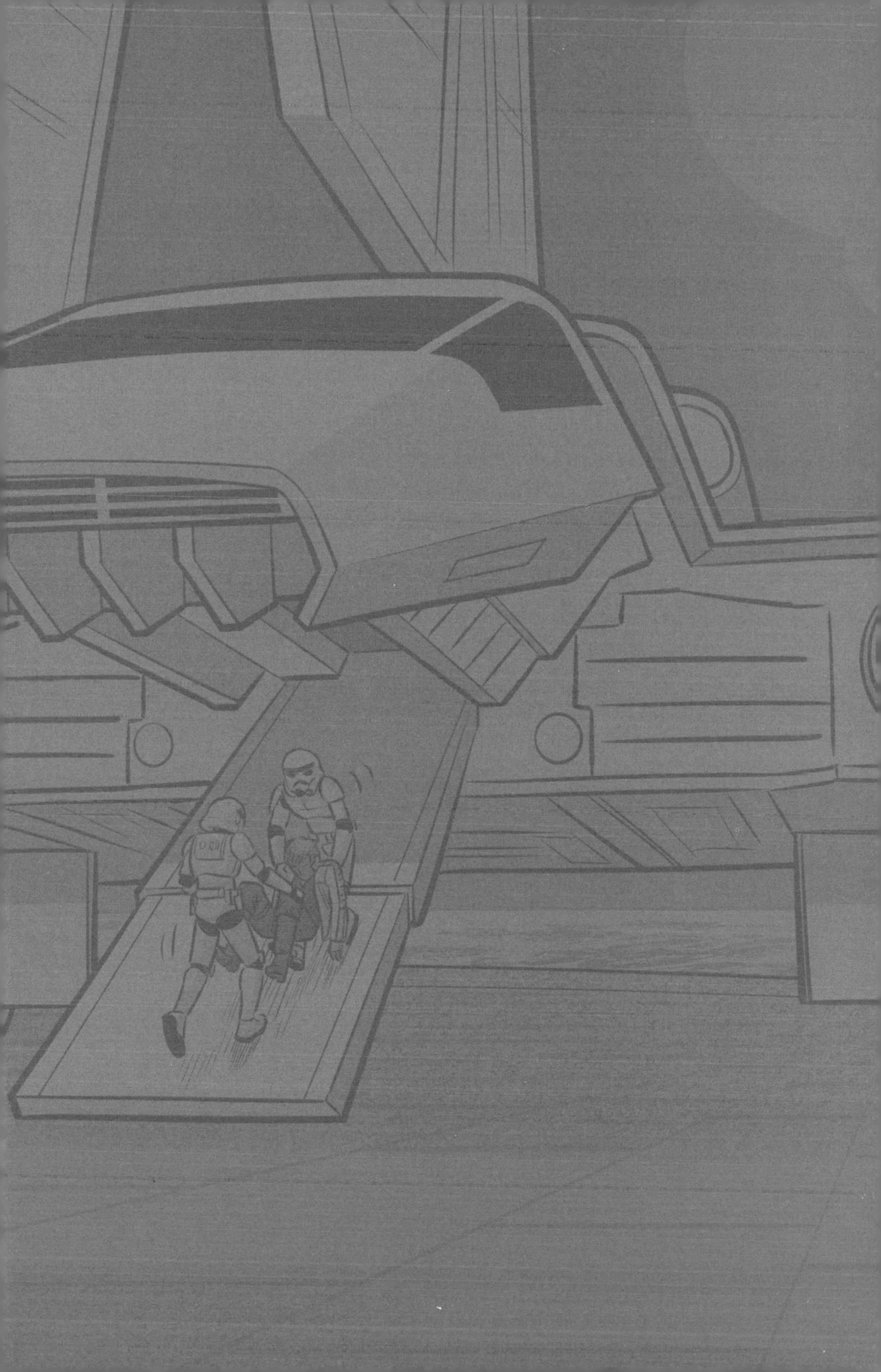

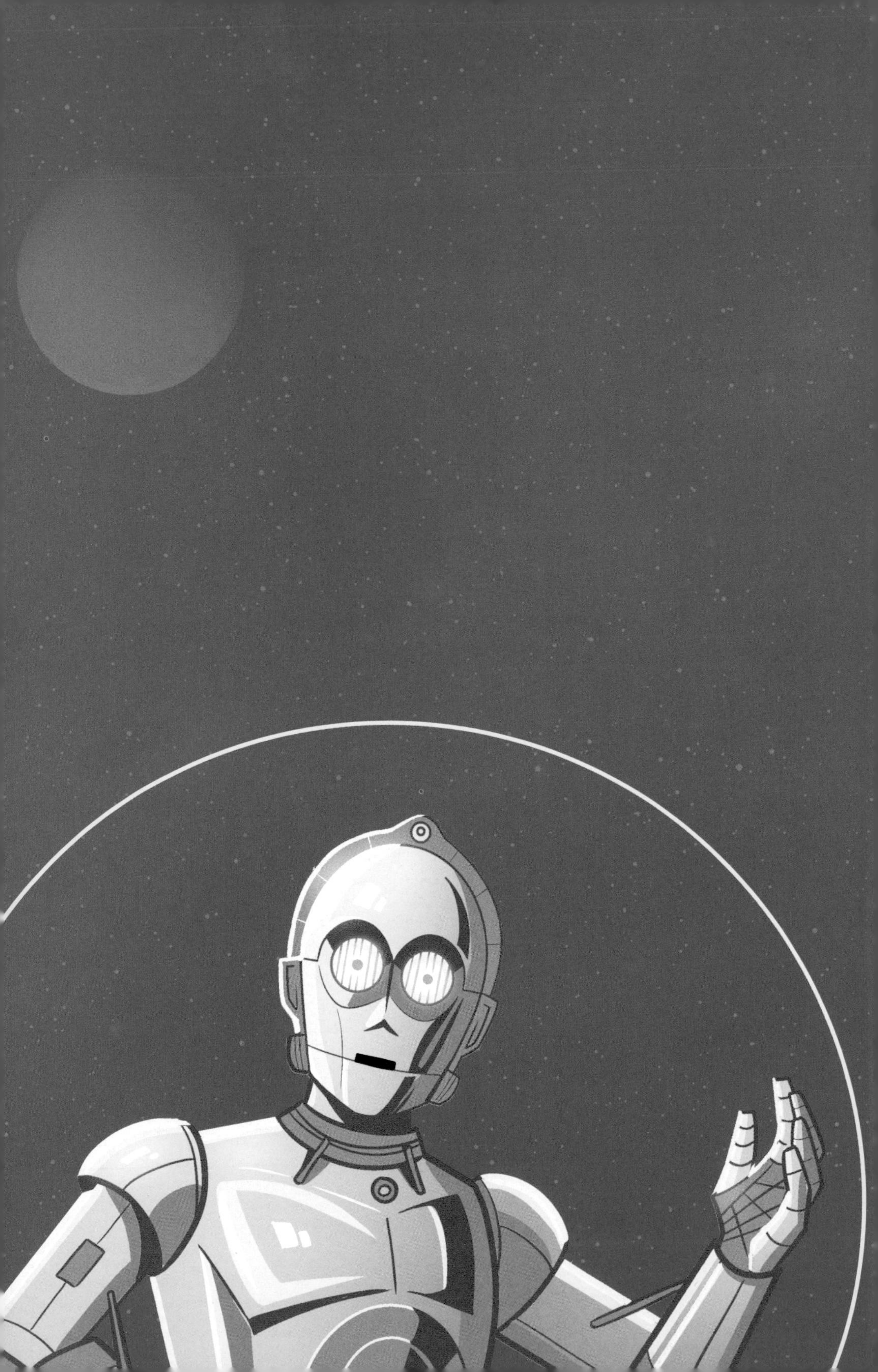

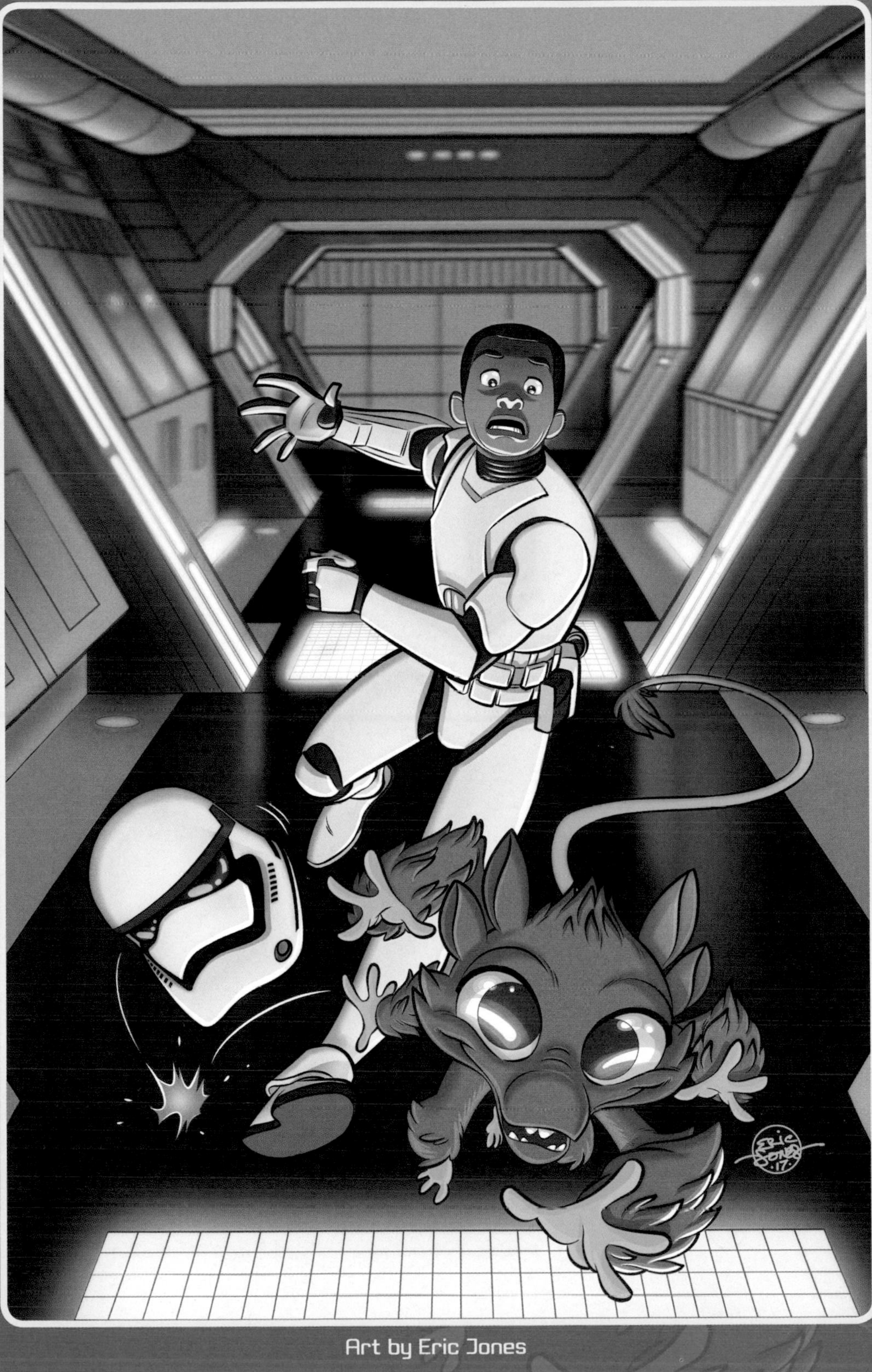
ERIC JONES 17

Art by Eric Jones

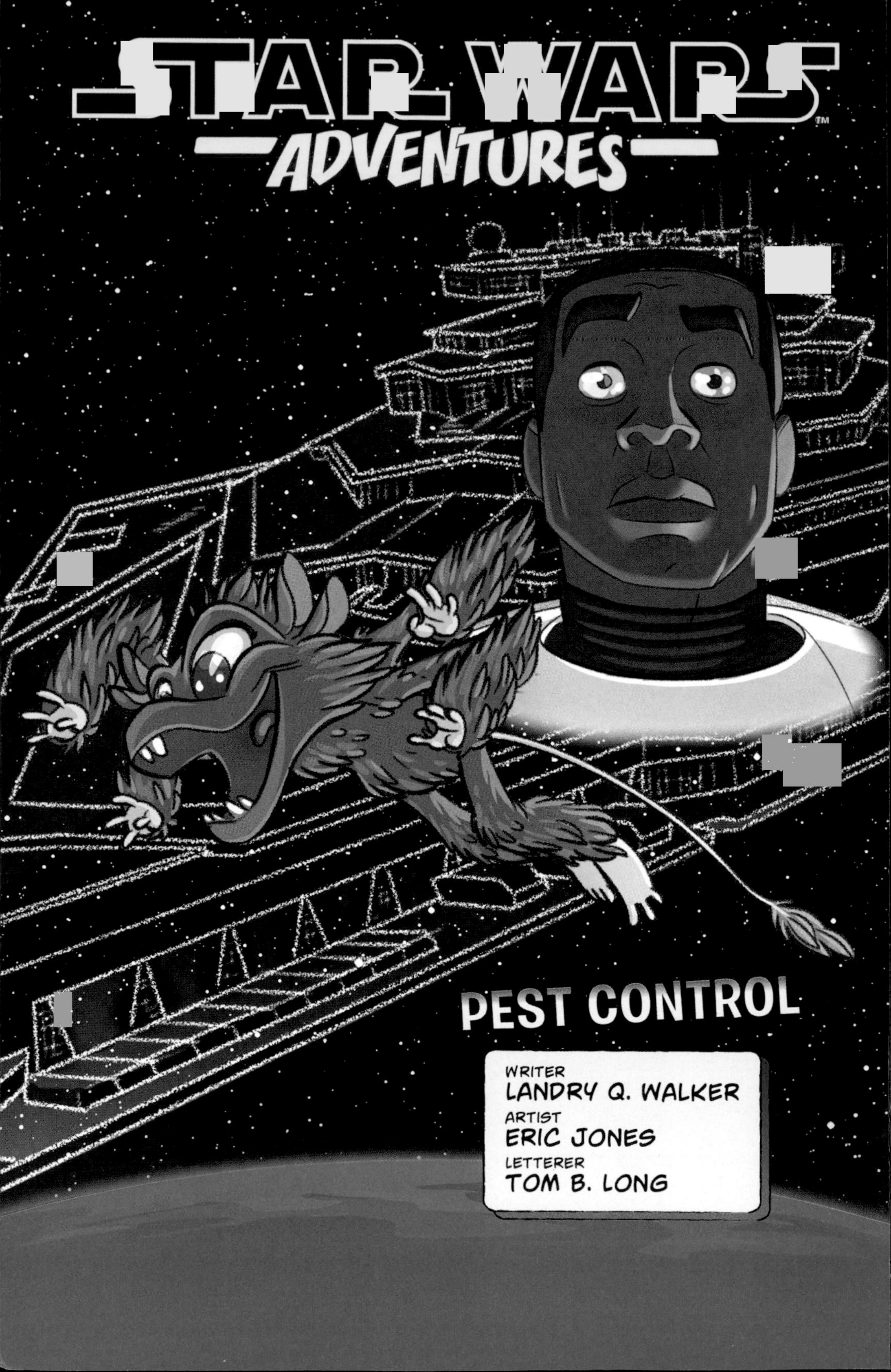
STAR WARS
ADVENTURES
PEST CONTROL
WRITER
LANDRY Q. WALKER
ARTIST
ERIC JONES
LETTERER
TOM B. LONG

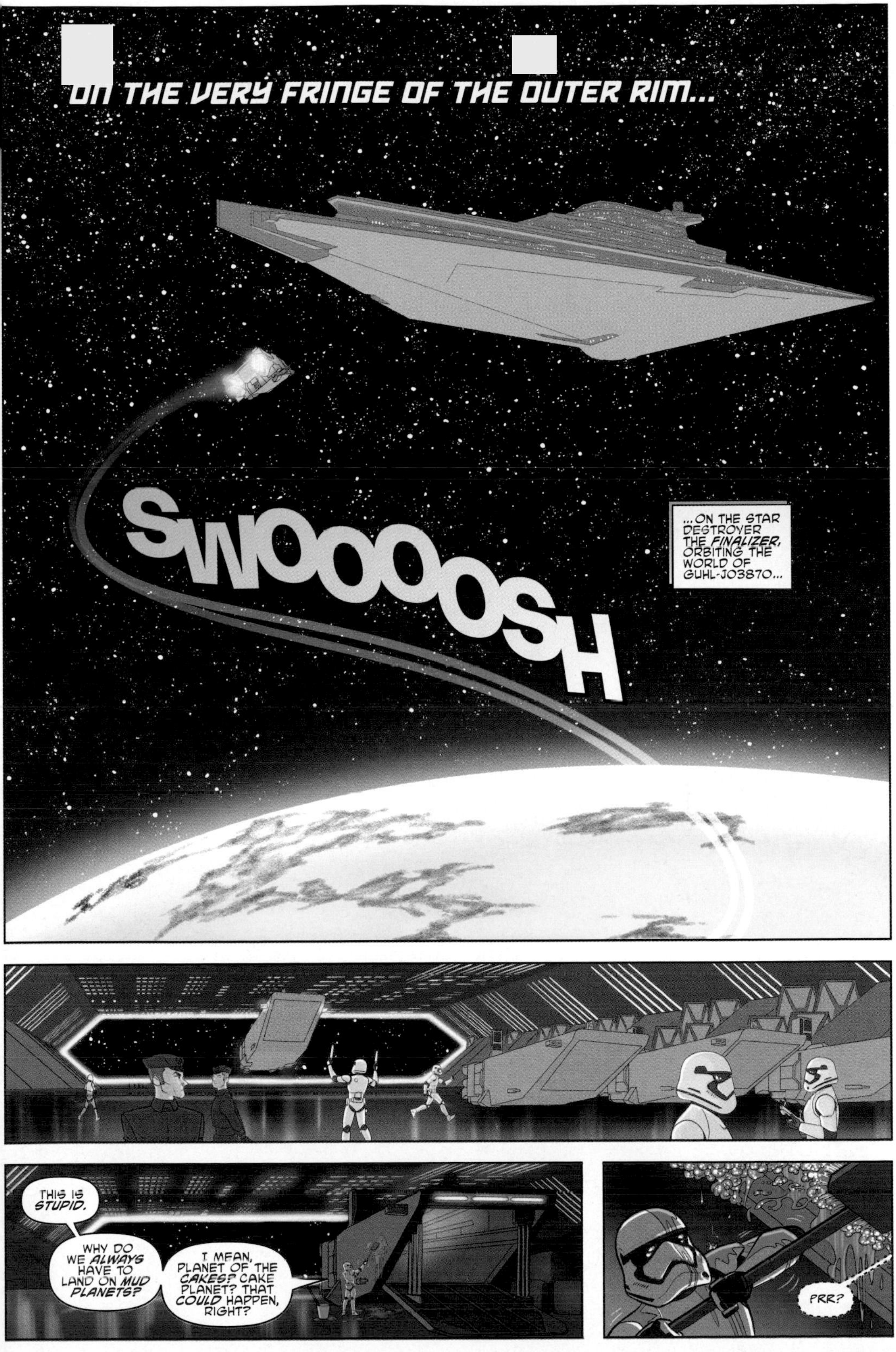
ON THE VERY FRINGE OF THE OUTER RIM...
SWOOOOSH
...ON THE STAR DESTROYER THE FINALIZER, ORBITING THE WORLD OF GUHL-JO3870...
THIS IS STUPID.
WHY DO WE ALWAYS HAVE TO LAND ON MUD PLANETS?
I MEAN, PLANET OF THE CAKES? CAKE PLANET? THAT COULD HAPPEN, RIGHT?
PRR?

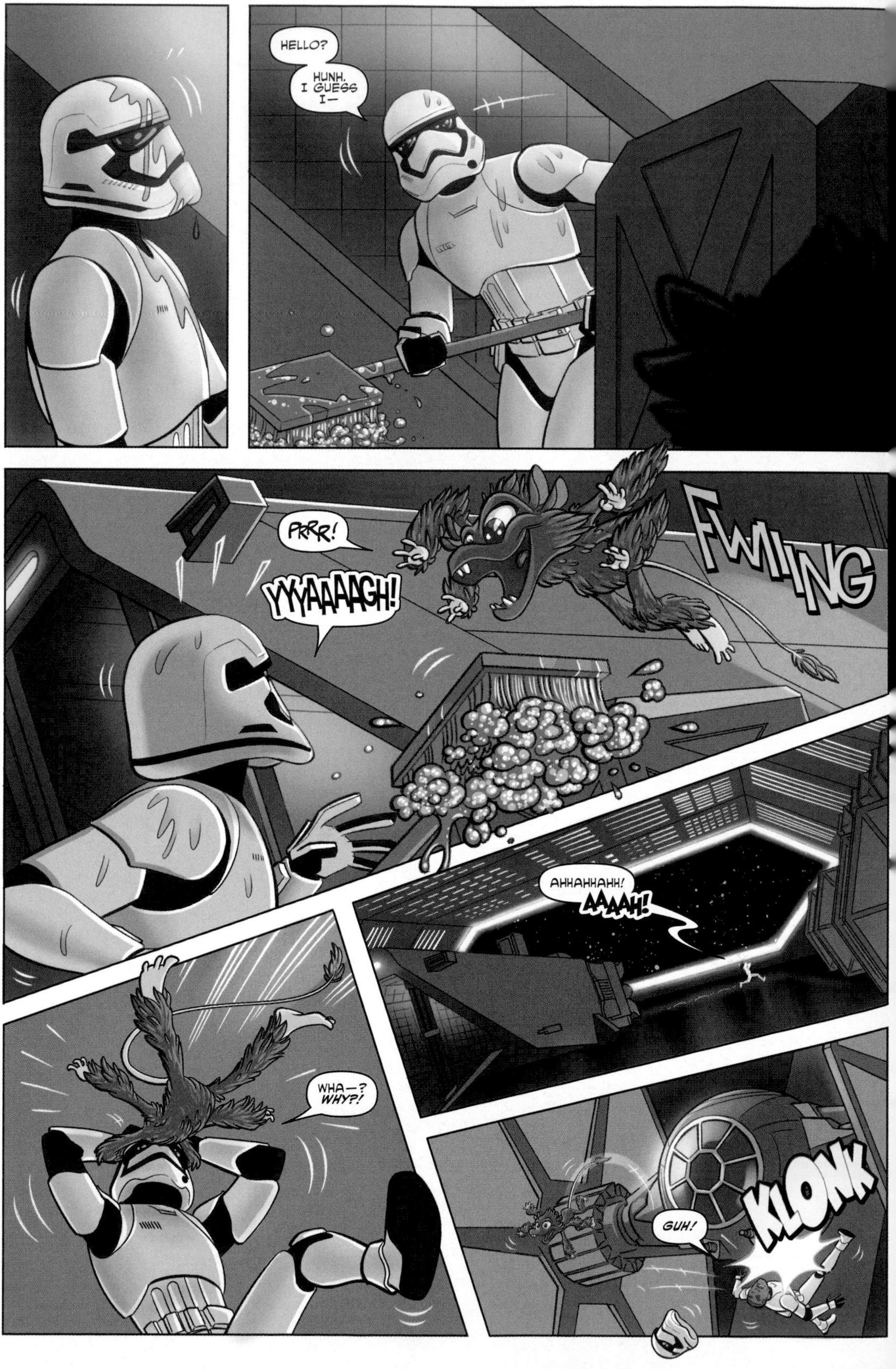
HELLO?
HUNH. I GUESS I—
PRRR!
YYYAAAAGH!
FWIIING
AHHAHHAHH! AAAAH!
WHA—? WHY?!
GUH!
KLONK

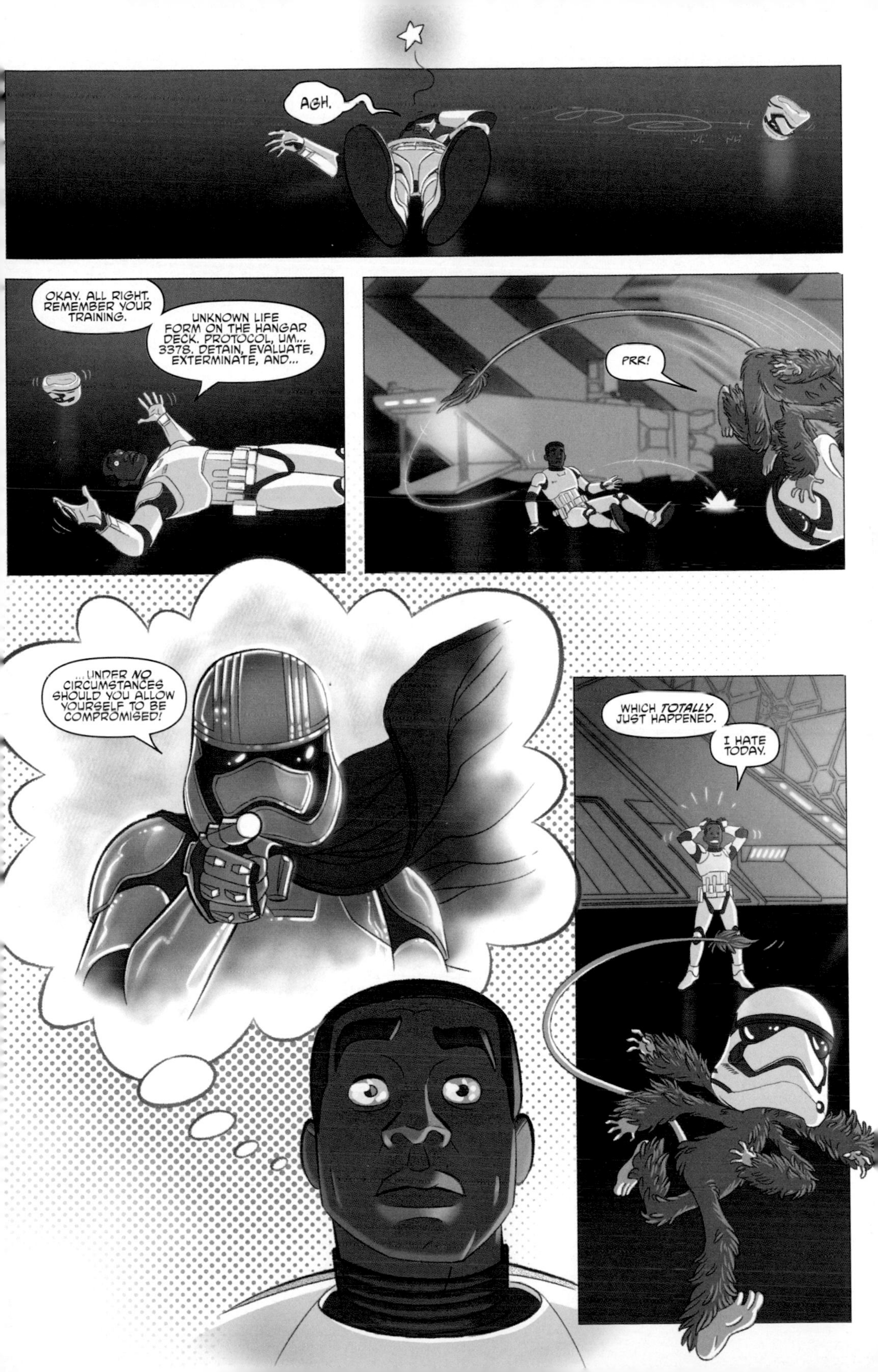
AGH.
OKAY. ALL RIGHT. REMEMBER YOUR TRAINING.
UNKNOWN LIFE FORM ON THE HANGAR DECK. PROTOCOL, UM... 3378. DETAIN, EVALUATE, EXTERMINATE, AND...
PRR!
...UNDER *NO* CIRCUMSTANCES SHOULD YOU ALLOW YOURSELF TO BE COMPROMISED!
WHICH *TOTALLY* JUST HAPPENED.
I HATE TODAY.

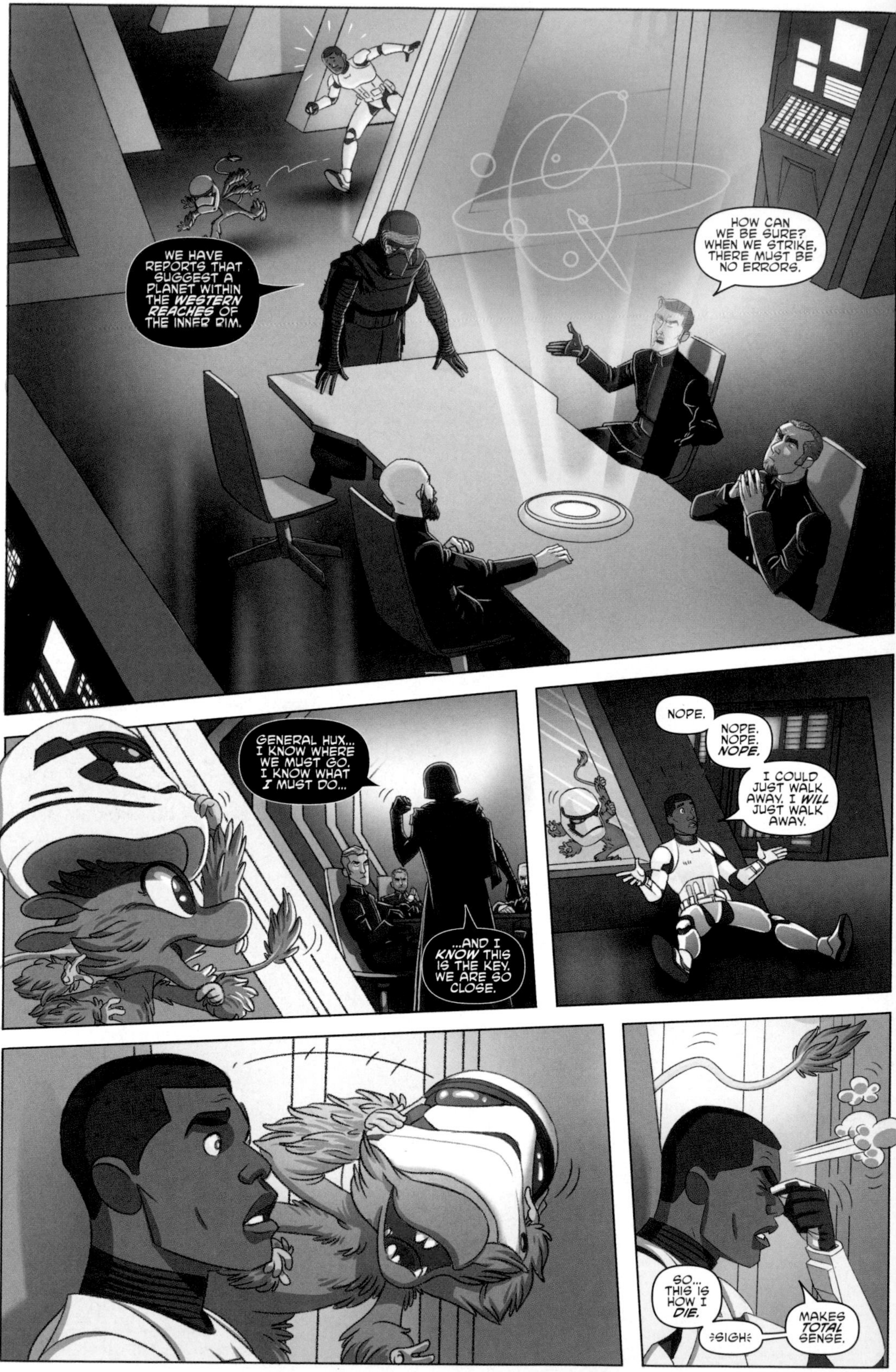
WE HAVE REPORTS THAT SUGGEST A PLANET WITHIN THE WESTERN REACHES OF THE INNER RIM.
HOW CAN WE BE SURE? WHEN WE STRIKE, THERE MUST BE NO ERRORS.
GENERAL HUX... I KNOW WHERE WE MUST GO. I KNOW WHAT I MUST DO...
...AND I KNOW THIS IS THE KEY. WE ARE SO CLOSE.
NOPE.
NOPE. NOPE. NOPE.
I COULD JUST WALK AWAY. I WILL JUST WALK AWAY.
SO... THIS IS HOW I DIE.
SIGH
MAKES TOTAL SENSE.

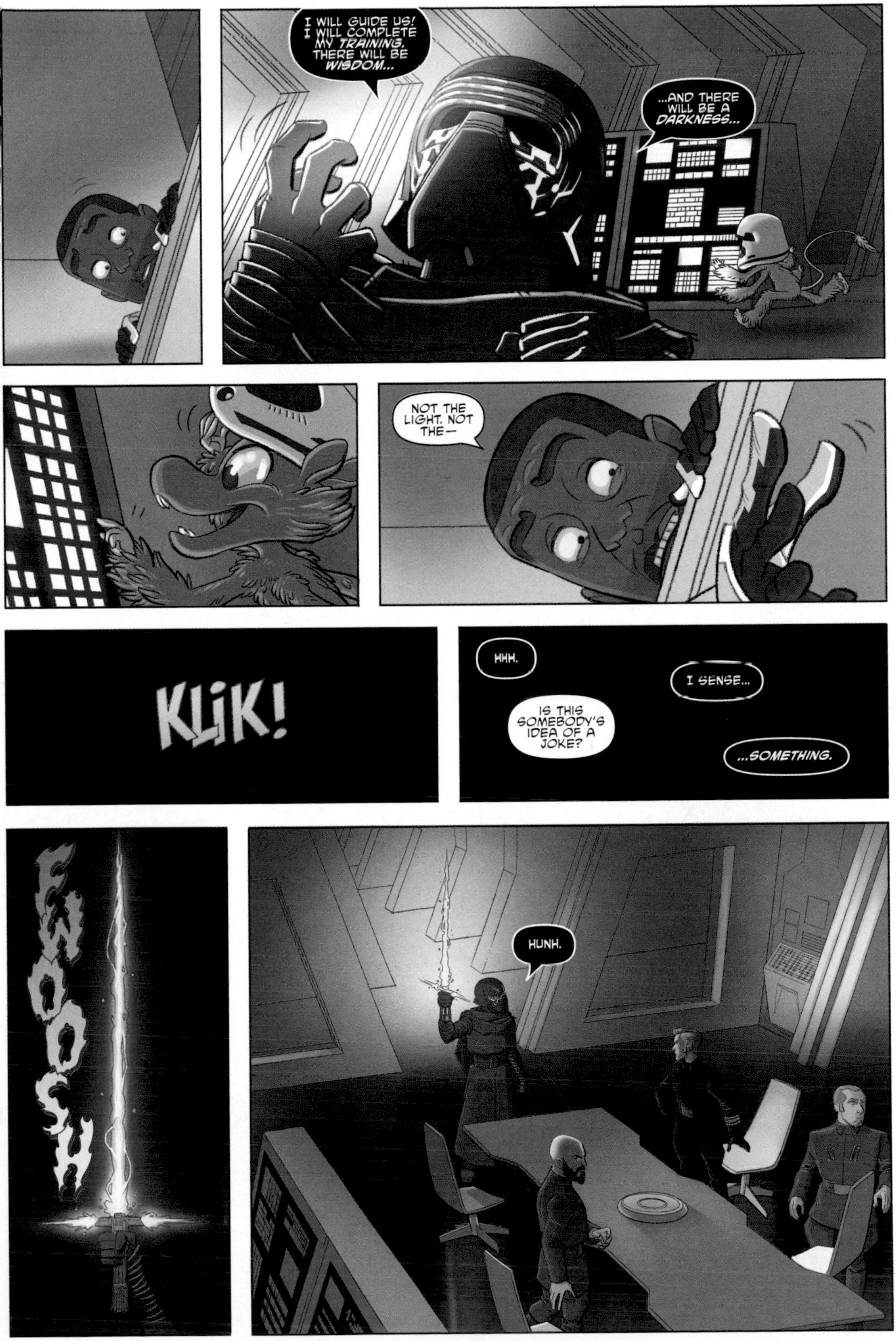
I WILL GUIDE US! I WILL COMPLETE MY TRAINING. THERE WILL BE WISDOM...
...AND THERE WILL BE A DARKNESS...
NOT THE LIGHT. NOT THE—
KLIK!
HHH.
I SENSE...
IS THIS SOMEBODY'S IDEA OF A JOKE?
...SOMETHING.
FWOOSH
HUNH.

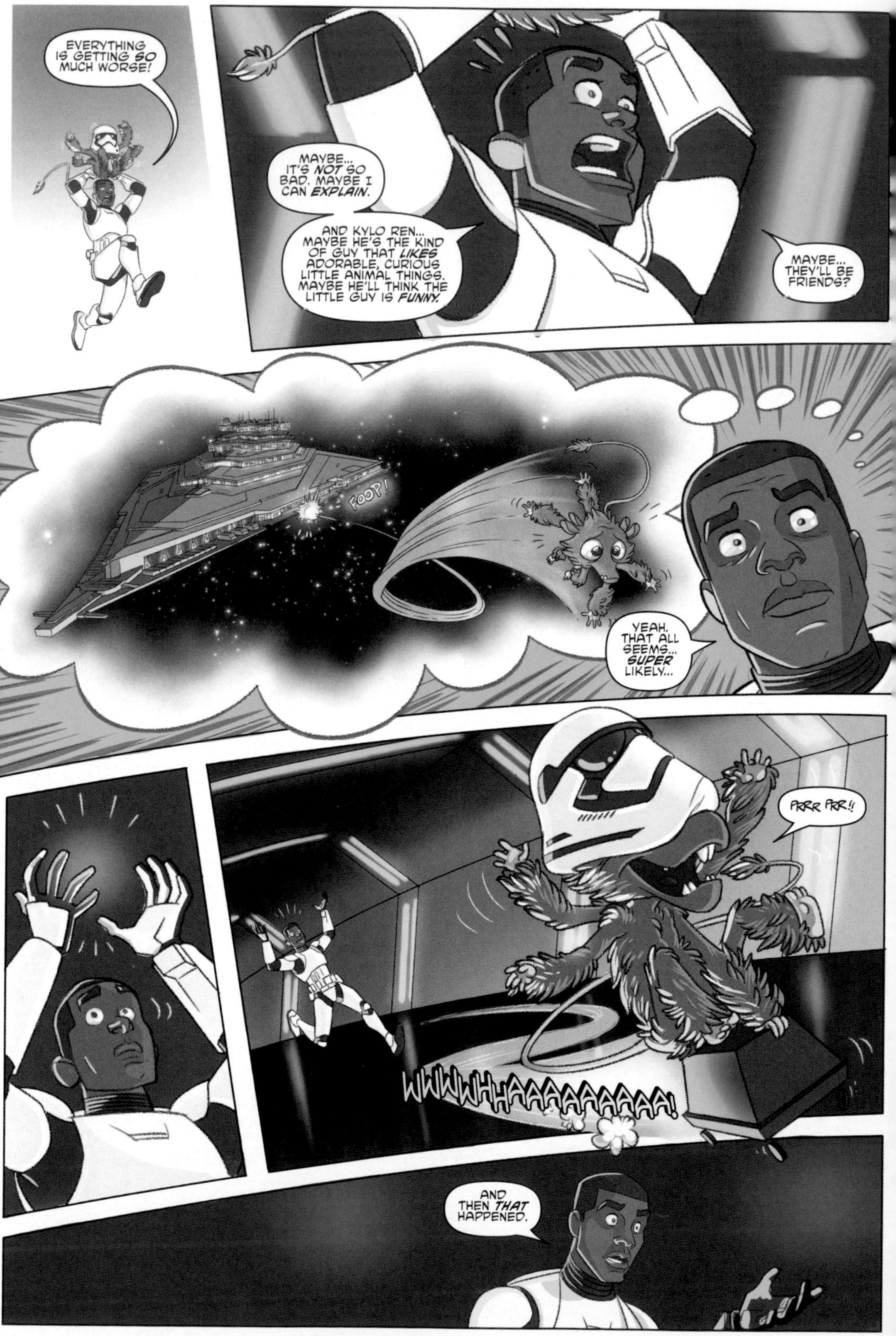
EVERYTHING IS GETTING SO MUCH WORSE!
MAYBE... IT'S NOT SO BAD. MAYBE I CAN EXPLAIN.
AND KYLO REN... MAYBE HE'S THE KIND OF GUY THAT LIKES ADORABLE, CURIOUS LITTLE ANIMAL THINGS. MAYBE HE'LL THINK THE LITTLE GUY IS FUNNY.
MAYBE... THEY'LL BE FRIENDS?
FOOP!
YEAH. THAT ALL SEEMS... SUPER LIKELY...
PRRR PRR!!
WWWWHHAAAAAAAAAA!
AND THEN THAT HAPPENED.

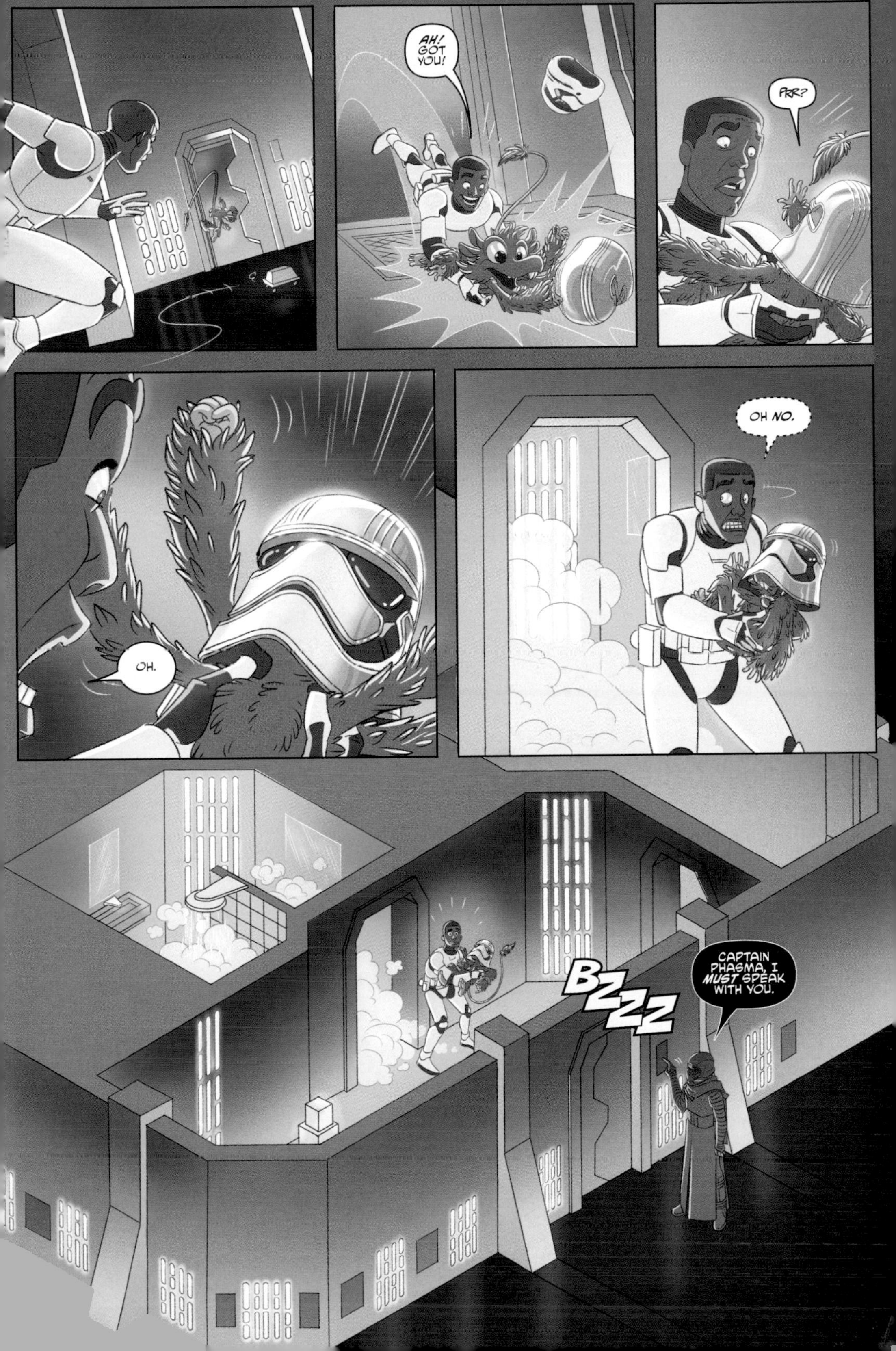
AH! GOT YOU!
PRR?
OH.
OH NO.
BZZZ
CAPTAIN PHASMA, I MUST SPEAK WITH YOU.

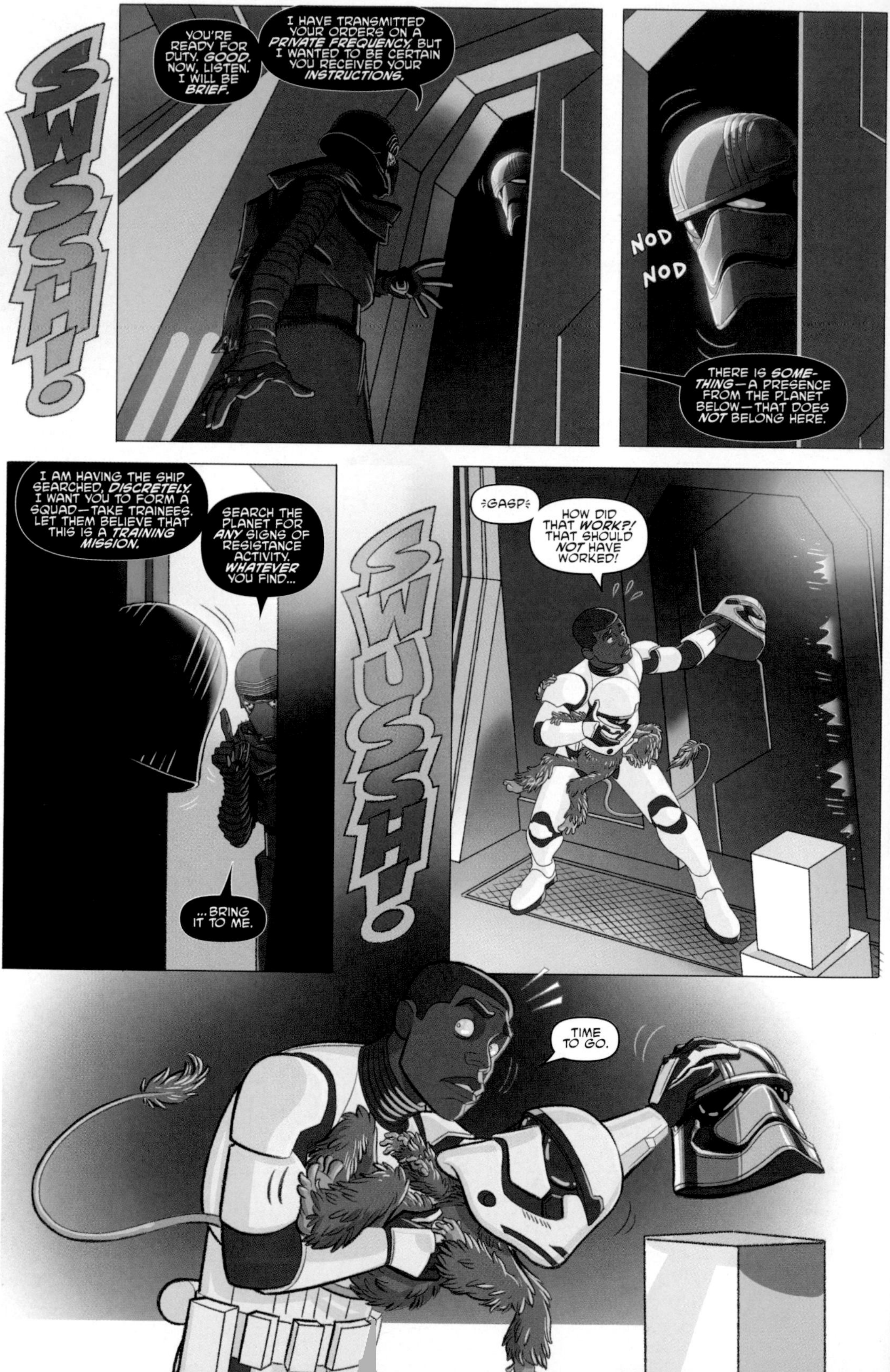
SWSSH!
YOU'RE READY FOR DUTY. GOOD. NOW, LISTEN. I WILL BE BRIEF.
I HAVE TRANSMITTED YOUR ORDERS ON A PRIVATE FREQUENCY, BUT I WANTED TO BE CERTAIN YOU RECEIVED YOUR INSTRUCTIONS.
NOD NOD
THERE IS SOME-THING—A PRESENCE FROM THE PLANET BELOW—THAT DOES NOT BELONG HERE.
I AM HAVING THE SHIP SEARCHED, DISCRETELY. I WANT YOU TO FORM A SQUAD—TAKE TRAINEES. LET THEM BELIEVE THAT THIS IS A TRAINING MISSION.
SEARCH THE PLANET FOR ANY SIGNS OF RESISTANCE ACTIVITY. WHATEVER YOU FIND...
...BRING IT TO ME.
SWUSSH!
GASP
HOW DID THAT WORK?! THAT SHOULD NOT HAVE WORKED!
TIME TO GO.

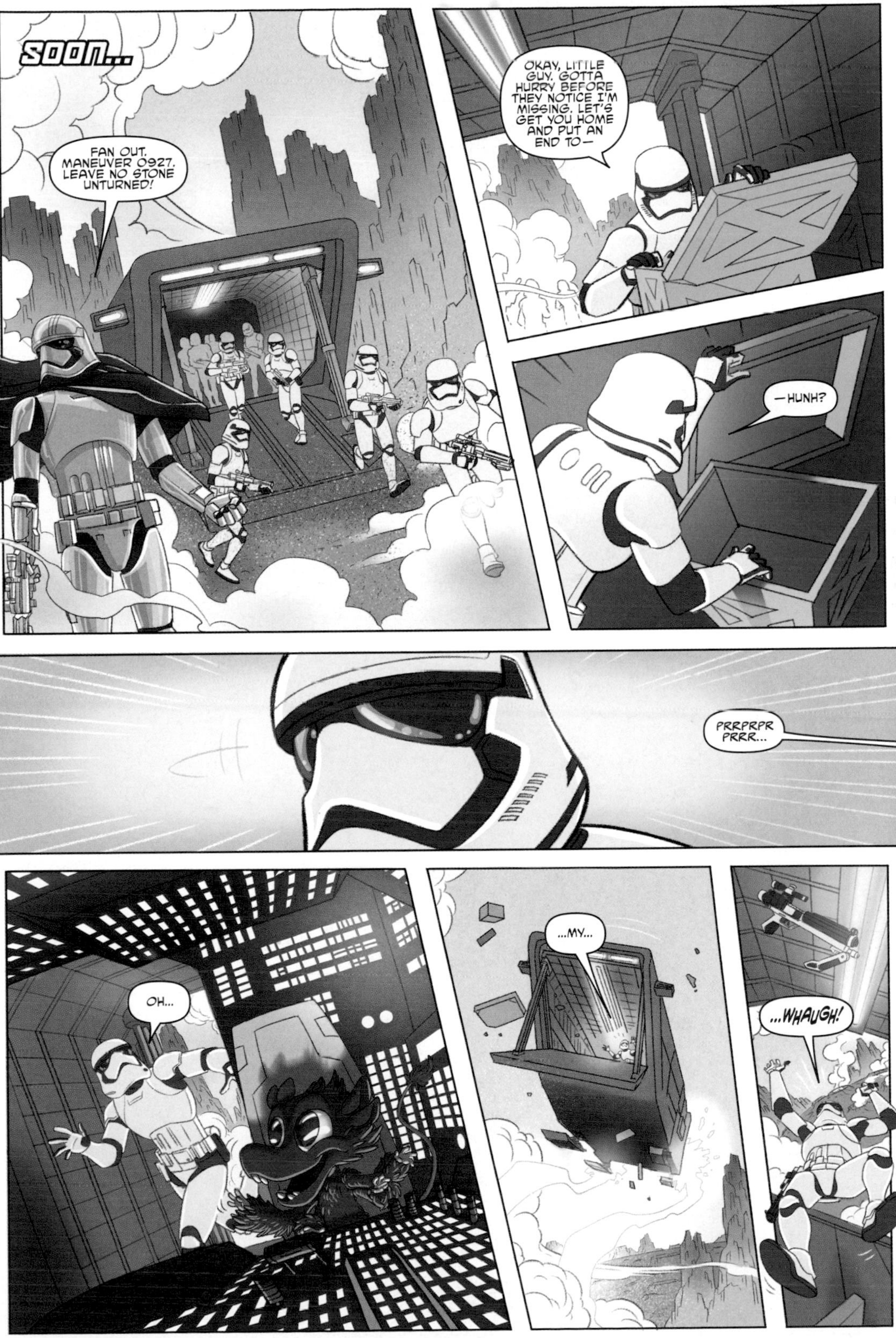
SOON...
FAN OUT. MANEUVER 0927. LEAVE NO STONE UNTURNED!
OKAY, LITTLE GUY. GOTTA HURRY BEFORE THEY NOTICE I'M MISSING. LET'S GET YOU HOME AND PUT AN END TO—
—HUNH?
PRRPRPR PRRR...
OH...
...MY...
...WHAUGH!

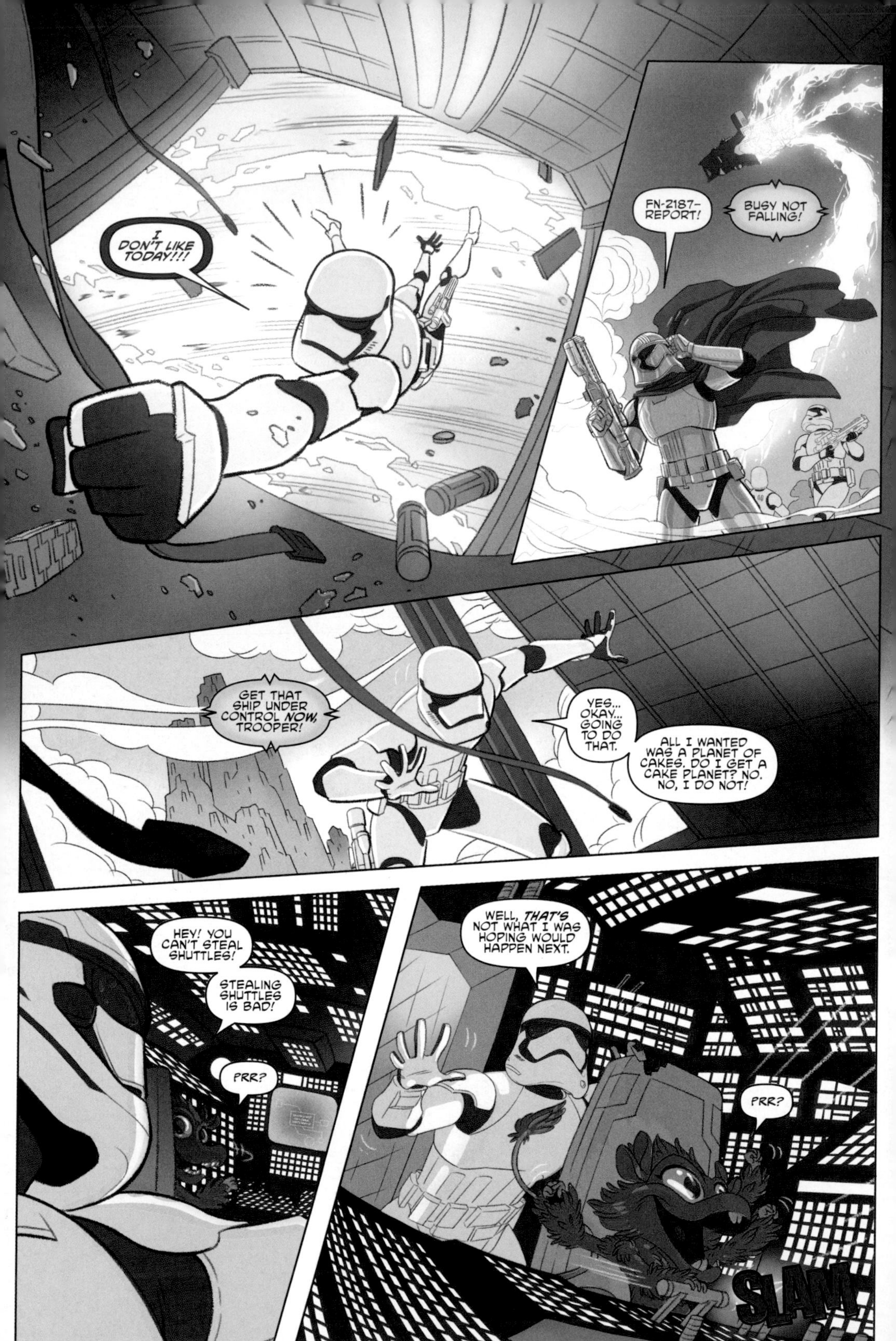
I DON'T LIKE TODAY!!!
FN-2187-- REPORT!
BUSY NOT FALLING!
GET THAT SHIP UNDER CONTROL NOW, TROOPER!
YES... OKAY... GOING TO DO THAT.
ALL I WANTED WAS A PLANET OF CAKES. DO I GET A CAKE PLANET? NO. NO, I DO NOT!
HEY! YOU CAN'T STEAL SHUTTLES!
STEALING SHUTTLES IS BAD!
PRR?
WELL, THAT'S NOT WHAT I WAS HOPING WOULD HAPPEN NEXT.
PRR?
SLAM

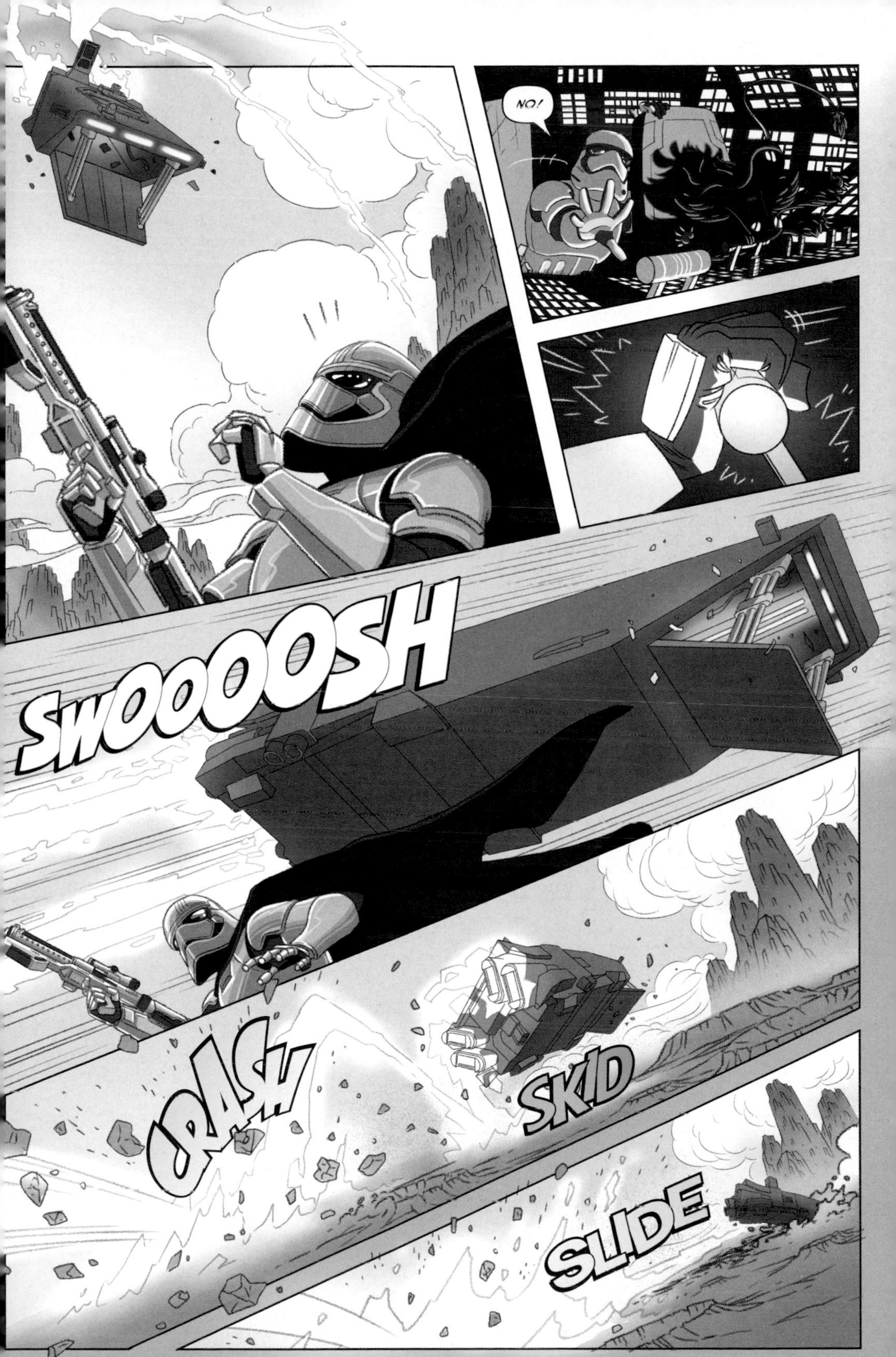

NO!
SWOOOOSH
CRASH
SKID
SLIDE

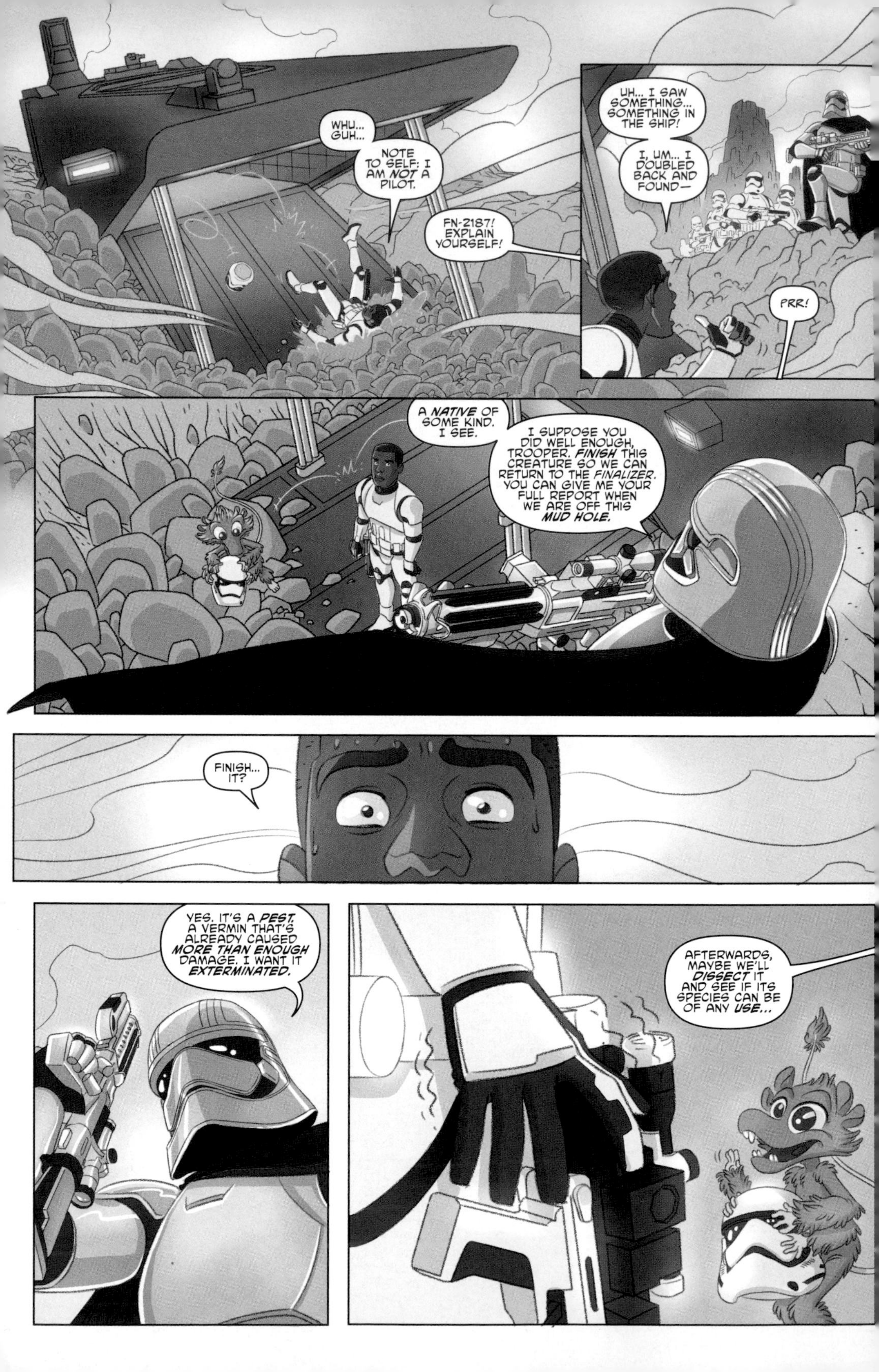
WHU... GUH...
NOTE TO SELF: I AM NOT A PILOT.
FN-2187! EXPLAIN YOURSELF!
UH... I SAW SOMETHING... SOMETHING IN THE SHIP!
I, UM... I DOUBLED BACK AND FOUND—
PRR!
A NATIVE OF SOME KIND. I SEE.
I SUPPOSE YOU DID WELL ENOUGH, TROOPER. FINISH THIS CREATURE SO WE CAN RETURN TO THE FINALIZER. YOU CAN GIVE ME YOUR FULL REPORT WHEN WE ARE OFF THIS MUD HOLE.
FINISH... IT?
YES. IT'S A PEST. A VERMIN THAT'S ALREADY CAUSED MORE THAN ENOUGH DAMAGE. I WANT IT EXTERMINATED.
AFTERWARDS, MAYBE WE'LL DISSECT IT AND SEE IF ITS SPECIES CAN BE OF ANY USE...

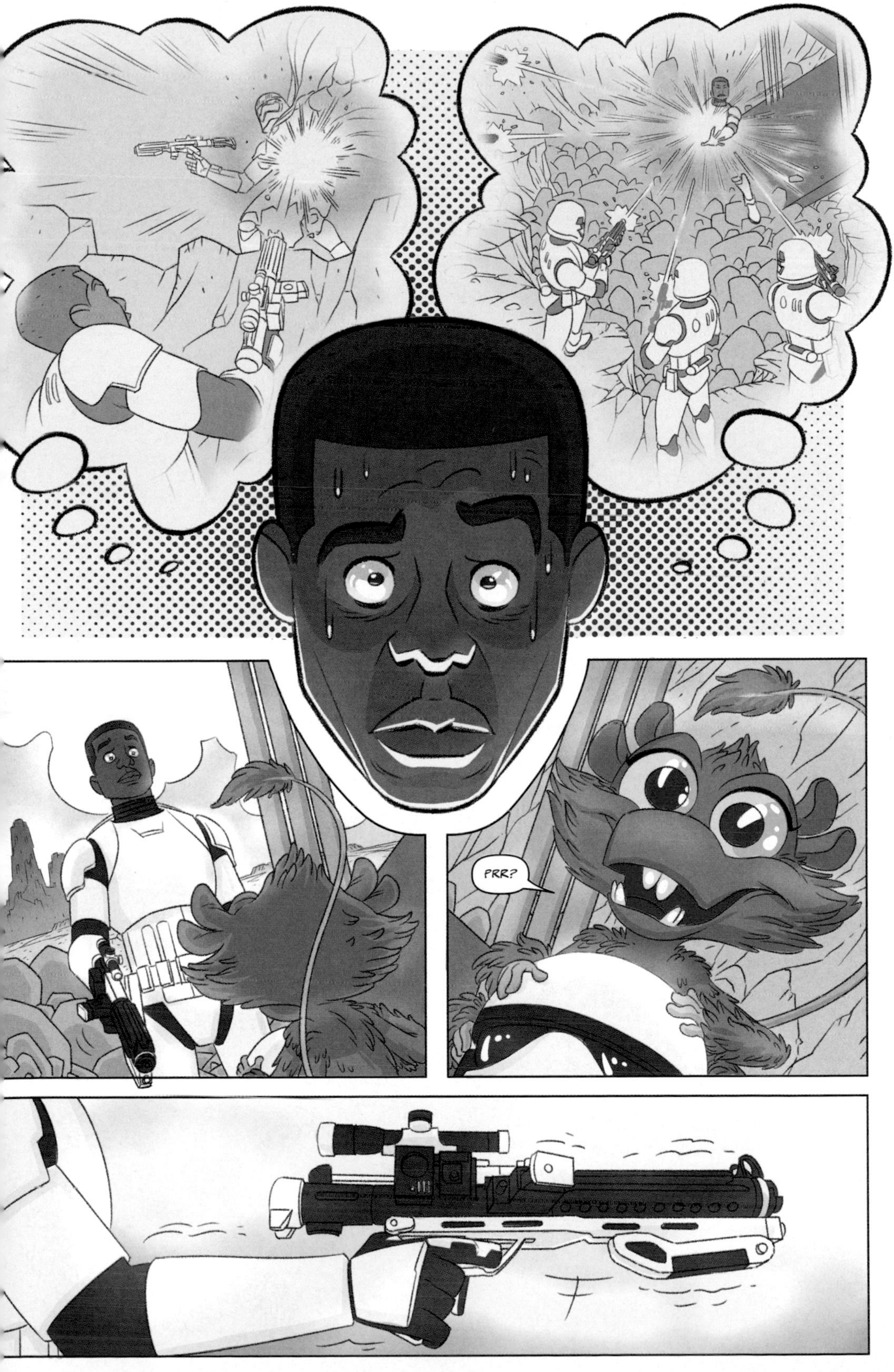
PRR?

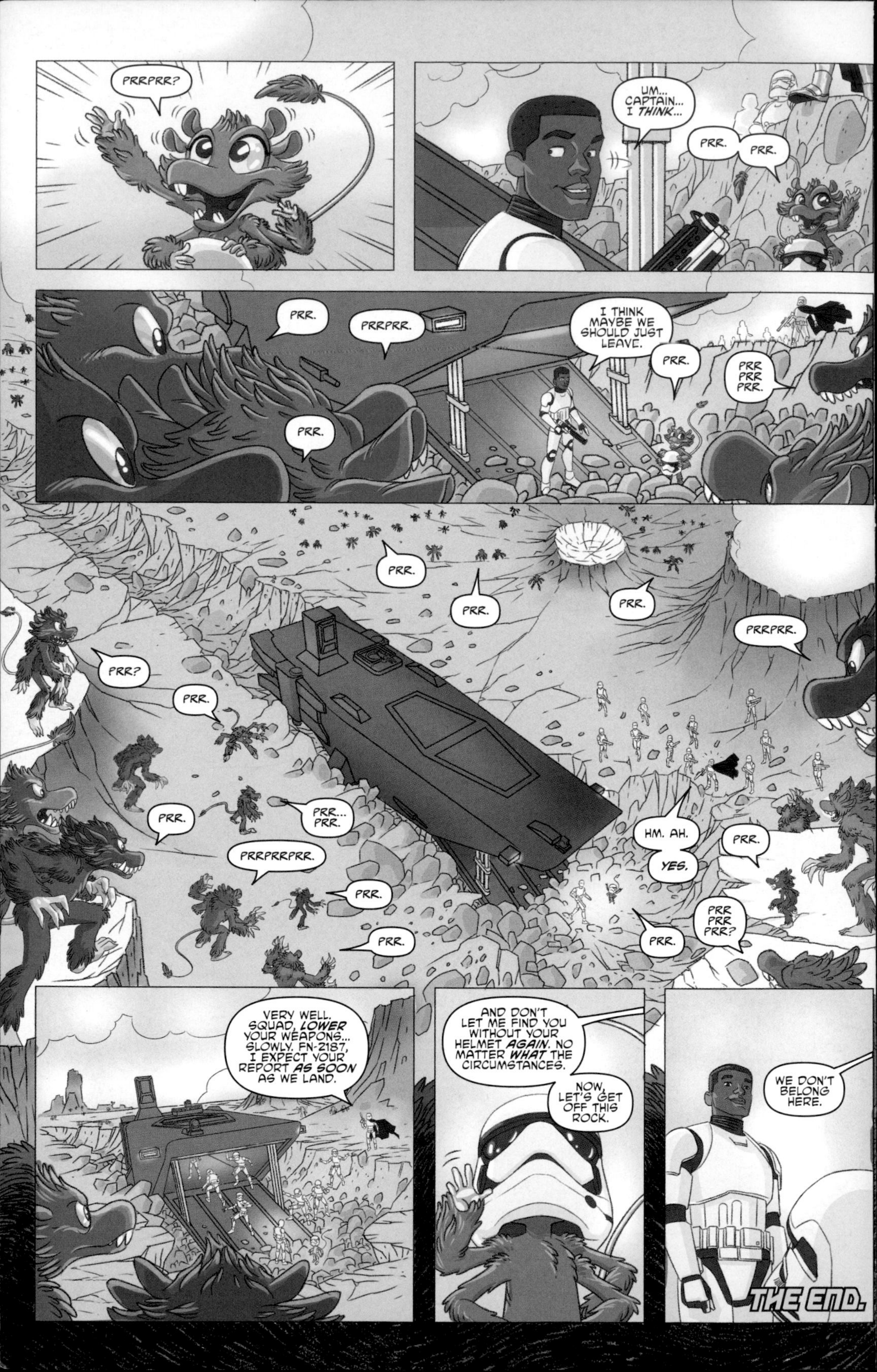
PRRPRR?
UM... CAPTAIN... I *THINK*...
PRR.
PRR.
PRR.
PRRPRR.
I THINK MAYBE WE SHOULD JUST LEAVE.
PRR.
PRR PRR PRR.
PRR.
PRR.
PRR.
PRR.
PRRPRR.
PRR?
PRR.
PRR.
PRR... PRR.
PRRPRRPRR.
PRR.
PRR.
HM. AH. *YES.*
PRR.
PRR.
PRR PRR PRR?
VERY WELL. SQUAD, *LOWER* YOUR WEAPONS... SLOWLY. FN-2187, I EXPECT YOUR REPORT *AS SOON* AS WE LAND.
AND DON'T LET ME FIND YOU WITHOUT YOUR HELMET *AGAIN*. NO MATTER *WHAT* THE CIRCUMSTANCES.
NOW, LET'S GET OFF THIS ROCK.
WE DON'T BELONG HERE.
THE END.

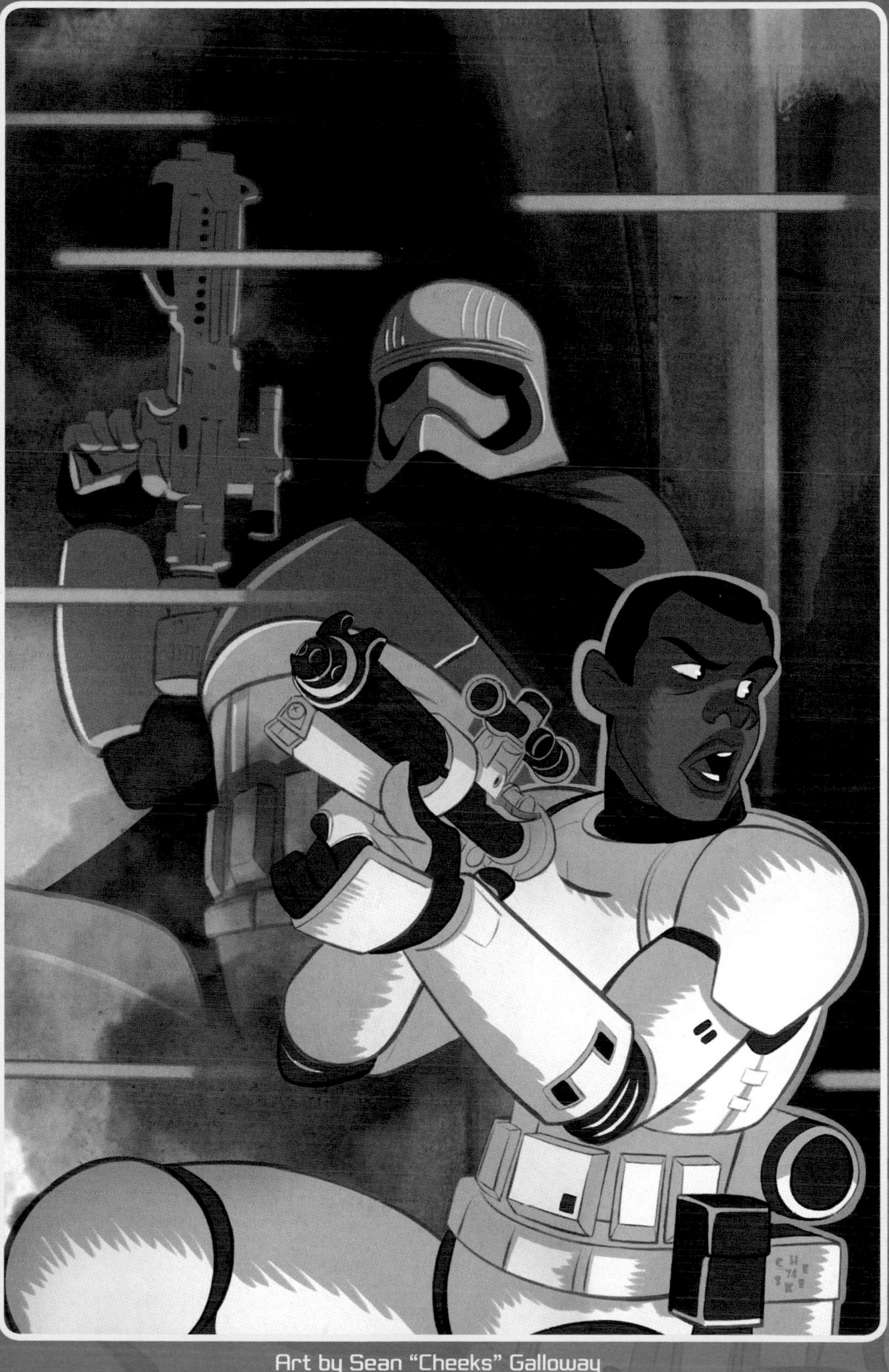
CHEEKS 74

Art by Sean "Cheeks" Galloway

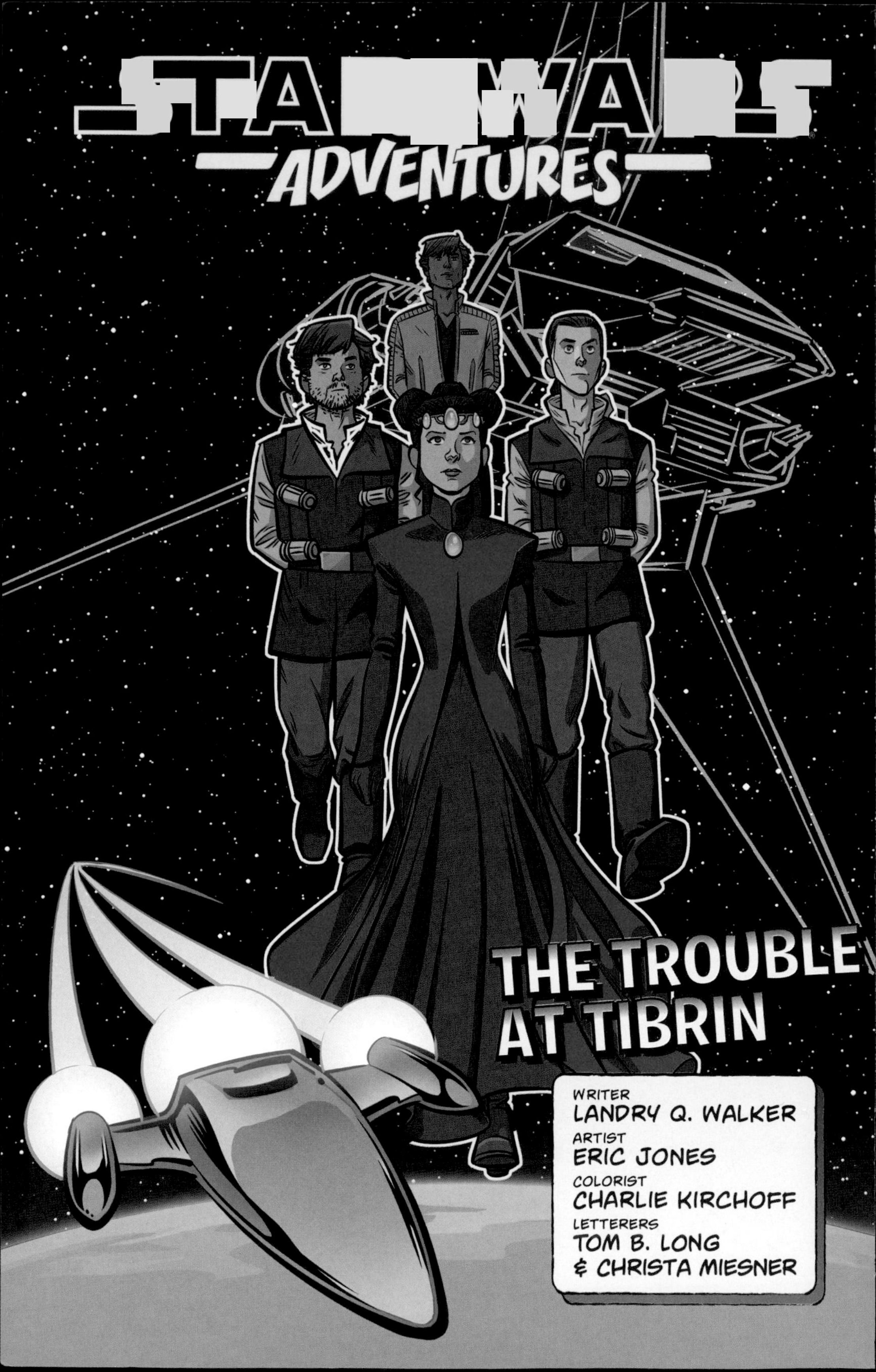
ADVENTURES
THE TROUBLE AT TIBRIN
WRITER
LANDRY Q. WALKER
ARTIST
ERIC JONES
COLORIST
CHARLIE KIRCHOFF
LETTERERS
TOM B. LONG
& CHRISTA MIESNER

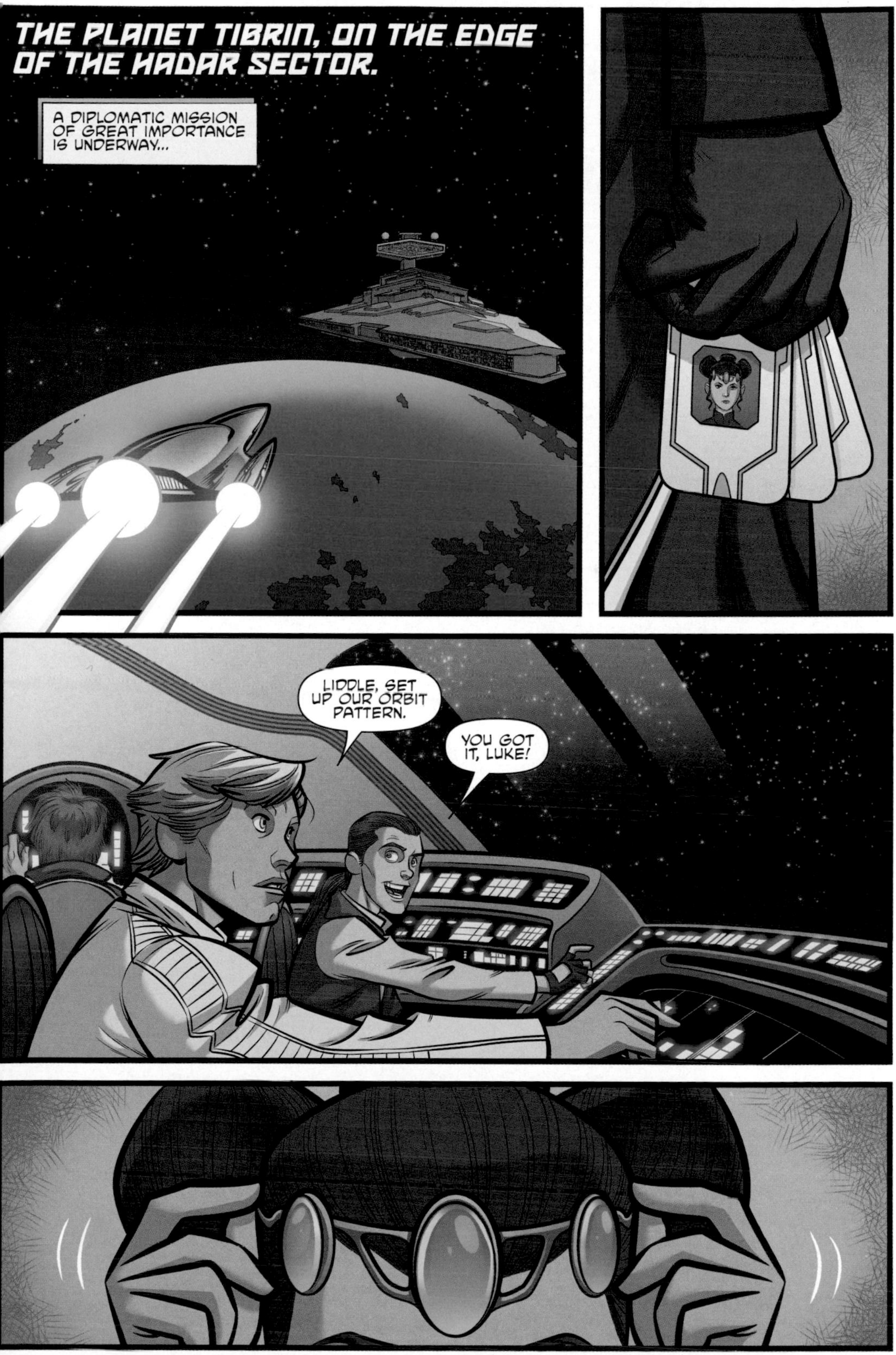
THE PLANET TIBRIN, ON THE EDGE OF THE HADAR SECTOR.
A DIPLOMATIC MISSION OF GREAT IMPORTANCE IS UNDERWAY...
LIDDLE, SET UP OUR ORBIT PATTERN.
YOU GOT IT, LUKE!

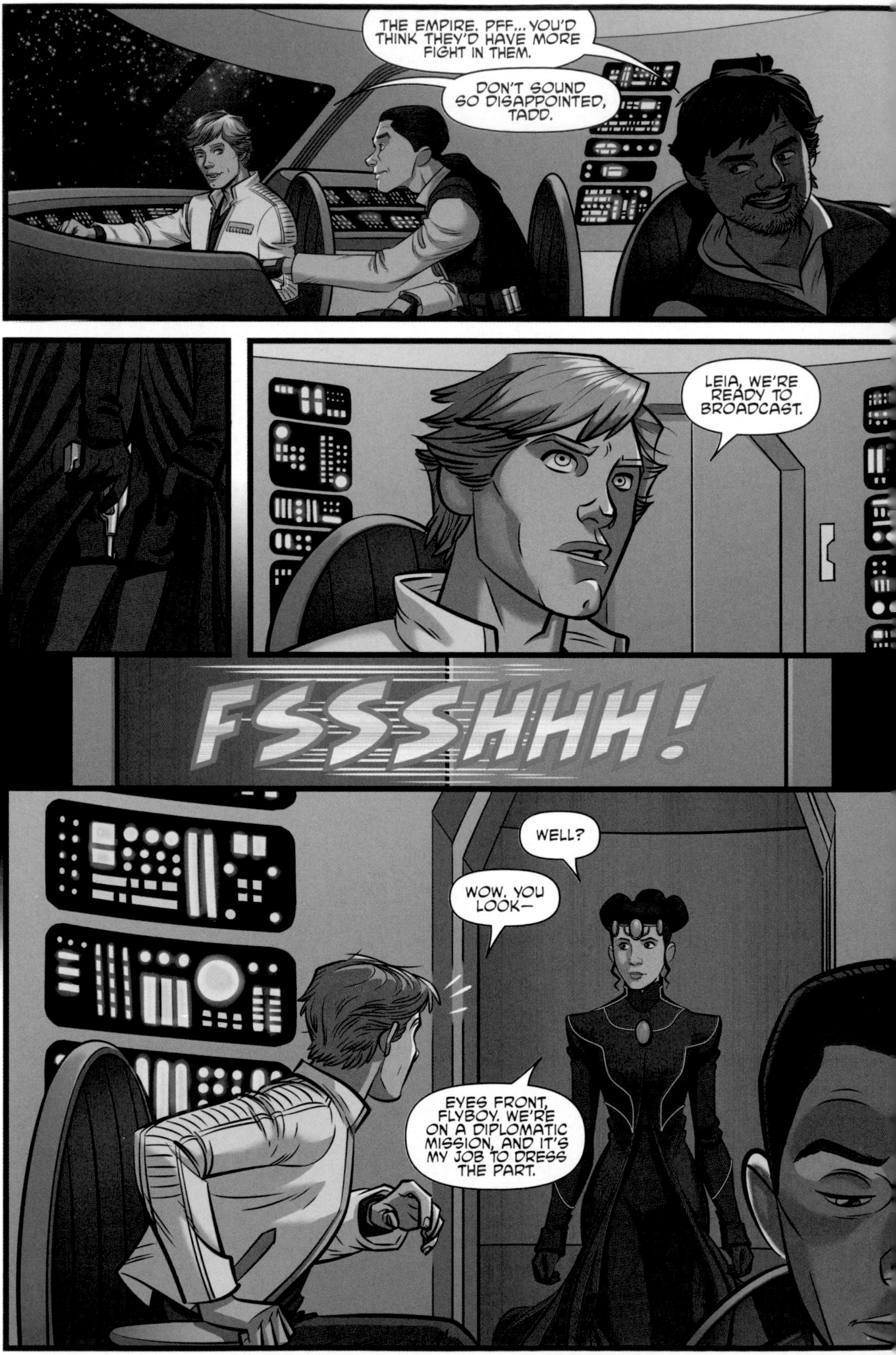
THE EMPIRE. PFF... YOU'D THINK THEY'D HAVE MORE FIGHT IN THEM.
DON'T SOUND SO DISAPPOINTED, TADD.
LEIA, WE'RE READY TO BROADCAST.
FSSSHHH!
WELL?
WOW. YOU LOOK—
EYES FRONT, FLYBOY. WE'RE ON A DIPLOMATIC MISSION, AND IT'S MY JOB TO DRESS THE PART.

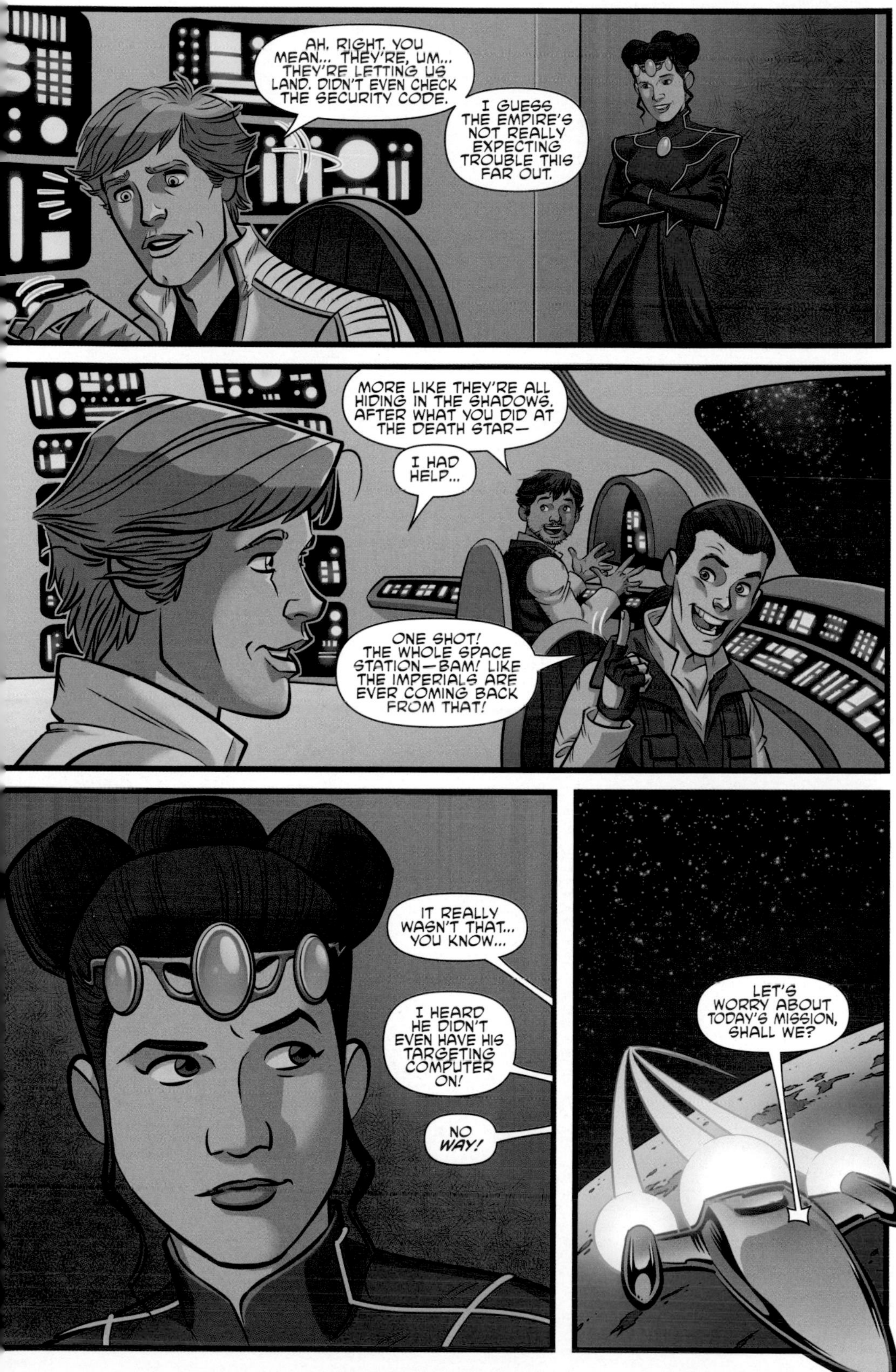
AH. RIGHT. YOU MEAN... THEY'RE, UM... THEY'RE LETTING US LAND. DIDN'T EVEN CHECK THE SECURITY CODE.
I GUESS THE EMPIRE'S NOT REALLY EXPECTING TROUBLE THIS FAR OUT.
MORE LIKE THEY'RE ALL HIDING IN THE SHADOWS. AFTER WHAT YOU DID AT THE DEATH STAR—
I HAD HELP...
ONE SHOT! THE WHOLE SPACE STATION—BAM! LIKE THE IMPERIALS ARE EVER COMING BACK FROM THAT!
IT REALLY WASN'T THAT... YOU KNOW...
I HEARD HE DIDN'T EVEN HAVE HIS TARGETING COMPUTER ON!
NO *WAY!*
LET'S WORRY ABOUT TODAY'S MISSION, SHALL WE?

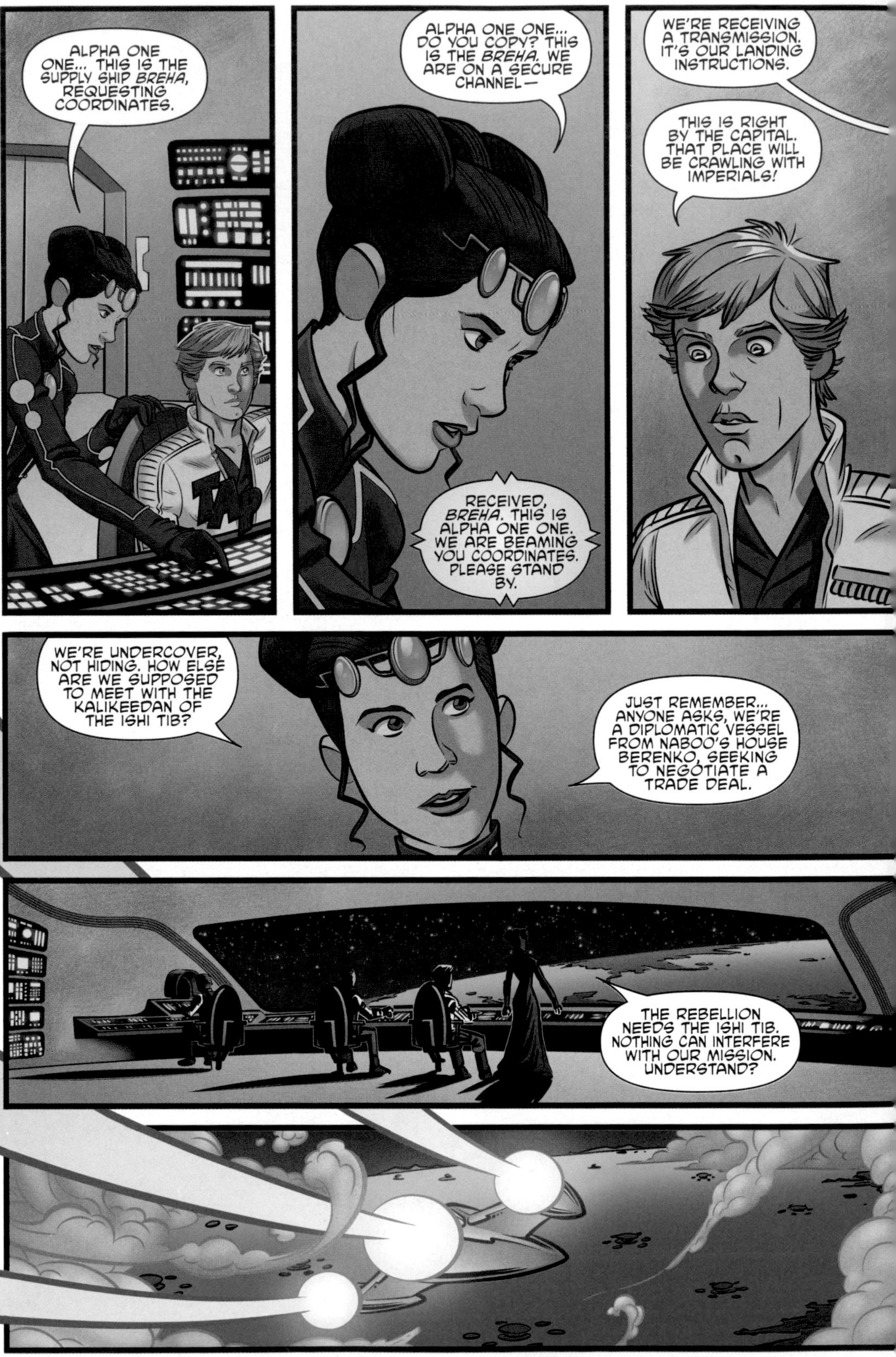
ALPHA ONE ONE... THIS IS THE SUPPLY SHIP *BREHA*, REQUESTING COORDINATES.
ALPHA ONE ONE... DO YOU COPY? THIS IS THE *BREHA*. WE ARE ON A SECURE CHANNEL—
RECEIVED, *BREHA*. THIS IS ALPHA ONE ONE. WE ARE BEAMING YOU COORDINATES. PLEASE STAND BY.
WE'RE RECEIVING A TRANSMISSION. IT'S OUR LANDING INSTRUCTIONS.
THIS IS RIGHT BY THE CAPITAL. THAT PLACE WILL BE CRAWLING WITH IMPERIALS!
WE'RE UNDERCOVER, NOT HIDING. HOW ELSE ARE WE SUPPOSED TO MEET WITH THE KALIKEEDAN OF THE ISHI TIB?
JUST REMEMBER... ANYONE ASKS, WE'RE A DIPLOMATIC VESSEL FROM NABOO'S HOUSE BERENKO, SEEKING TO NEGOTIATE A TRADE DEAL.
THE REBELLION NEEDS THE ISHI TIB. NOTHING CAN INTERFERE WITH OUR MISSION. UNDERSTAND?

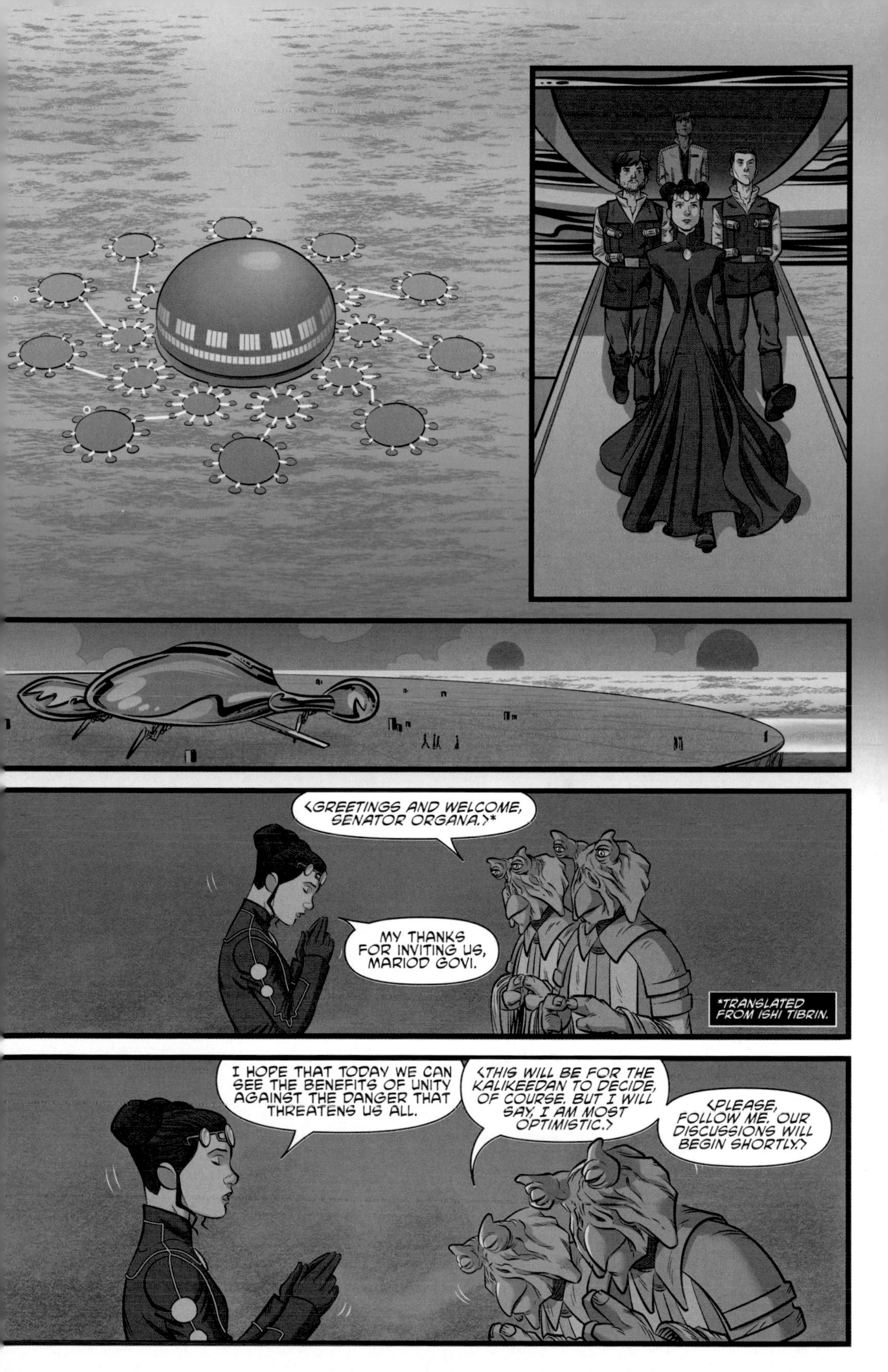

<GREETINGS AND WELCOME, SENATOR ORGANA.>*
MY THANKS FOR INVITING US, MARIOD GOVI.
*TRANSLATED FROM ISHI TIBRIN.
I HOPE THAT TODAY WE CAN SEE THE BENEFITS OF UNITY AGAINST THE DANGER THAT THREATENS US ALL.
<THIS WILL BE FOR THE KALIKEEDAN TO DECIDE, OF COURSE. BUT I WILL SAY, I AM MOST OPTIMISTIC.>
<PLEASE, FOLLOW ME. OUR DISCUSSIONS WILL BEGIN SHORTLY.>

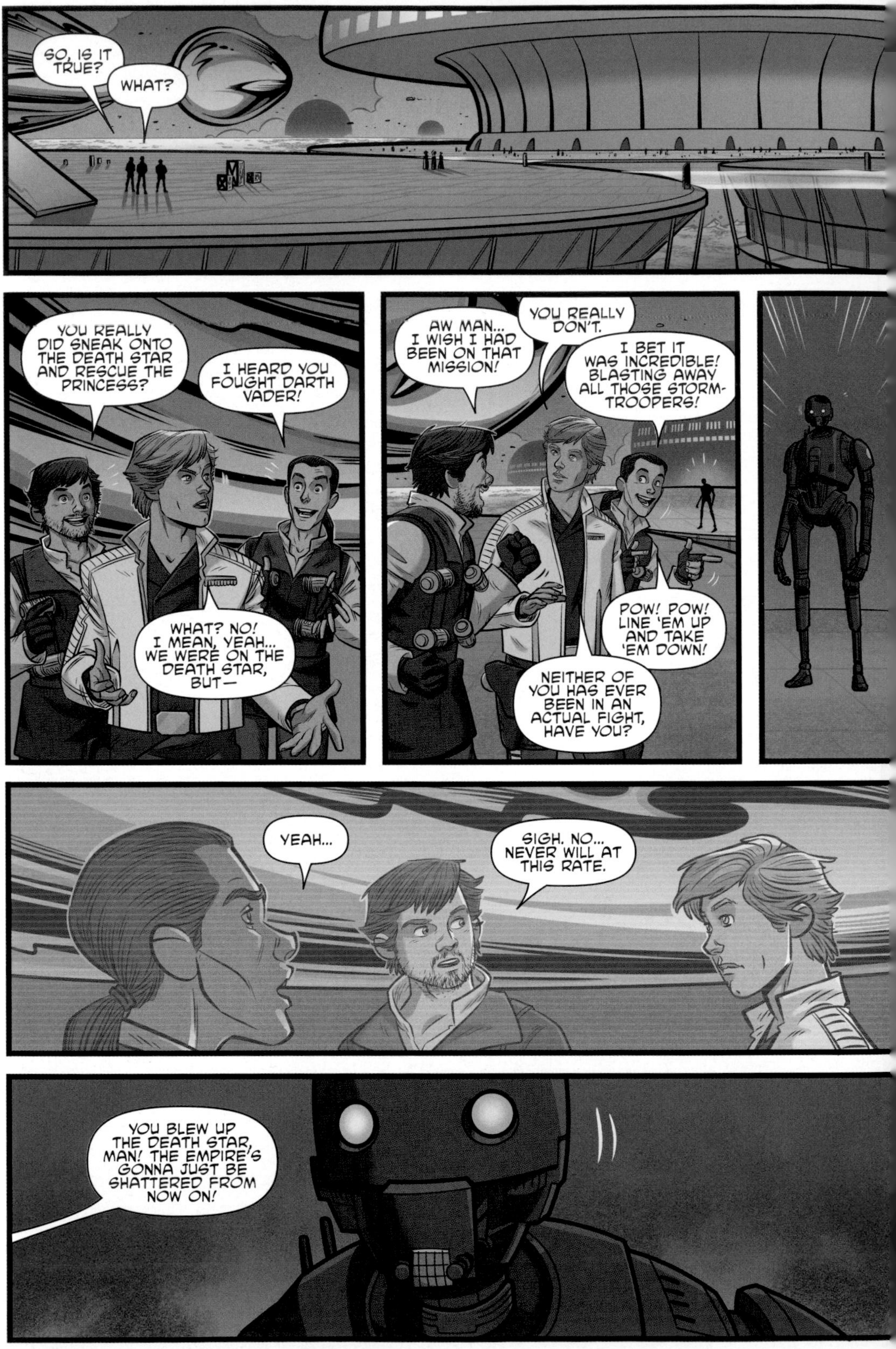
SO, IS IT TRUE?
WHAT?
YOU REALLY DID SNEAK ONTO THE DEATH STAR AND RESCUE THE PRINCESS?
I HEARD YOU FOUGHT DARTH VADER!
WHAT? NO! I MEAN, YEAH... WE WERE ON THE DEATH STAR, BUT—
AW MAN... I WISH I HAD BEEN ON THAT MISSION!
YOU REALLY DON'T.
I BET IT WAS INCREDIBLE! BLASTING AWAY ALL THOSE STORM-TROOPERS!
POW! POW! LINE 'EM UP AND TAKE 'EM DOWN!
NEITHER OF YOU HAS EVER BEEN IN AN ACTUAL FIGHT, HAVE YOU?
YEAH...
SIGH. NO... NEVER WILL AT THIS RATE.
YOU BLEW UP THE DEATH STAR, MAN! THE EMPIRE'S GONNA JUST BE SHATTERED FROM NOW ON!

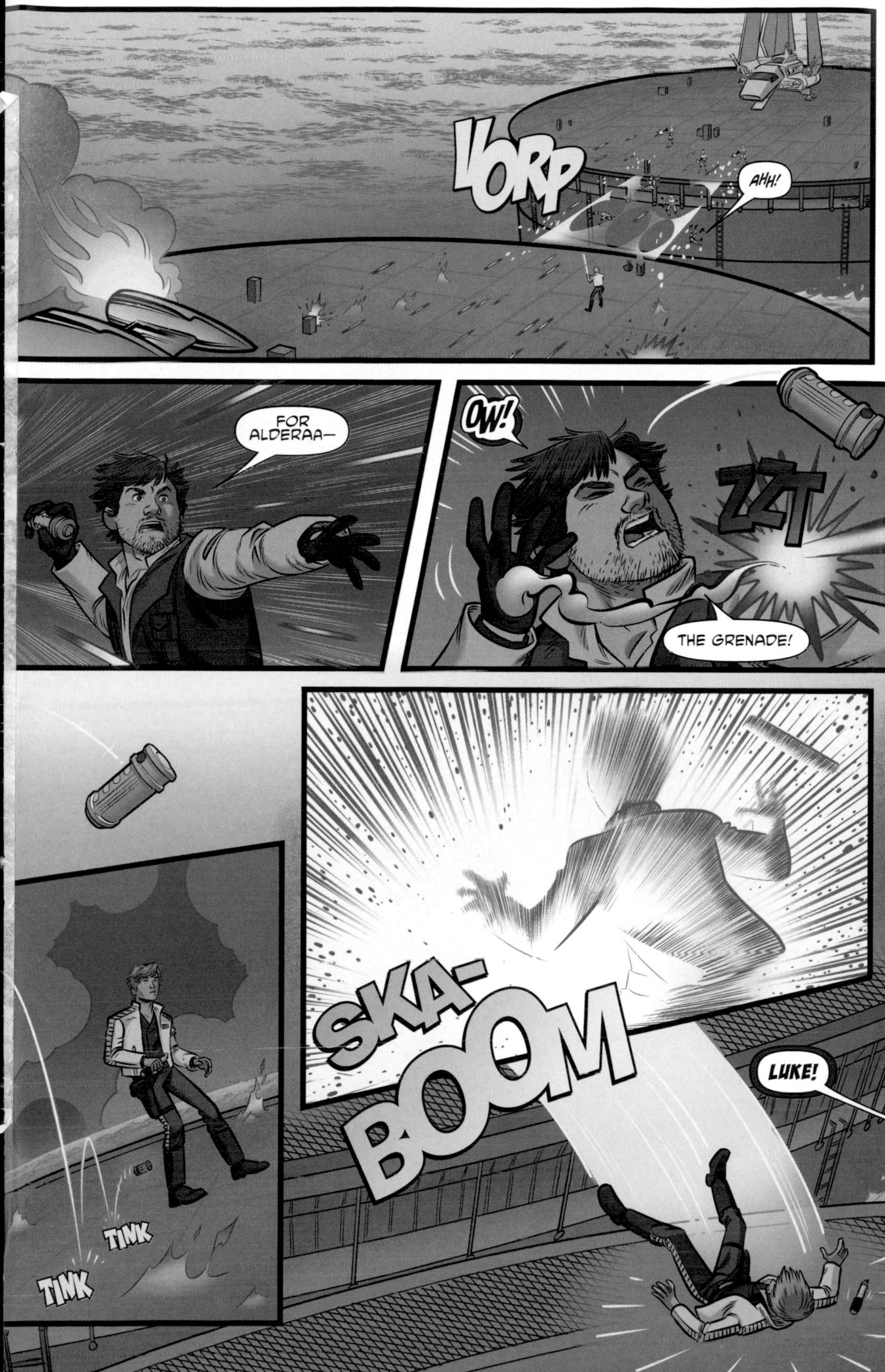
VORP
AHH!
FOR ALDERAA—
OW!
ZZT
THE GRENADE!
SKA-BOOM
LUKE!
TINK
TINK

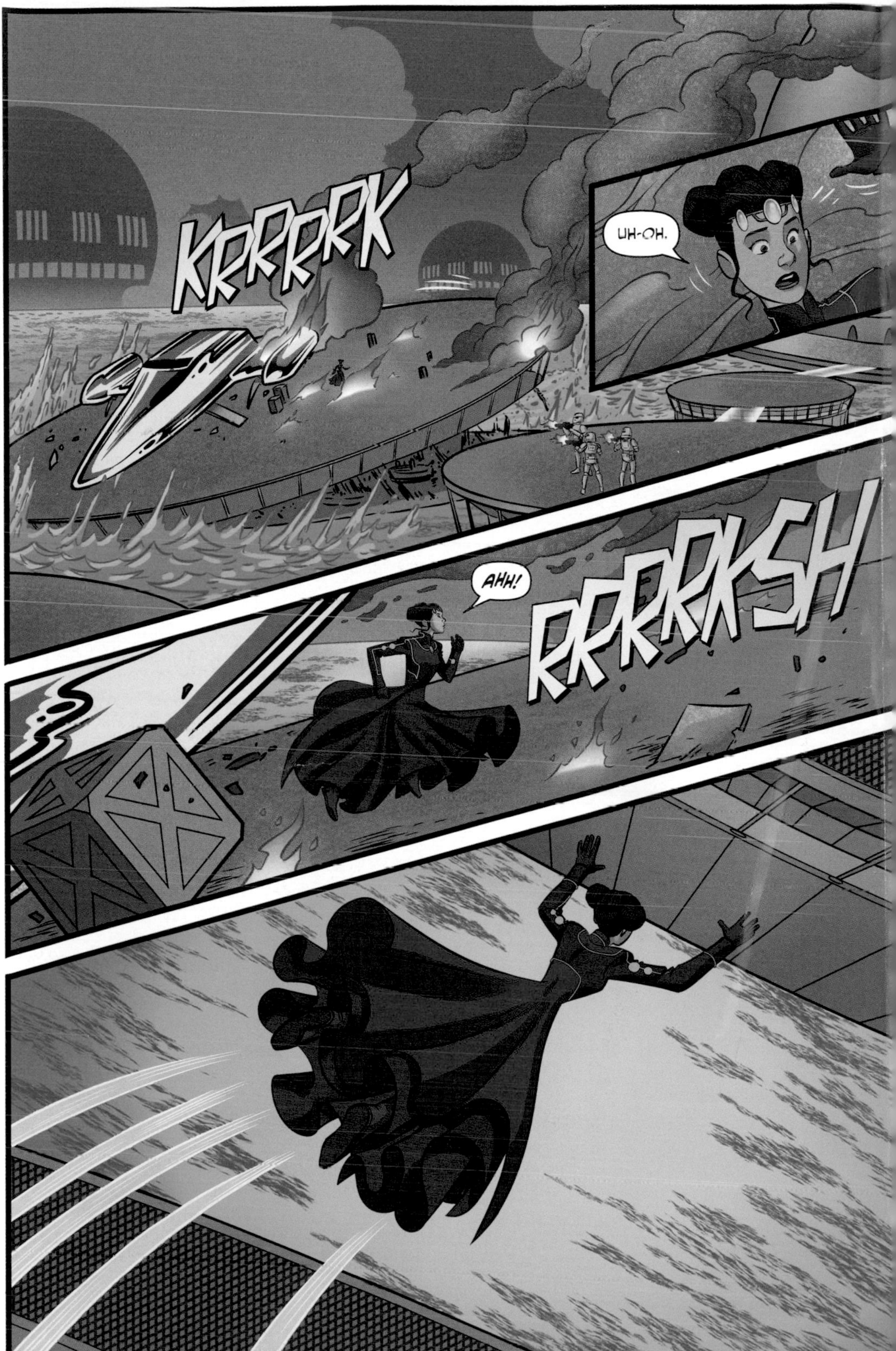
KRRRRK
UH-OH.
AHH!
RRRRRKSH

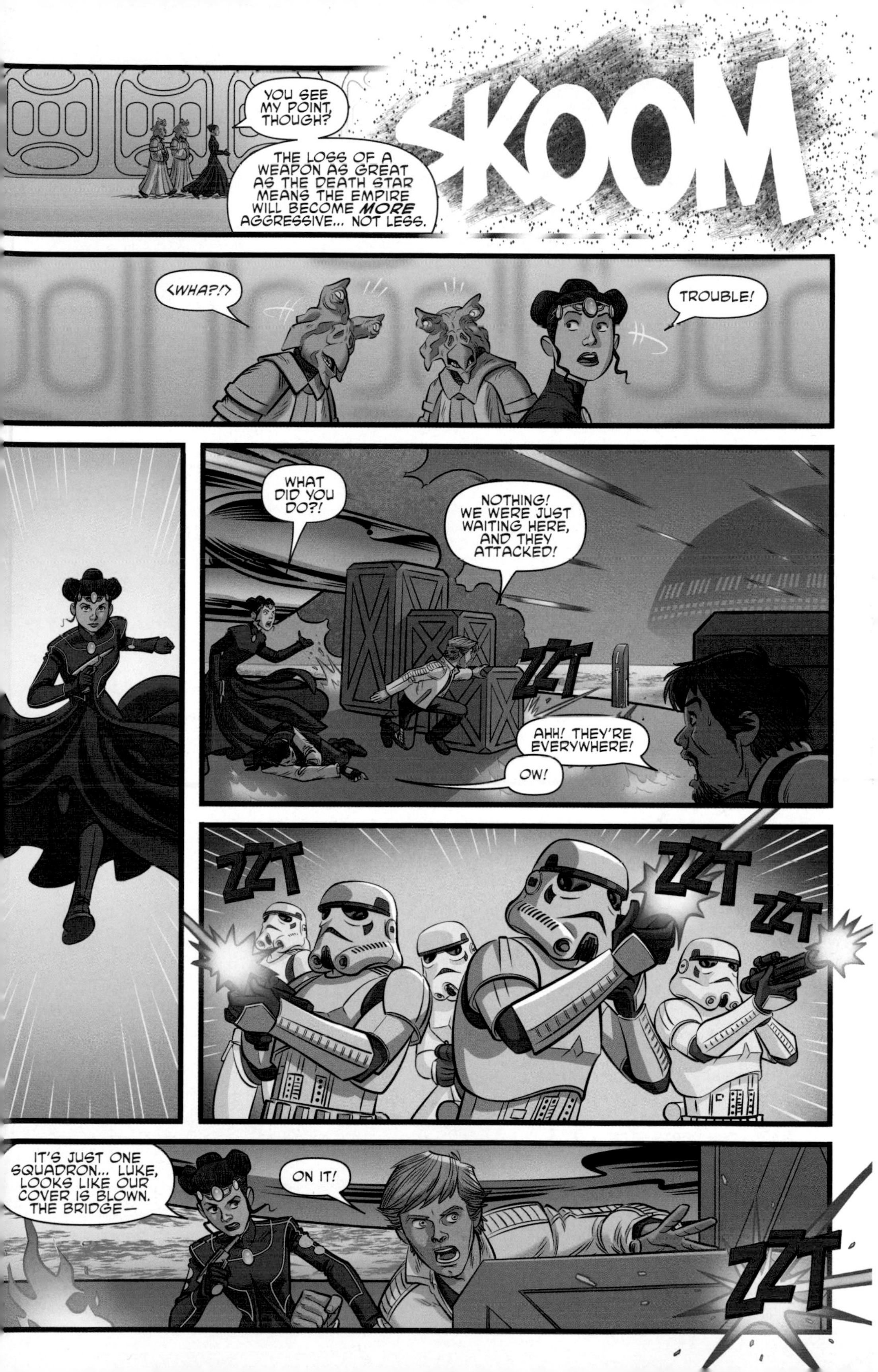
YOU SEE MY POINT, THOUGH?
THE LOSS OF A WEAPON AS GREAT AS THE DEATH STAR MEANS THE EMPIRE WILL BECOME *MORE* AGGRESSIVE... NOT LESS.
SKOOM
<WHA?!>
TROUBLE!
WHAT DID YOU DO?!
NOTHING! WE WERE JUST WAITING HERE, AND THEY ATTACKED!
ZZT
AHH! THEY'RE EVERYWHERE!
OW!
ZZT
ZZT
ZZT
IT'S JUST ONE SQUADRON... LUKE, LOOKS LIKE OUR COVER IS BLOWN. THE BRIDGE—
ON IT!
ZZT

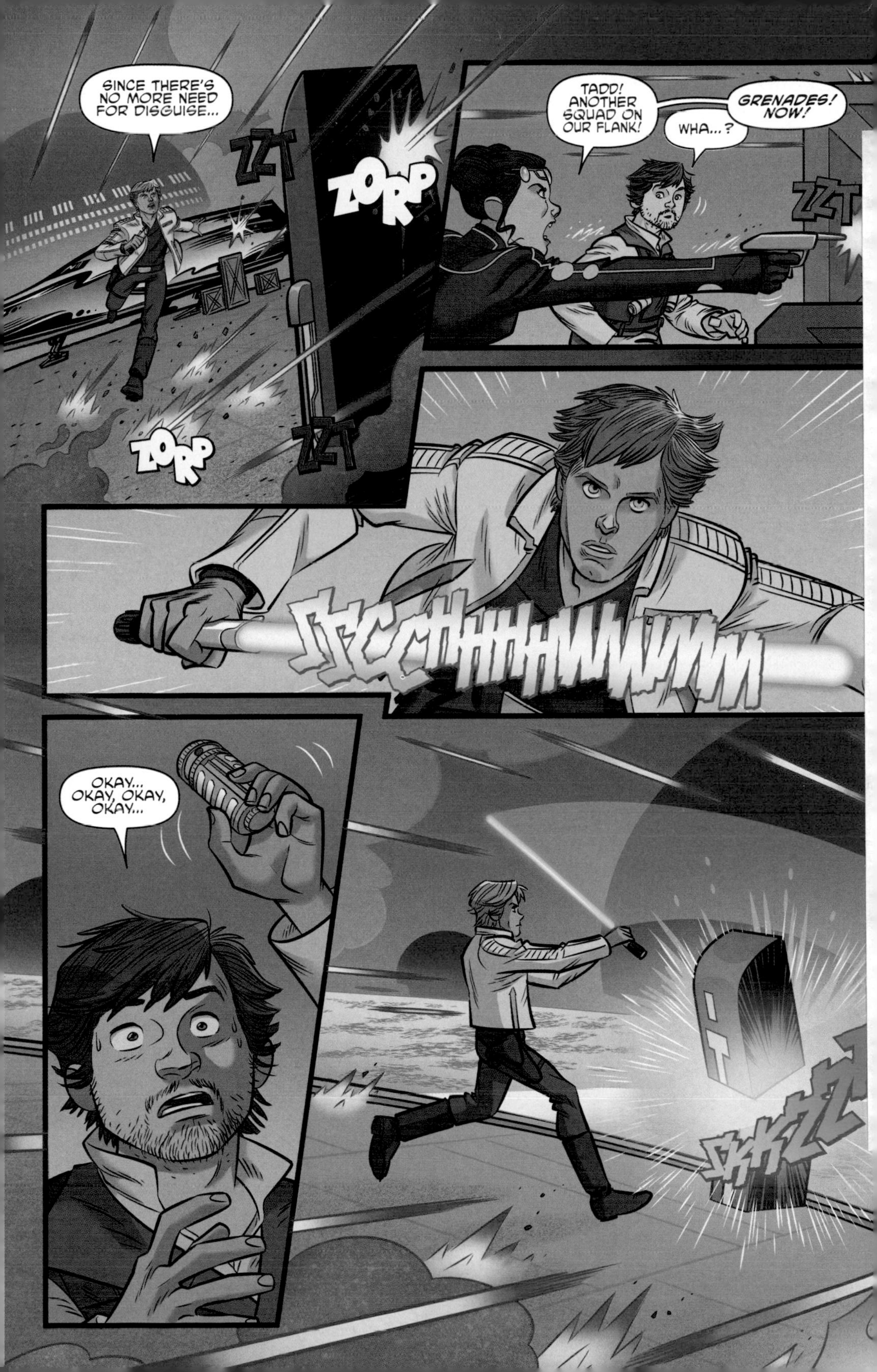
SINCE THERE'S NO MORE NEED FOR DISGUISE...
ZZT
ZORP
ZORP
ZZT
TADD! ANOTHER SQUAD ON OUR FLANK!
WHA...?
GRENADES! NOW!
ZZT
TSCCHHHHMMMMMM
OKAY... OKAY, OKAY, OKAY...
SKKZZ

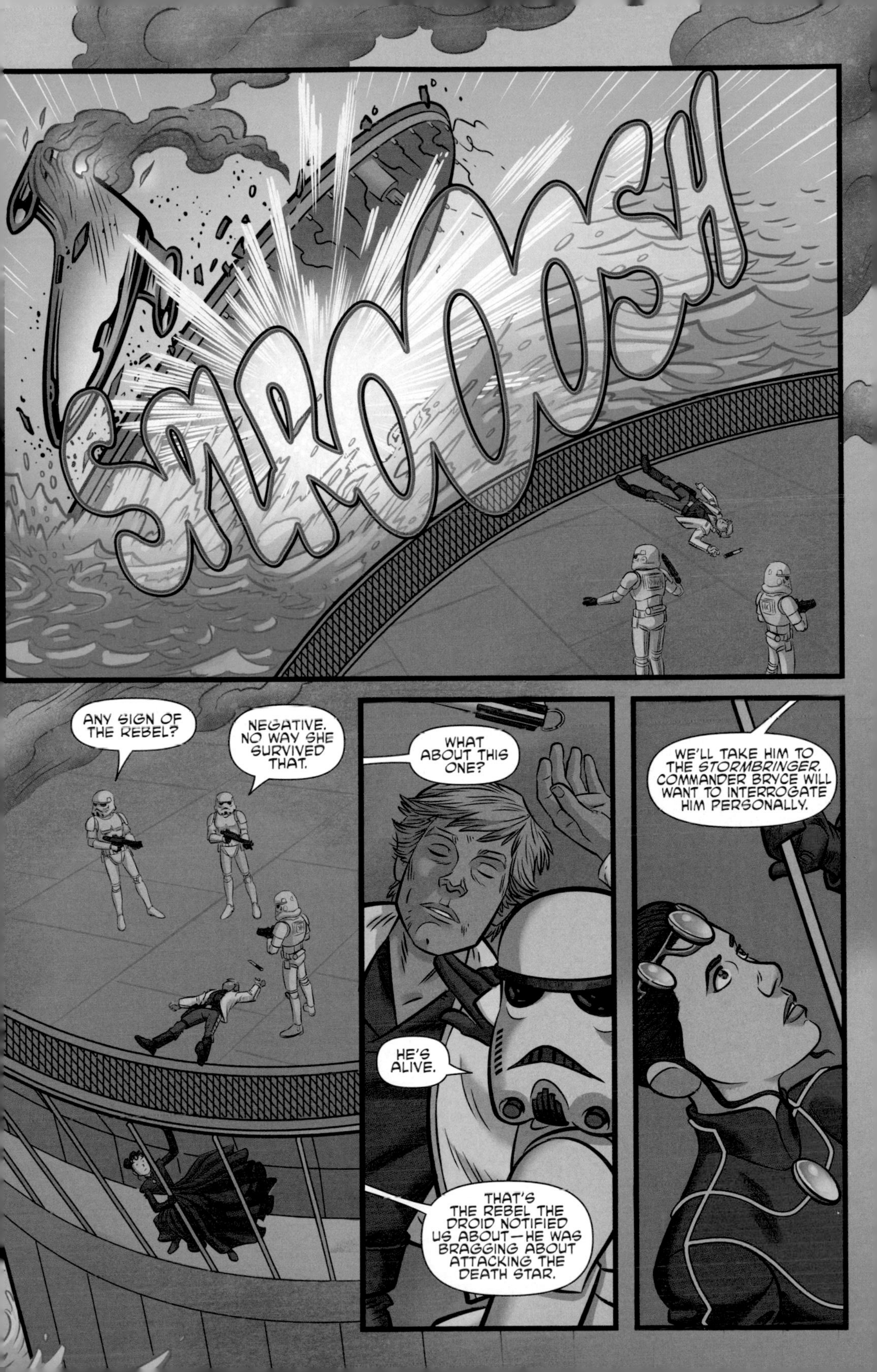
SHROOOSH
ANY SIGN OF THE REBEL?
NEGATIVE. NO WAY SHE SURVIVED THAT.
WHAT ABOUT THIS ONE?
HE'S ALIVE.
THAT'S THE REBEL THE DROID NOTIFIED US ABOUT—HE WAS BRAGGING ABOUT ATTACKING THE DEATH STAR.
WE'LL TAKE HIM TO THE *STORMBRINGER.* COMMANDER BRYCE WILL WANT TO INTERROGATE HIM PERSONALLY.

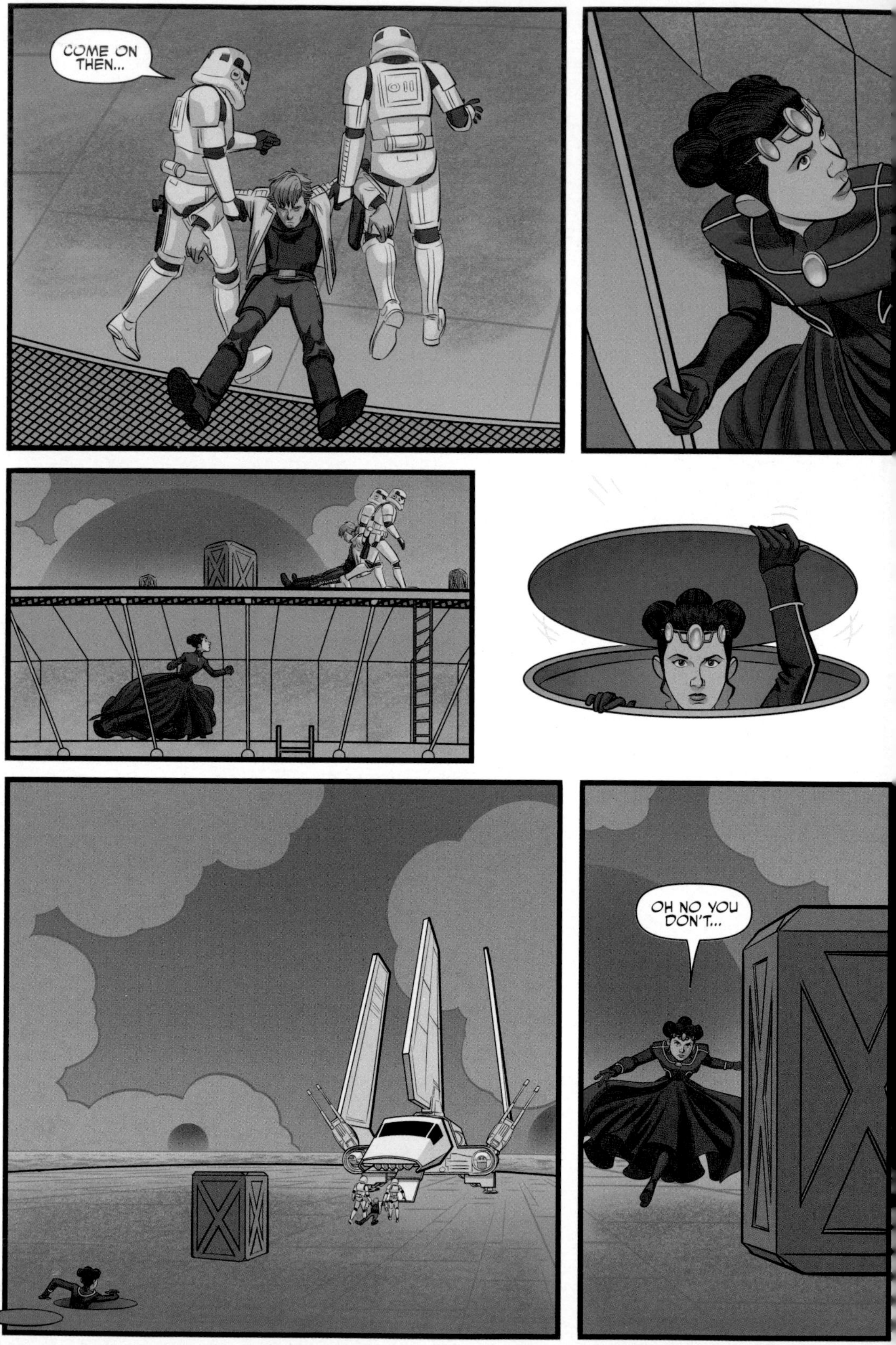
COME ON THEN...
OH NO YOU DON'T...

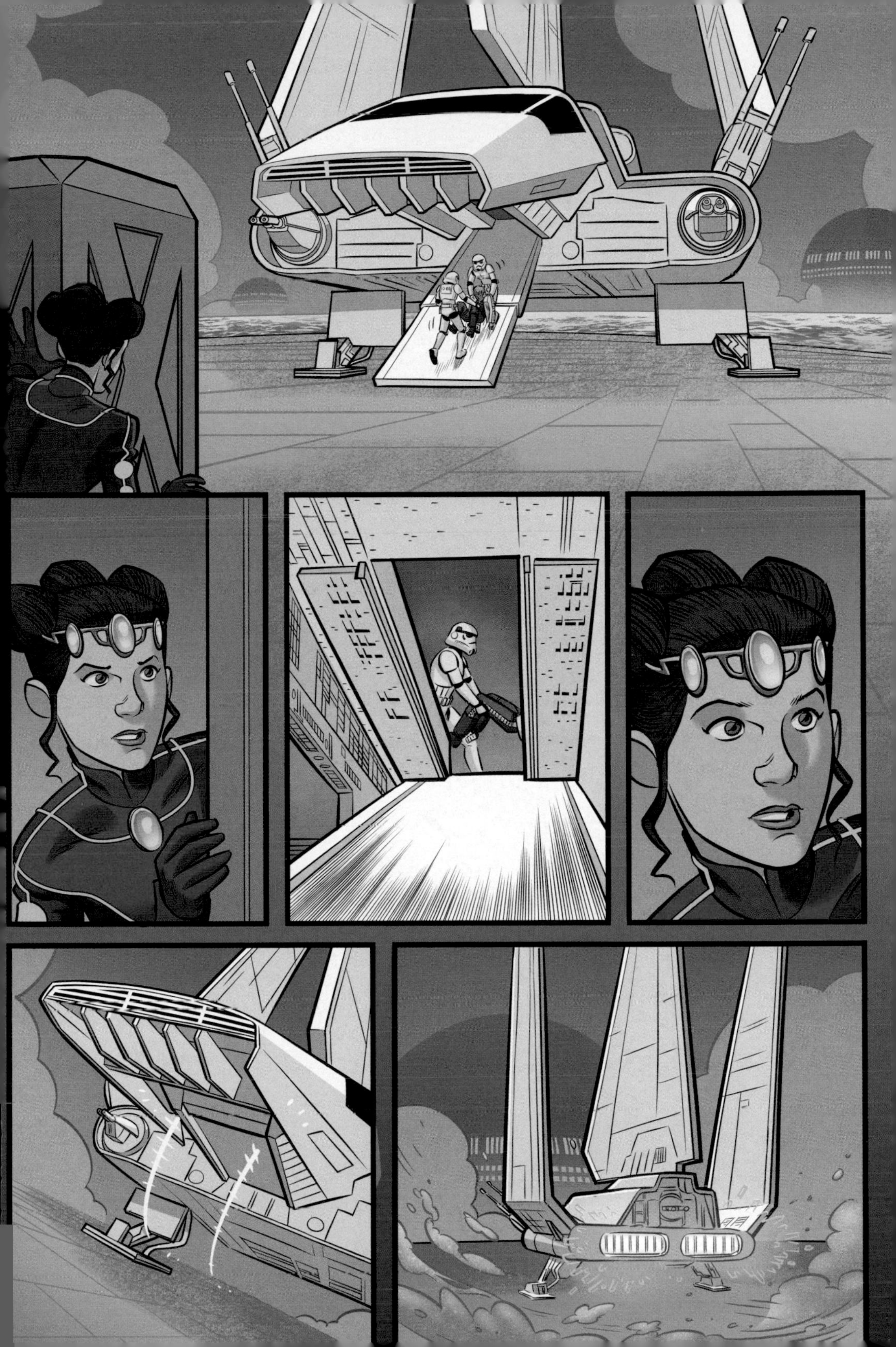

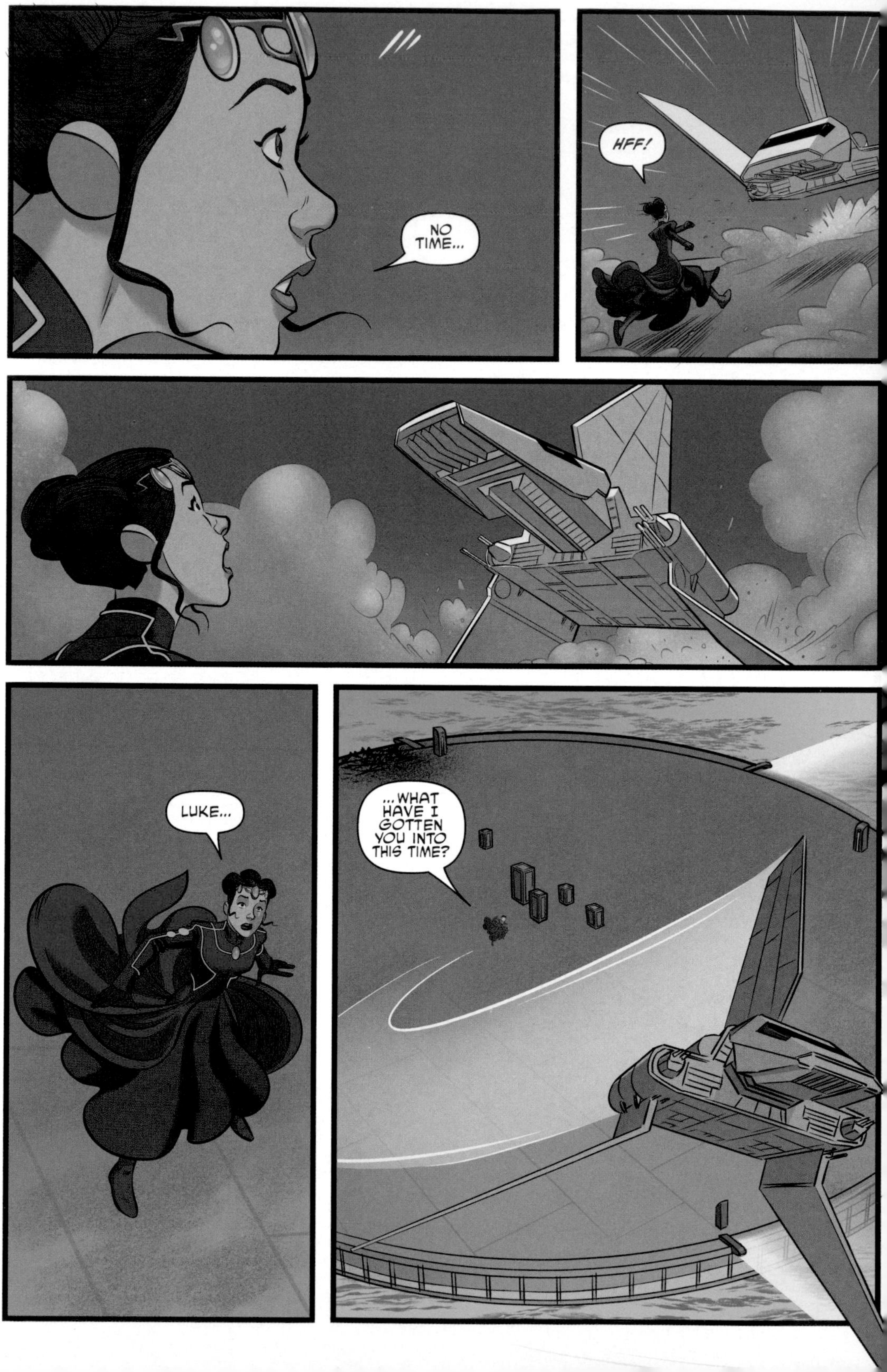

NO TIME...
HFF!
LUKE...
...WHAT HAVE I GOTTEN YOU INTO THIS TIME?

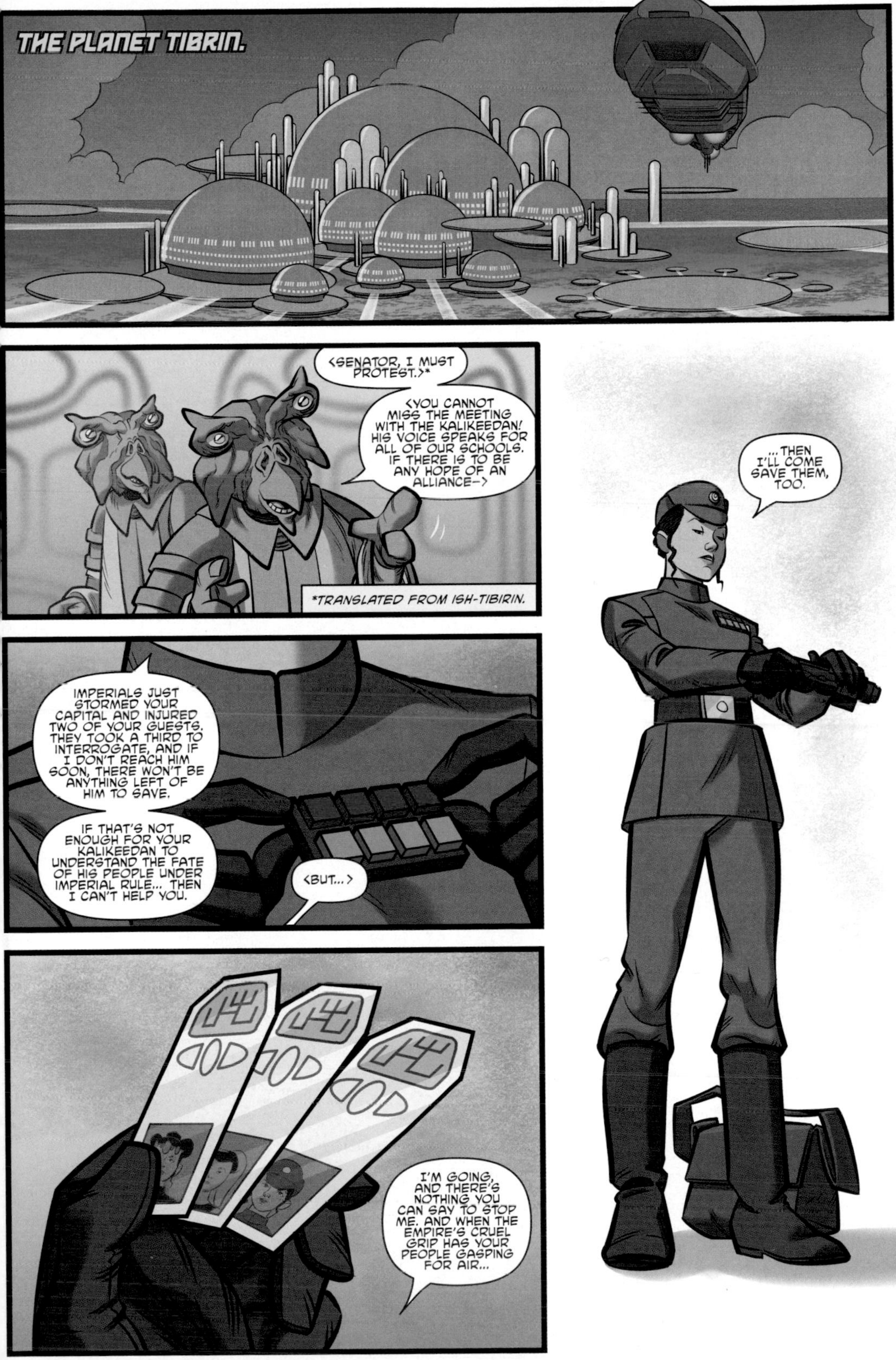
THE PLANET TIBRIN.
<SENATOR, I MUST PROTEST.>*
<YOU CANNOT MISS THE MEETING WITH THE KALIKEEDAN! HIS VOICE SPEAKS FOR ALL OF OUR SCHOOLS. IF THERE IS TO BE ANY HOPE OF AN ALLIANCE–>
*TRANSLATED FROM ISH-TIBIRIN.
IMPERIALS JUST STORMED YOUR CAPITAL AND INJURED TWO OF YOUR GUESTS. THEY TOOK A THIRD TO INTERROGATE, AND IF I DON'T REACH HIM SOON, THERE WON'T BE ANYTHING LEFT OF HIM TO SAVE.
IF THAT'S NOT ENOUGH FOR YOUR KALIKEEDAN TO UNDERSTAND THE FATE OF HIS PEOPLE UNDER IMPERIAL RULE... THEN I CAN'T HELP YOU.
<BUT...>
I'M GOING, AND THERE'S NOTHING YOU CAN SAY TO STOP ME. AND WHEN THE EMPIRE'S CRUEL GRIP HAS YOUR PEOPLE GASPING FOR AIR...
...THEN I'LL COME SAVE THEM, TOO.

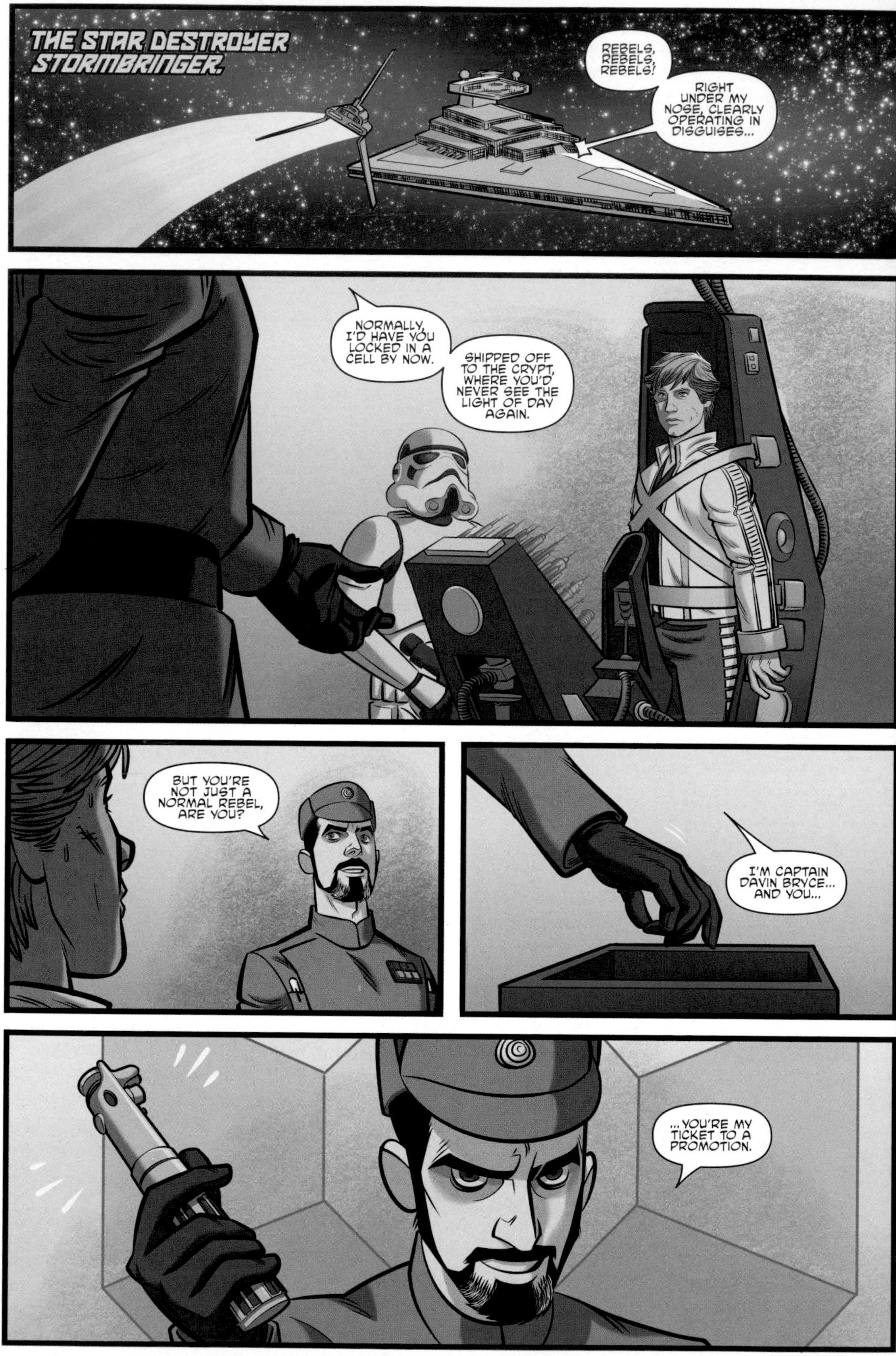
THE STAR DESTROYER STORMBRINGER.
REBELS, REBELS, REBELS!
RIGHT UNDER MY NOSE, CLEARLY OPERATING IN DISGUISES...
NORMALLY, I'D HAVE YOU LOCKED IN A CELL BY NOW.
SHIPPED OFF TO THE CRYPT, WHERE YOU'D NEVER SEE THE LIGHT OF DAY AGAIN.
BUT YOU'RE NOT JUST A NORMAL REBEL, ARE YOU?
I'M CAPTAIN DAVIN BRYCE... AND YOU...
...YOU'RE MY TICKET TO A PROMOTION.

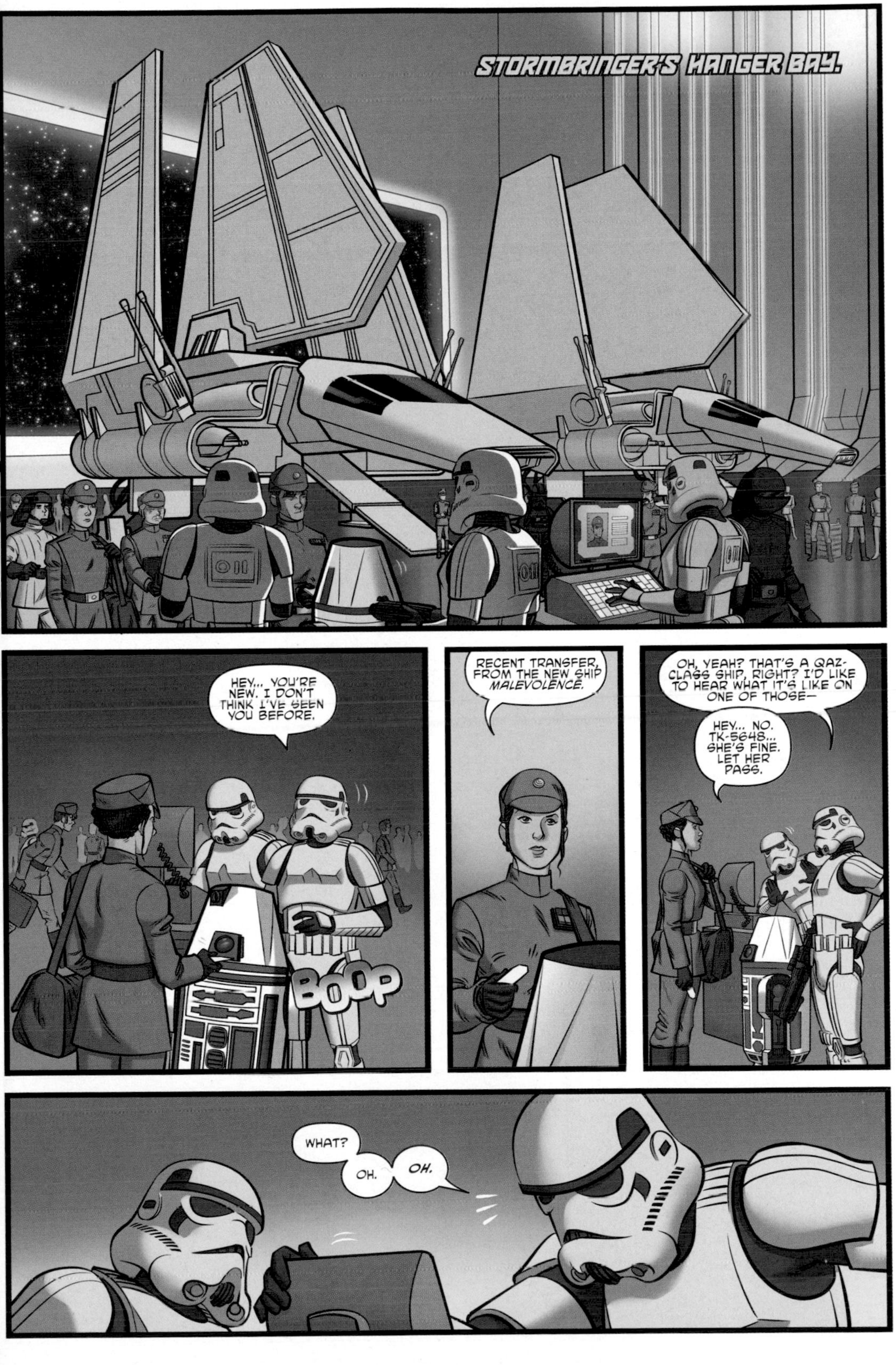
STORMBRINGER'S HANGER BAY.
HEY... YOU'RE NEW. I DON'T THINK I'VE SEEN YOU BEFORE.
BOOP
RECENT TRANSFER, FROM THE NEW SHIP *MALEVOLENCE.*
OH, YEAH? THAT'S A QAZ-CLASS SHIP, RIGHT? I'D LIKE TO HEAR WHAT IT'S LIKE ON ONE OF THOSE—
HEY... NO. TK-5648... SHE'S FINE. LET HER PASS.
WHAT?
OH.
OH.

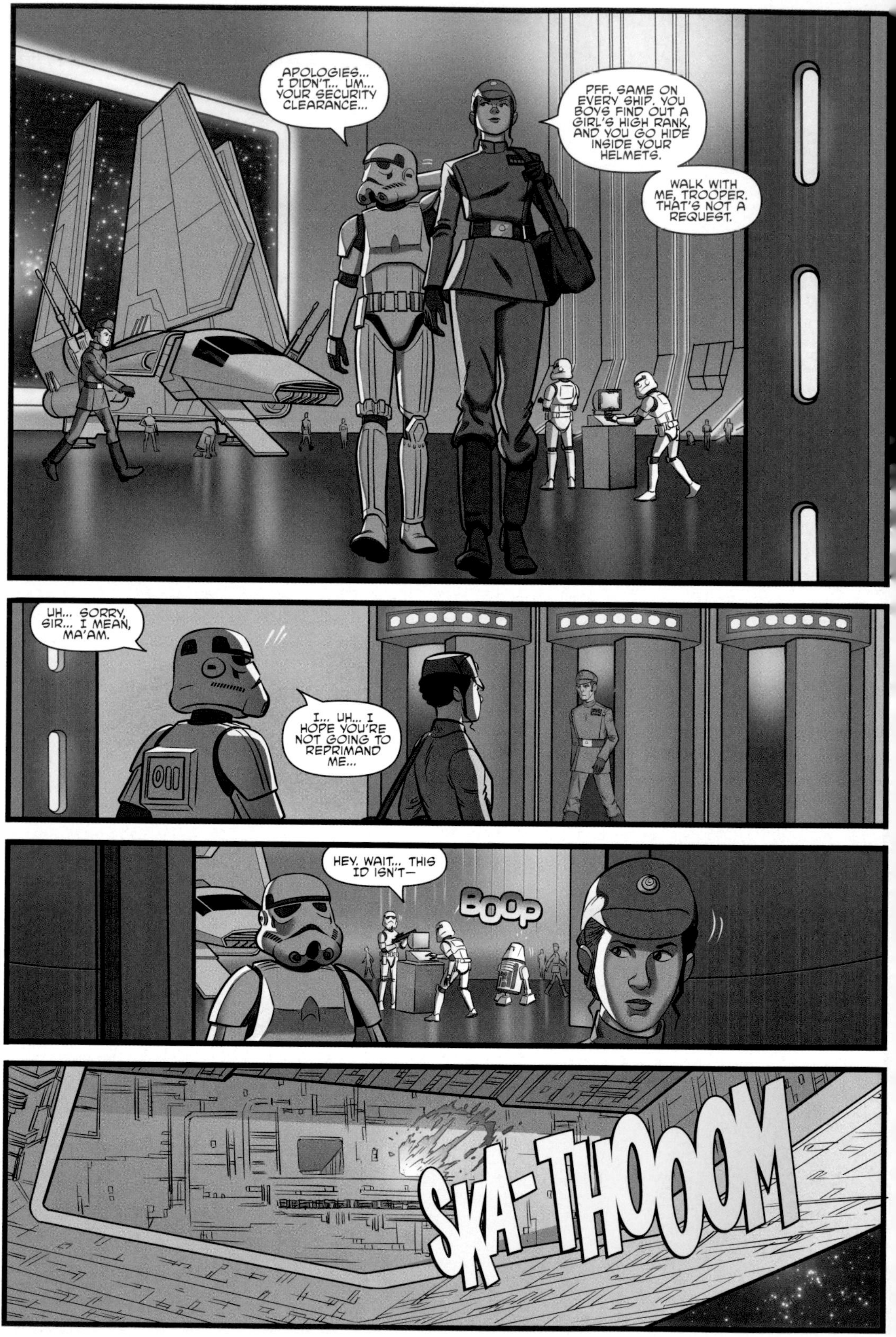
APOLOGIES... I DIDN'T... UM... YOUR SECURITY CLEARANCE...
PFF. SAME ON EVERY SHIP. YOU BOYS FIND OUT A GIRL'S HIGH RANK, AND YOU GO HIDE INSIDE YOUR HELMETS.
WALK WITH ME, TROOPER. THAT'S NOT A REQUEST.
UH... SORRY, SIR... I MEAN, MA'AM.
I... UH... I HOPE YOU'RE NOT GOING TO REPRIMAND ME...
HEY. WAIT... THIS ID ISN'T—
BOOP
SKA-THOOOM

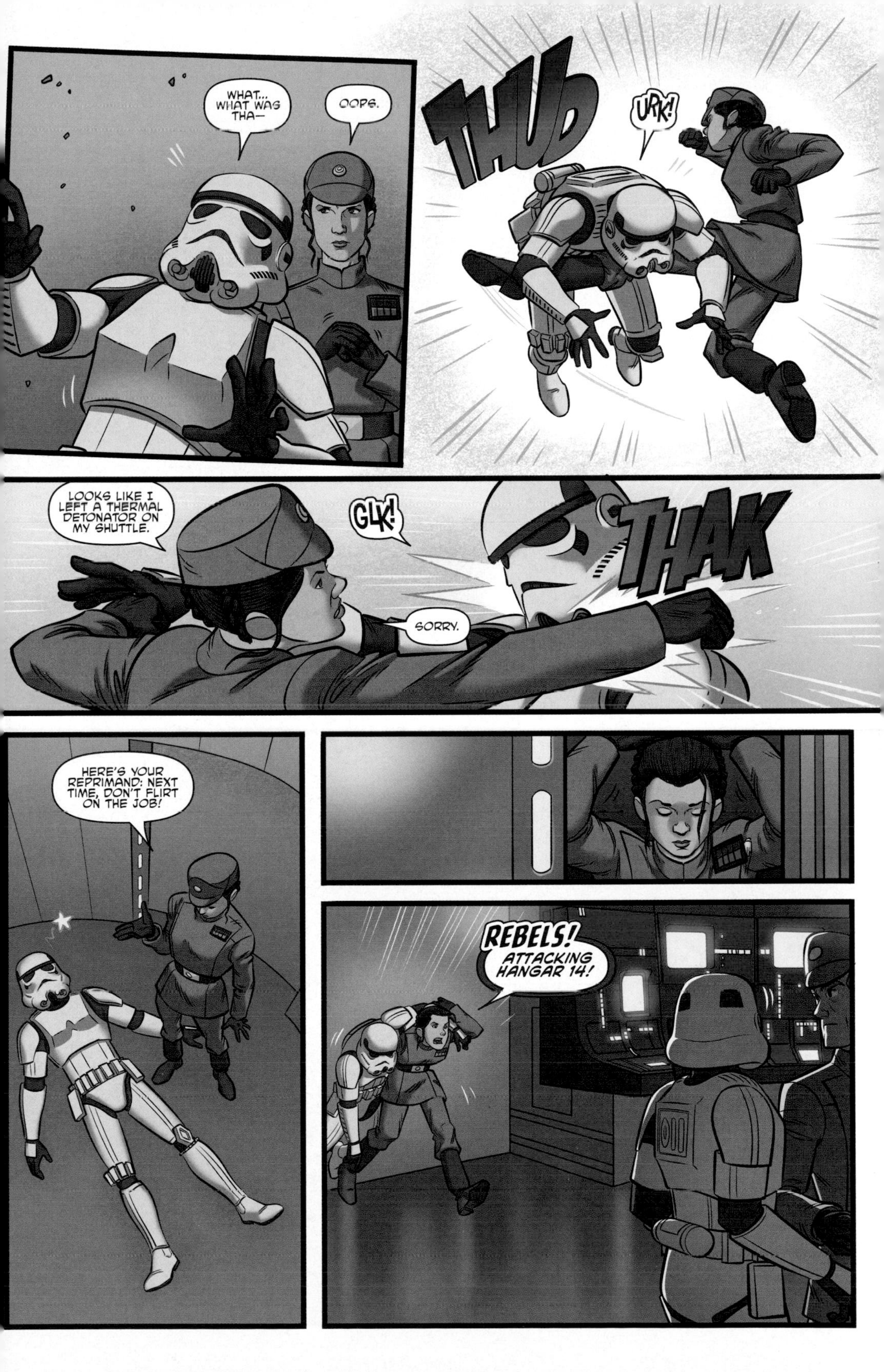
WHAT... WHAT WAS THA—
OOPS.
THUD
URK!
LOOKS LIKE I LEFT A THERMAL DETONATOR ON MY SHUTTLE.
GLK!
THAK
SORRY.
HERE'S YOUR REPRIMAND: NEXT TIME, DON'T FLIRT ON THE JOB!
REBELS! ATTACKING HANGAR 14!

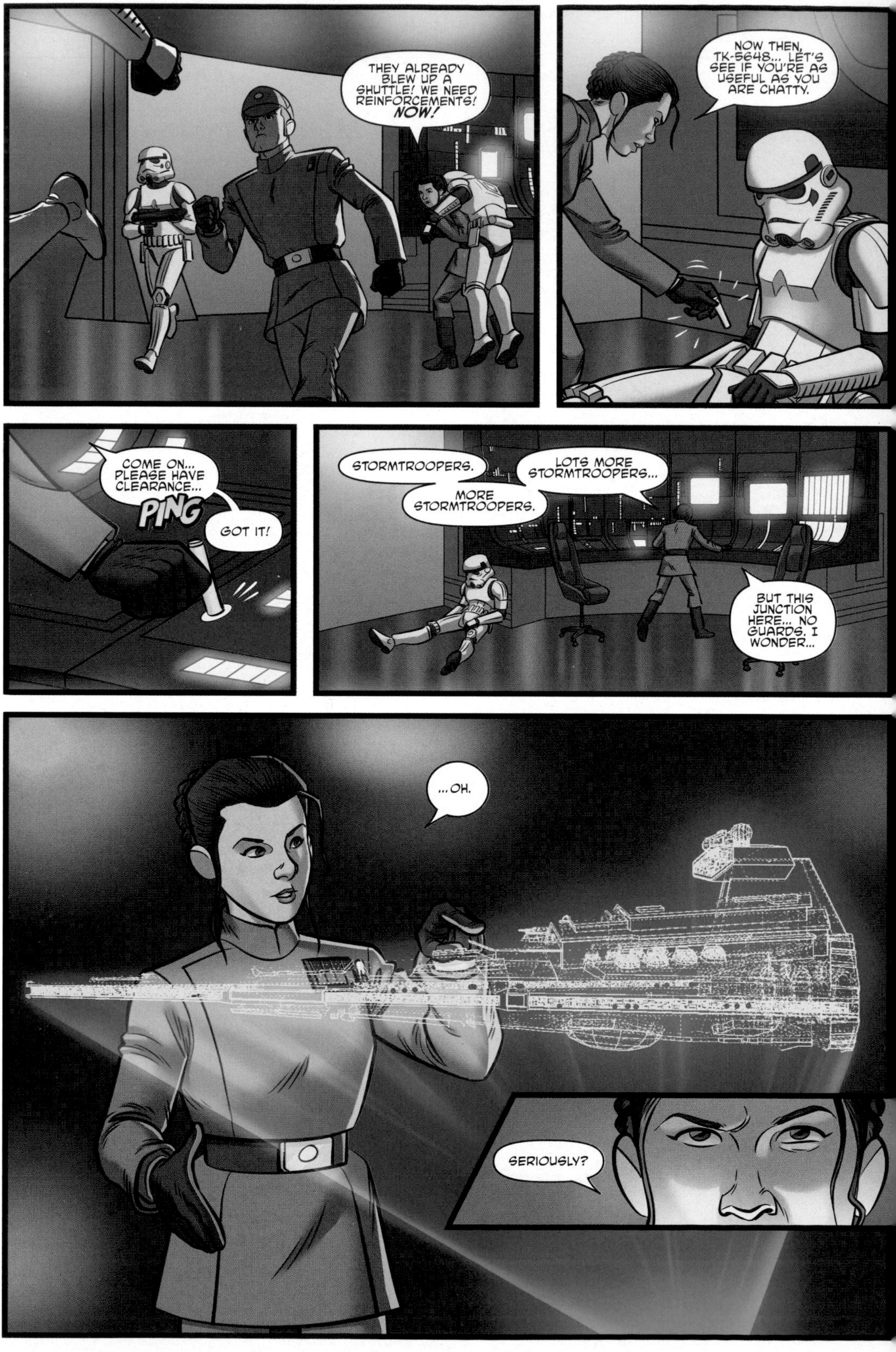
THEY ALREADY BLEW UP A SHUTTLE! WE NEED REINFORCEMENTS! NOW!
NOW THEN, TK-5648... LET'S SEE IF YOU'RE AS USEFUL AS YOU ARE CHATTY.
COME ON... PLEASE HAVE CLEARANCE...
PING
GOT IT!
STORMTROOPERS.
MORE STORMTROOPERS.
LOTS MORE STORMTROOPERS...
BUT THIS JUNCTION HERE... NO GUARDS. I WONDER...
...OH.
SERIOUSLY?

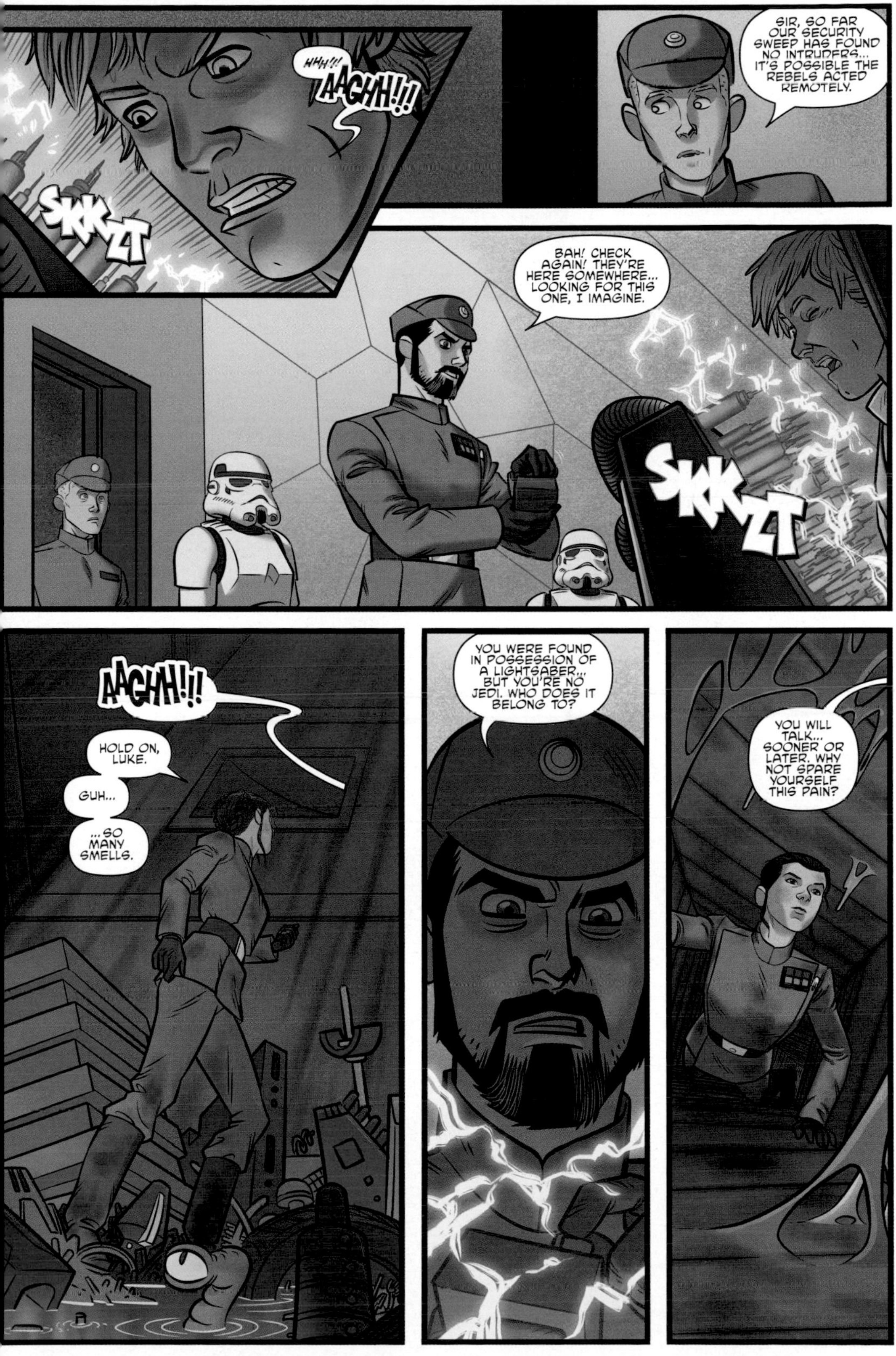
HHH!!!
AAGHH!!!
SKKZZT
SIR, SO FAR OUR SECURITY SWEEP HAS FOUND NO INTRUDERS... IT'S POSSIBLE THE REBELS ACTED REMOTELY.
BAH! CHECK AGAIN! THEY'RE HERE SOMEWHERE... LOOKING FOR THIS ONE, I IMAGINE.
SKKZZT
AAGHH!!!
HOLD ON, LUKE.
GUH...
...SO MANY SMELLS.
YOU WERE FOUND IN POSSESSION OF A LIGHTSABER... BUT YOU'RE NO JEDI. WHO DOES IT BELONG TO?
YOU WILL TALK... SOONER OR LATER. WHY NOT SPARE YOURSELF THIS PAIN?

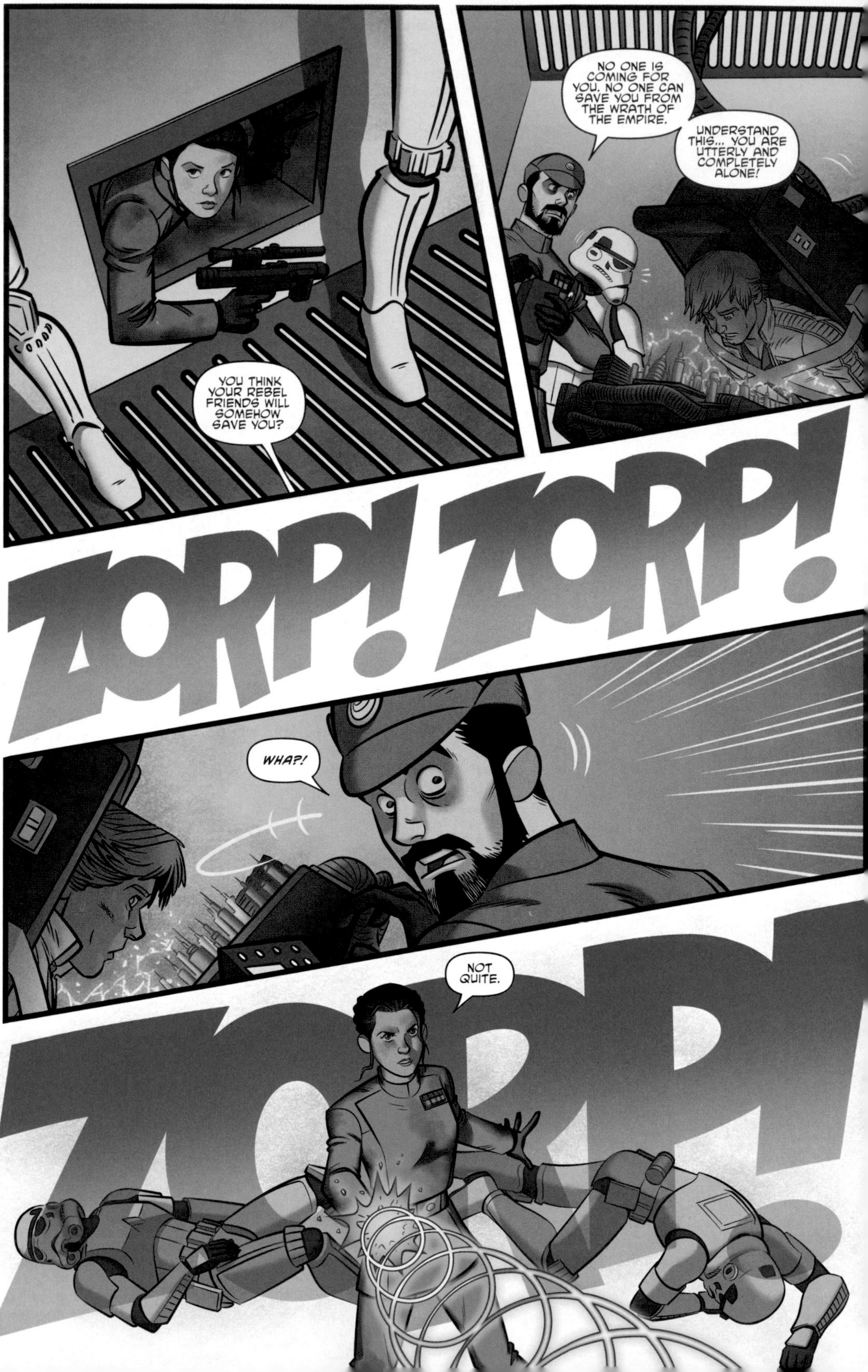
YOU THINK YOUR REBEL FRIENDS WILL SOMEHOW SAVE YOU?
NO ONE IS COMING FOR YOU. NO ONE CAN SAVE YOU FROM THE WRATH OF THE EMPIRE.
UNDERSTAND THIS... YOU ARE UTTERLY AND COMPLETELY ALONE!
ZORP! ZORP!
WHA?!
NOT QUITE.
ZORP!

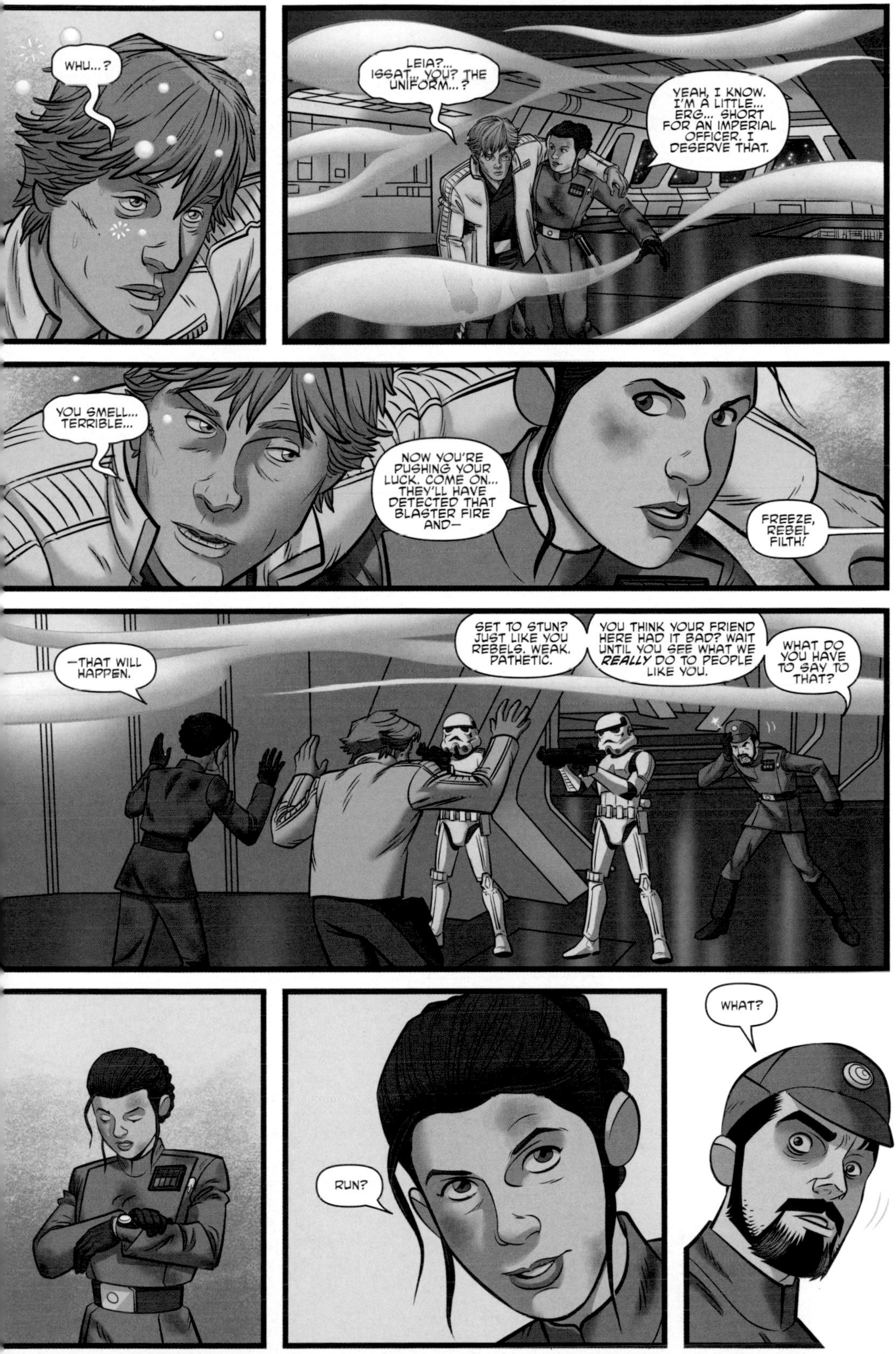
WHU...?
LEIA?... ISSAT... YOU? THE UNIFORM...?
YEAH, I KNOW. I'M A LITTLE... ERG... SHORT FOR AN IMPERIAL OFFICER. I DESERVE THAT.
YOU SMELL... TERRIBLE...
NOW YOU'RE PUSHING YOUR LUCK. COME ON... THEY'LL HAVE DETECTED THAT BLASTER FIRE AND—
FREEZE, REBEL FILTH!
—THAT WILL HAPPEN.
SET TO STUN? JUST LIKE YOU REBELS. WEAK. PATHETIC.
YOU THINK YOUR FRIEND HERE HAD IT BAD? WAIT UNTIL YOU SEE WHAT WE *REALLY* DO TO PEOPLE LIKE YOU.
WHAT DO YOU HAVE TO SAY TO THAT?
RUN?
WHAT?

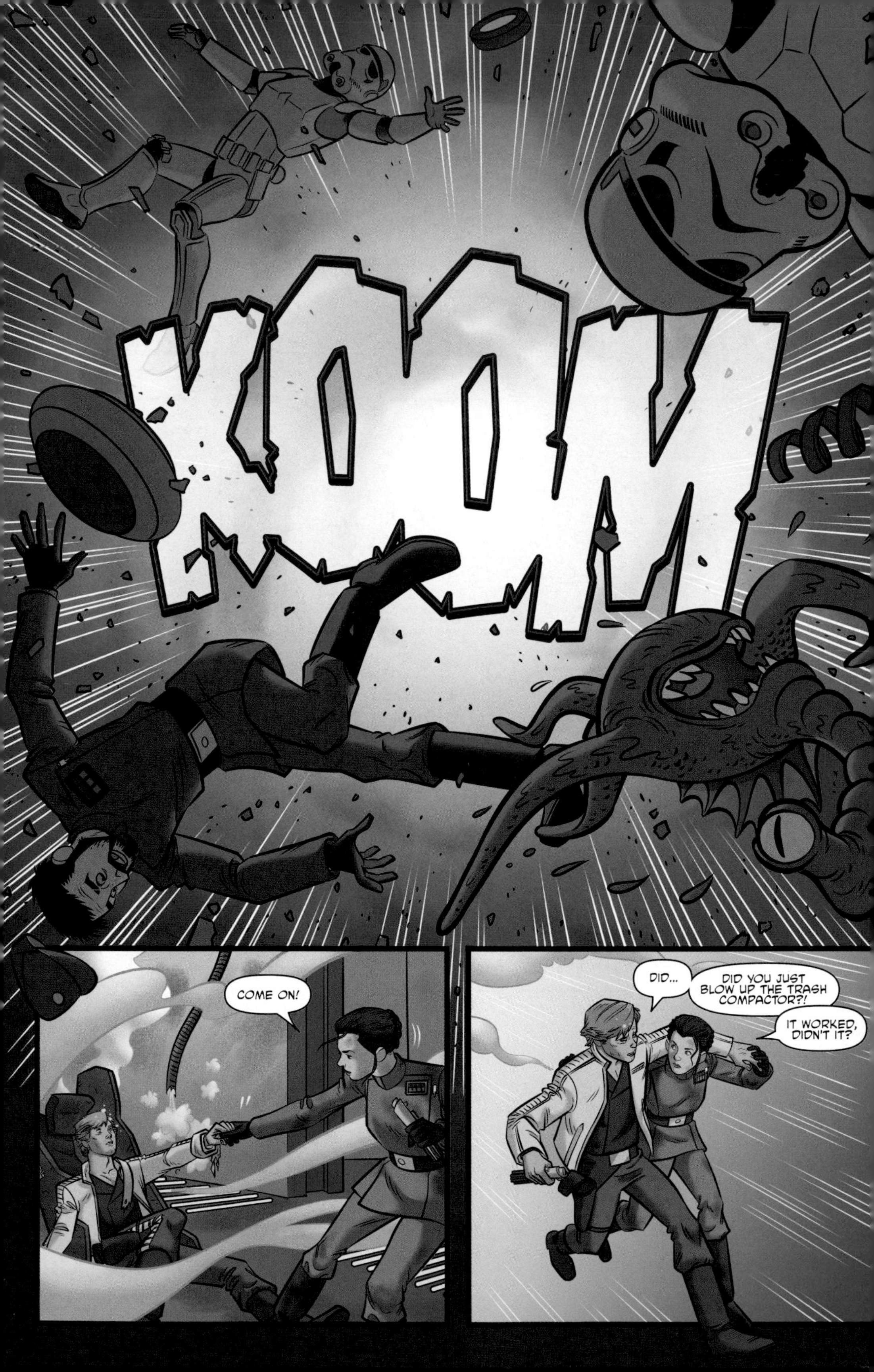
KOOM
COME ON!
DID...
DID YOU JUST BLOW UP THE TRASH COMPACTOR?!
IT WORKED, DIDN'T IT?

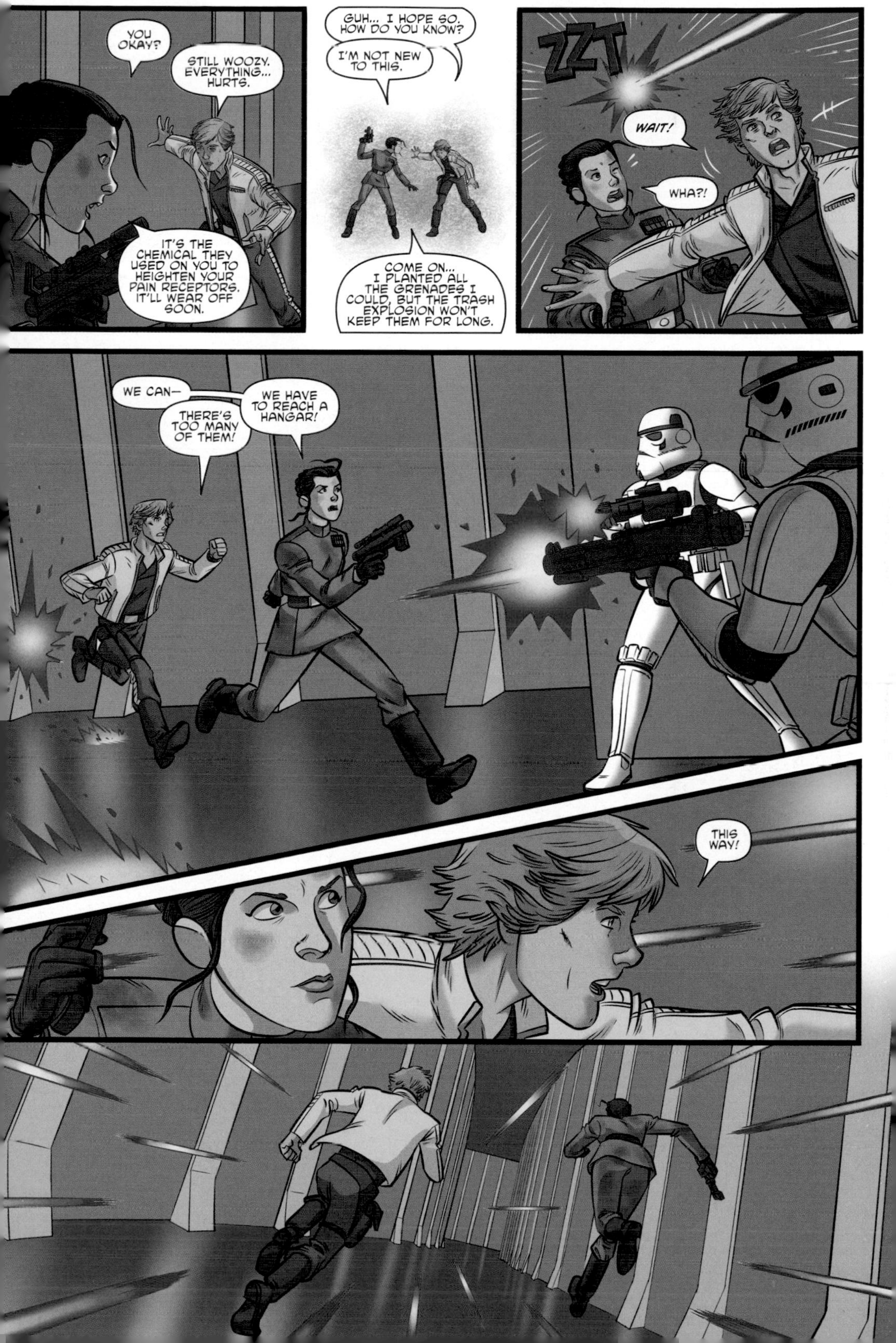
YOU OKAY?
STILL WOOZY. EVERYTHING... HURTS.
IT'S THE CHEMICAL THEY USED ON YOU TO HEIGHTEN YOUR PAIN RECEPTORS. IT'LL WEAR OFF SOON.
GUH... I HOPE SO. HOW DO YOU KNOW?
I'M NOT NEW TO THIS.
COME ON... I PLANTED ALL THE GRENADES I COULD, BUT THE TRASH EXPLOSION WON'T KEEP THEM FOR LONG.
ZZT
WAIT!
WHA?!
WE CAN—
WE HAVE TO REACH A HANGAR!
THERE'S TOO MANY OF THEM!
THIS WAY!

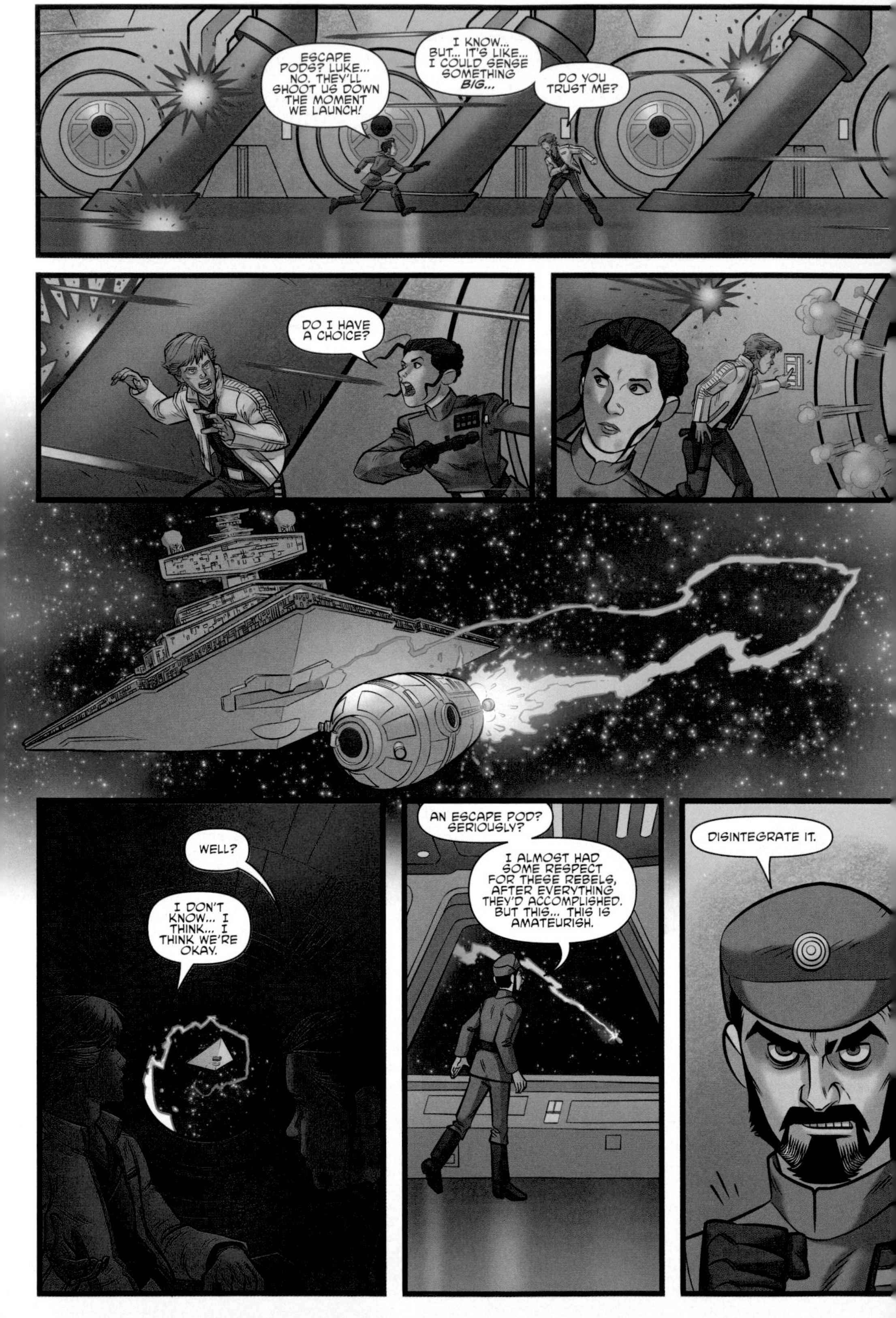
ESCAPE PODS? LUKE... NO. THEY'LL SHOOT US DOWN THE MOMENT WE LAUNCH!
I KNOW... BUT... IT'S LIKE... I COULD SENSE SOMETHING BIG...
DO YOU TRUST ME?
DO I HAVE A CHOICE?
WELL?
I DON'T KNOW... I THINK... I THINK WE'RE OKAY.
AN ESCAPE POD? SERIOUSLY?
I ALMOST HAD SOME RESPECT FOR THESE REBELS, AFTER EVERYTHING THEY'D ACCOMPLISHED. BUT THIS... THIS IS AMATEURISH.
DISINTEGRATE IT.

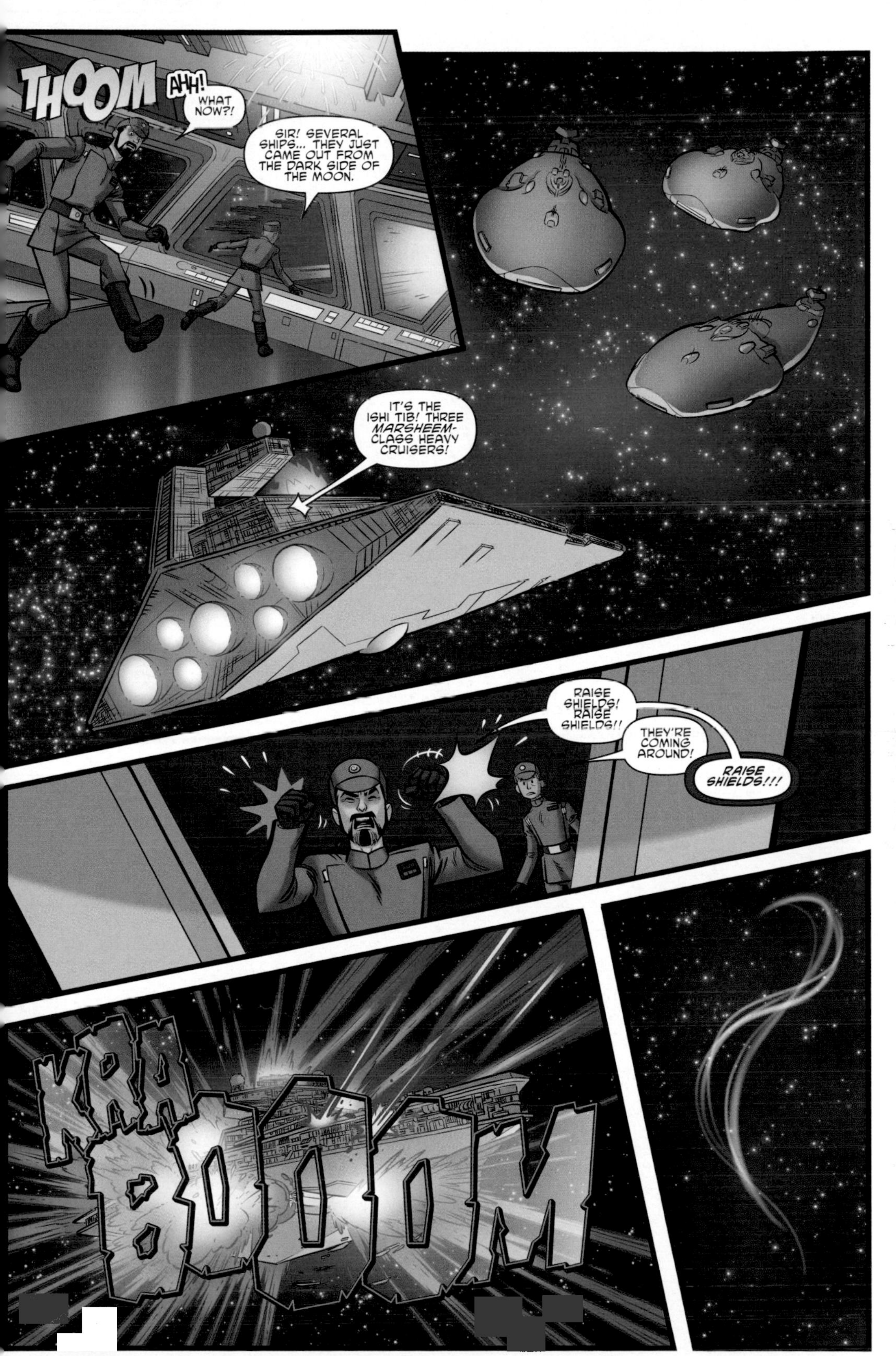
THOOM
AHH! WHAT NOW?!
SIR! SEVERAL SHIPS... THEY JUST CAME OUT FROM THE DARK SIDE OF THE MOON.
IT'S THE ISHI TIB! THREE *MARSHEEM*-CLASS HEAVY CRUISERS!
RAISE SHIELDS! RAISE SHIELDS!!
THEY'RE COMING AROUND!
RAISE SHIELDS!!!
KRA BOOOM
[redacted]

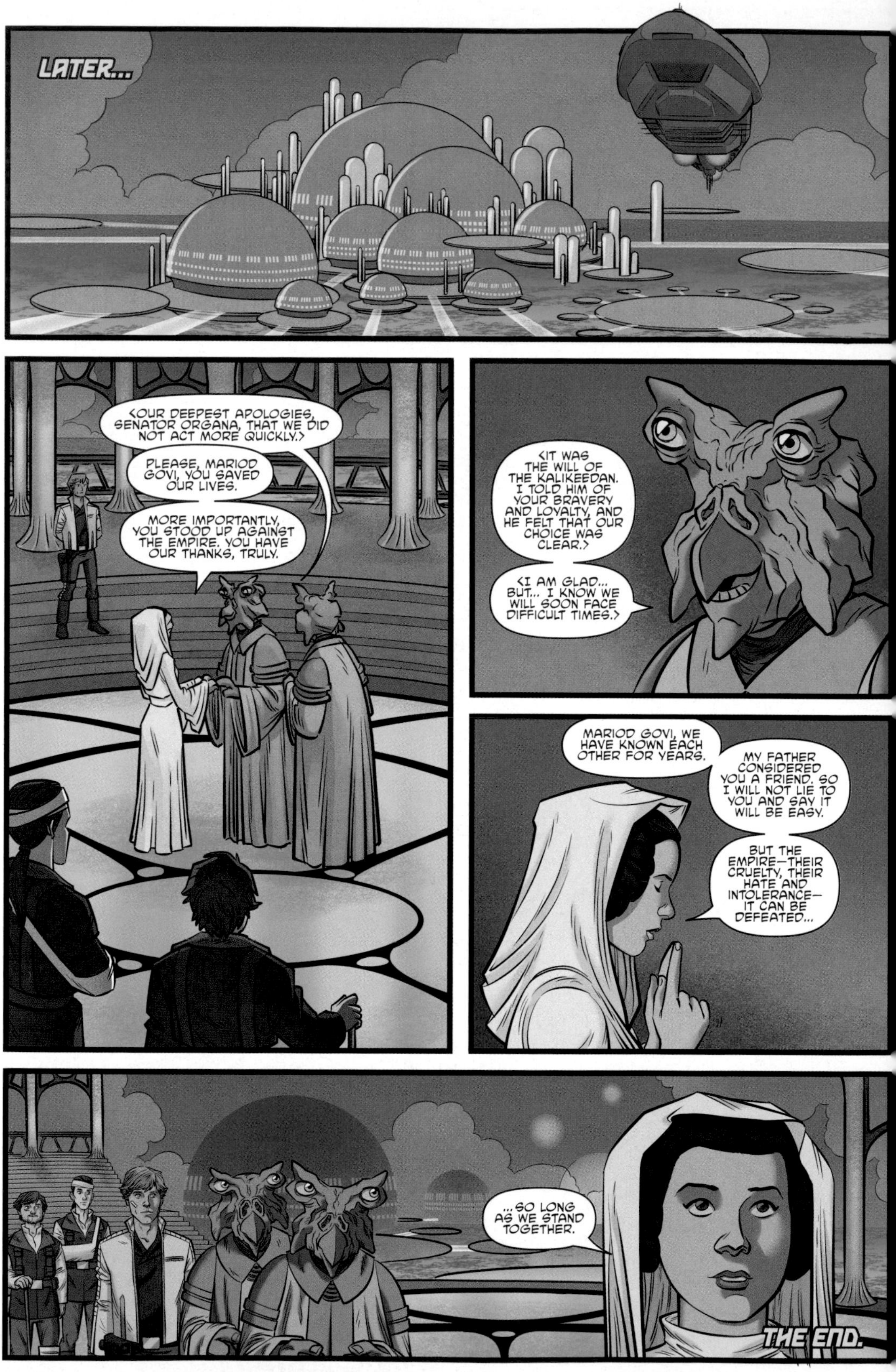
LATER...
<OUR DEEPEST APOLOGIES, SENATOR ORGANA, THAT WE DID NOT ACT MORE QUICKLY.>
PLEASE, MARIOD GOVI, YOU SAVED OUR LIVES.
MORE IMPORTANTLY, YOU STOOD UP AGAINST THE EMPIRE. YOU HAVE OUR THANKS, TRULY.
<IT WAS THE WILL OF THE KALIKEEDAN. I TOLD HIM OF YOUR BRAVERY AND LOYALTY, AND HE FELT THAT OUR CHOICE WAS CLEAR.>
<I AM GLAD... BUT... I KNOW WE WILL SOON FACE DIFFICULT TIMES.>
MARIOD GOVI, WE HAVE KNOWN EACH OTHER FOR YEARS.
MY FATHER CONSIDERED YOU A FRIEND. SO I WILL NOT LIE TO YOU AND SAY IT WILL BE EASY.
BUT THE EMPIRE—THEIR CRUELTY, THEIR HATE AND INTOLERANCE—IT CAN BE DEFEATED...
...SO LONG AS WE STAND TOGETHER.
THE END.

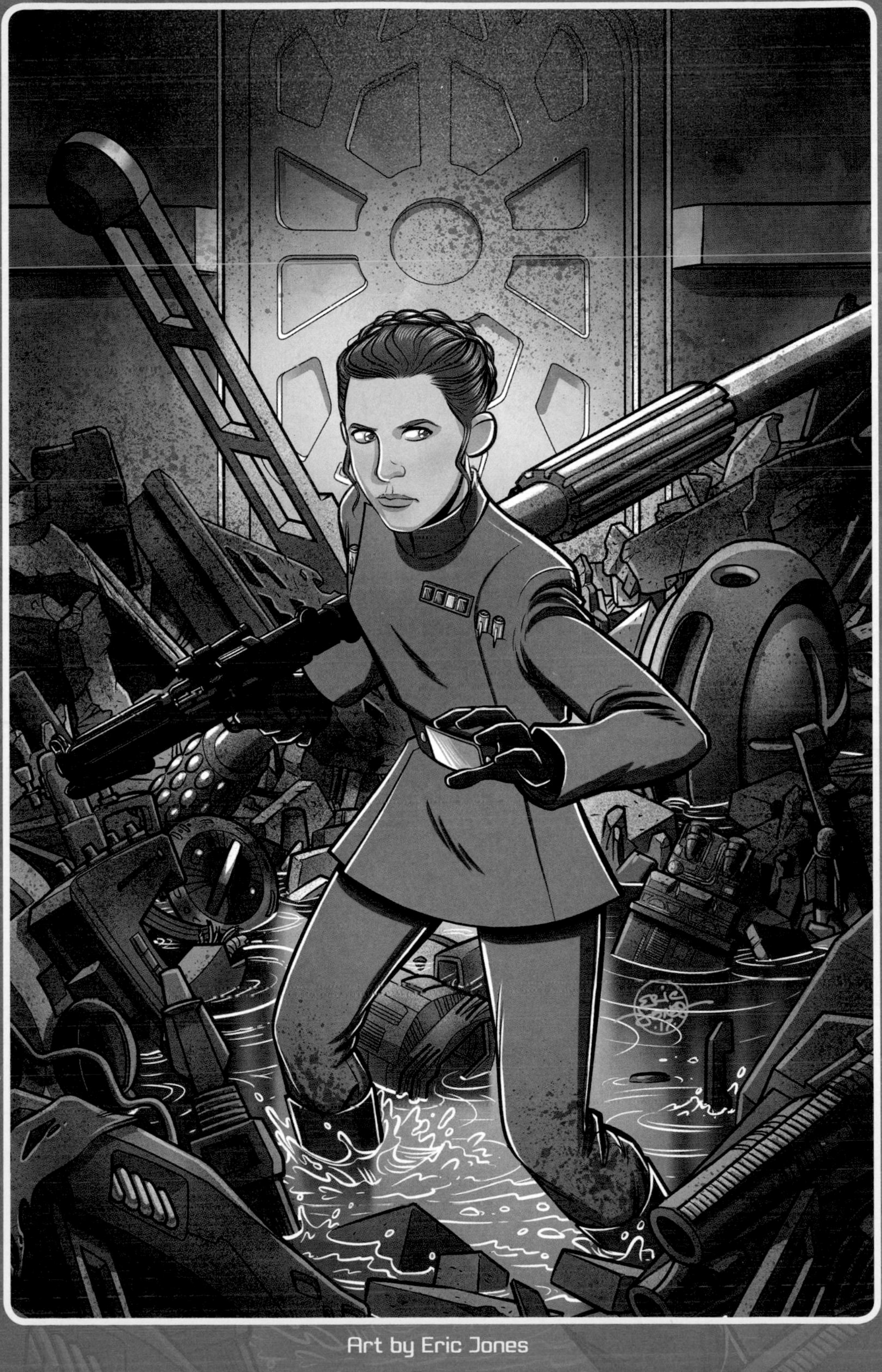

Art by Eric Jones

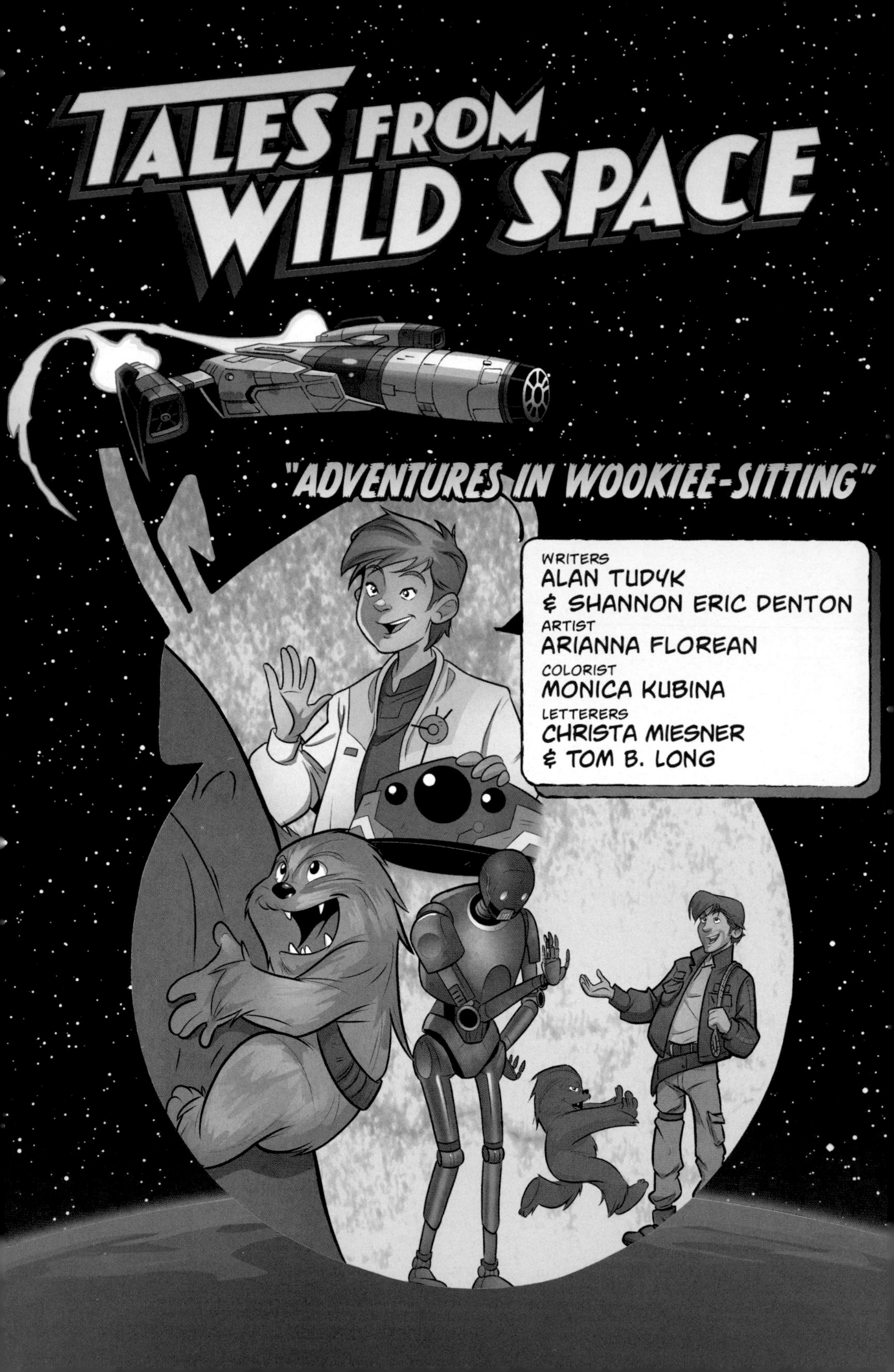

TALES FROM WILD SPACE
"ADVENTURES IN WOOKIEE-SITTING"
WRITERS
ALAN TUDYK
& SHANNON ERIC DENTON
ARTIST
ARIANNA FLOREAN
COLORIST
MONICA KUBINA
LETTERERS
CHRISTA MIESNER
& TOM B. LONG

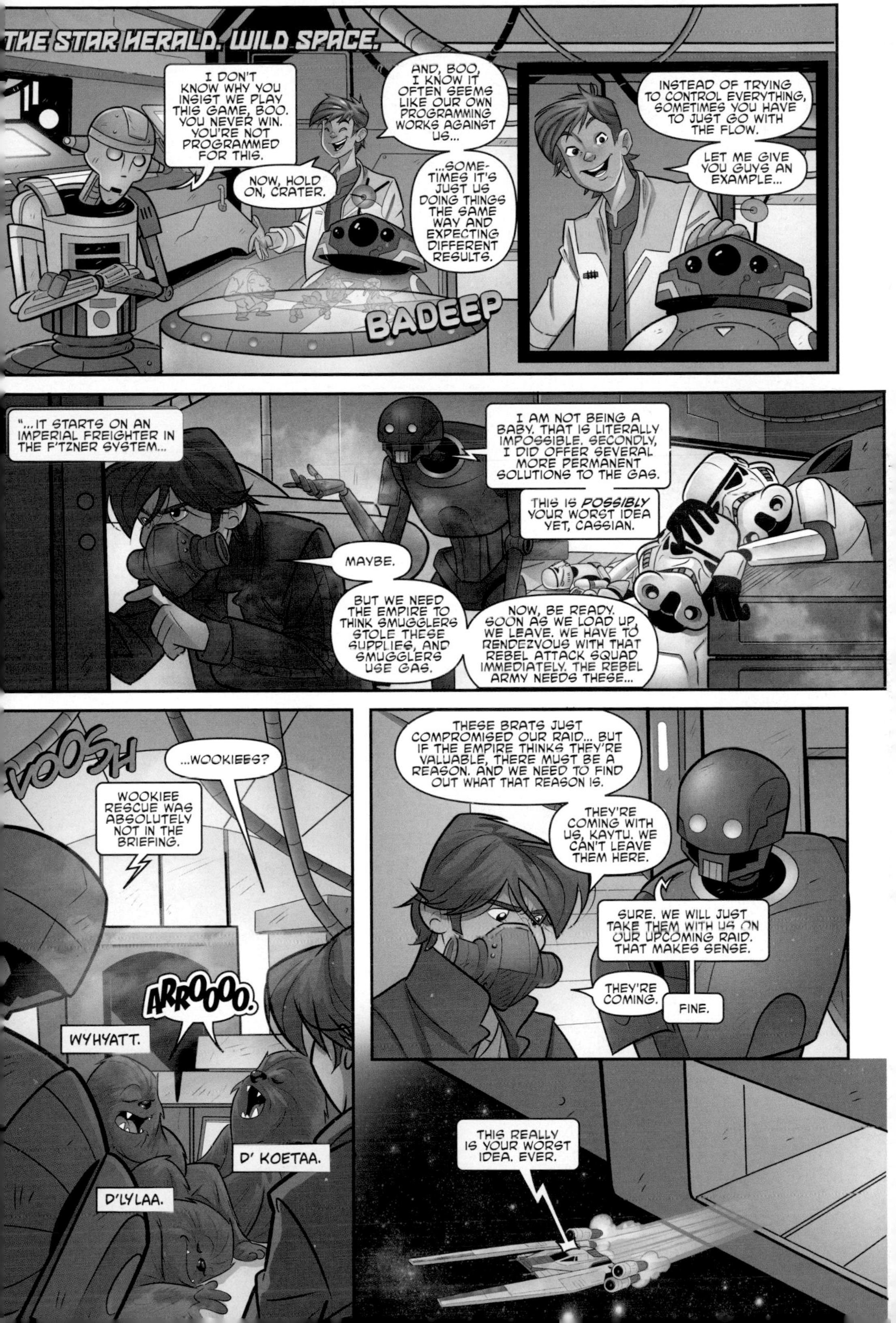
THE STAR HERALD. WILD SPACE.
I DON'T KNOW WHY YOU INSIST WE PLAY THIS GAME, BOO. YOU NEVER WIN. YOU'RE NOT PROGRAMMED FOR THIS.
NOW, HOLD ON, CRATER.
AND, BOO, I KNOW IT OFTEN SEEMS LIKE OUR OWN PROGRAMMING WORKS AGAINST US...
...SOMETIMES IT'S JUST US DOING THINGS THE SAME WAY AND EXPECTING DIFFERENT RESULTS.
BADEEP
INSTEAD OF TRYING TO CONTROL EVERYTHING, SOMETIMES YOU HAVE TO JUST GO WITH THE FLOW.
LET ME GIVE YOU GUYS AN EXAMPLE...
"...IT STARTS ON AN IMPERIAL FREIGHTER IN THE F'TZNER SYSTEM...
I AM NOT BEING A BABY. THAT IS LITERALLY IMPOSSIBLE. SECONDLY, I DID OFFER SEVERAL MORE PERMANENT SOLUTIONS TO THE GAS.
THIS IS *POSSIBLY* YOUR WORST IDEA YET, CASSIAN.
MAYBE.
BUT WE NEED THE EMPIRE TO THINK SMUGGLERS STOLE THESE SUPPLIES, AND SMUGGLERS USE GAS.
NOW, BE READY. SOON AS WE LOAD UP, WE LEAVE. WE HAVE TO RENDEZVOUS WITH THAT REBEL ATTACK SQUAD IMMEDIATELY. THE REBEL ARMY NEEDS THESE...
VOOSH
...WOOKIEES?
WOOKIEE RESCUE WAS ABSOLUTELY NOT IN THE BRIEFING.
ARROOOO.
WYHYATT.
D' KOETAA.
D'LYLAA.
THESE BRATS JUST COMPROMISED OUR RAID... BUT IF THE EMPIRE THINKS THEY'RE VALUABLE, THERE MUST BE A REASON. AND WE NEED TO FIND OUT WHAT THAT REASON IS.
THEY'RE COMING WITH US, KAYTU. WE CAN'T LEAVE THEM HERE.
SURE. WE WILL JUST TAKE THEM WITH US ON OUR UPCOMING RAID. THAT MAKES SENSE.
THEY'RE COMING.
FINE.
THIS REALLY IS YOUR WORST IDEA. EVER.

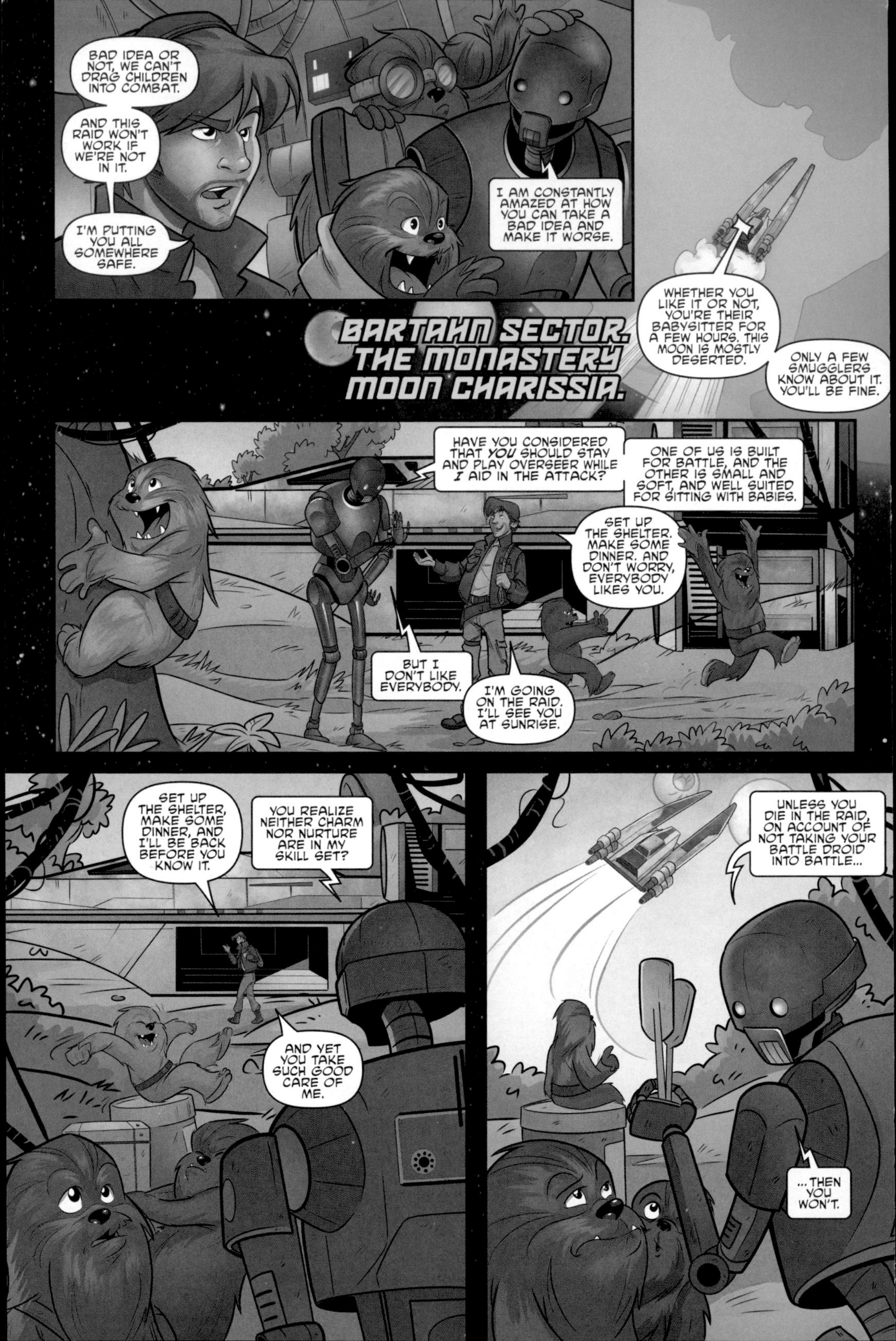
BAD IDEA OR NOT, WE CAN'T DRAG CHILDREN INTO COMBAT.
AND THIS RAID WON'T WORK IF WE'RE NOT IN IT.
I'M PUTTING YOU ALL SOMEWHERE SAFE.
I AM CONSTANTLY AMAZED AT HOW YOU CAN TAKE A BAD IDEA AND MAKE IT WORSE.
WHETHER YOU LIKE IT OR NOT, YOU'RE THEIR BABYSITTER FOR A FEW HOURS. THIS MOON IS MOSTLY DESERTED.
ONLY A FEW SMUGGLERS KNOW ABOUT IT. YOU'LL BE FINE.
BARTAHN SECTOR. THE MONASTERY MOON CHARISSIA.
HAVE YOU CONSIDERED THAT YOU SHOULD STAY AND PLAY OVERSEER WHILE I AID IN THE ATTACK?
ONE OF US IS BUILT FOR BATTLE, AND THE OTHER IS SMALL AND SOFT, AND WELL SUITED FOR SITTING WITH BABIES.
SET UP THE SHELTER. MAKE SOME DINNER. AND DON'T WORRY, EVERYBODY LIKES YOU.
BUT I DON'T LIKE EVERYBODY.
I'M GOING ON THE RAID. I'LL SEE YOU AT SUNRISE.
SET UP THE SHELTER, MAKE SOME DINNER, AND I'LL BE BACK BEFORE YOU KNOW IT.
YOU REALIZE NEITHER CHARM NOR NURTURE ARE IN MY SKILL SET?
AND YET YOU TAKE SUCH GOOD CARE OF ME.
UNLESS YOU DIE IN THE RAID, ON ACCOUNT OF NOT TAKING YOUR BATTLE DROID INTO BATTLE...
...THEN YOU WON'T.

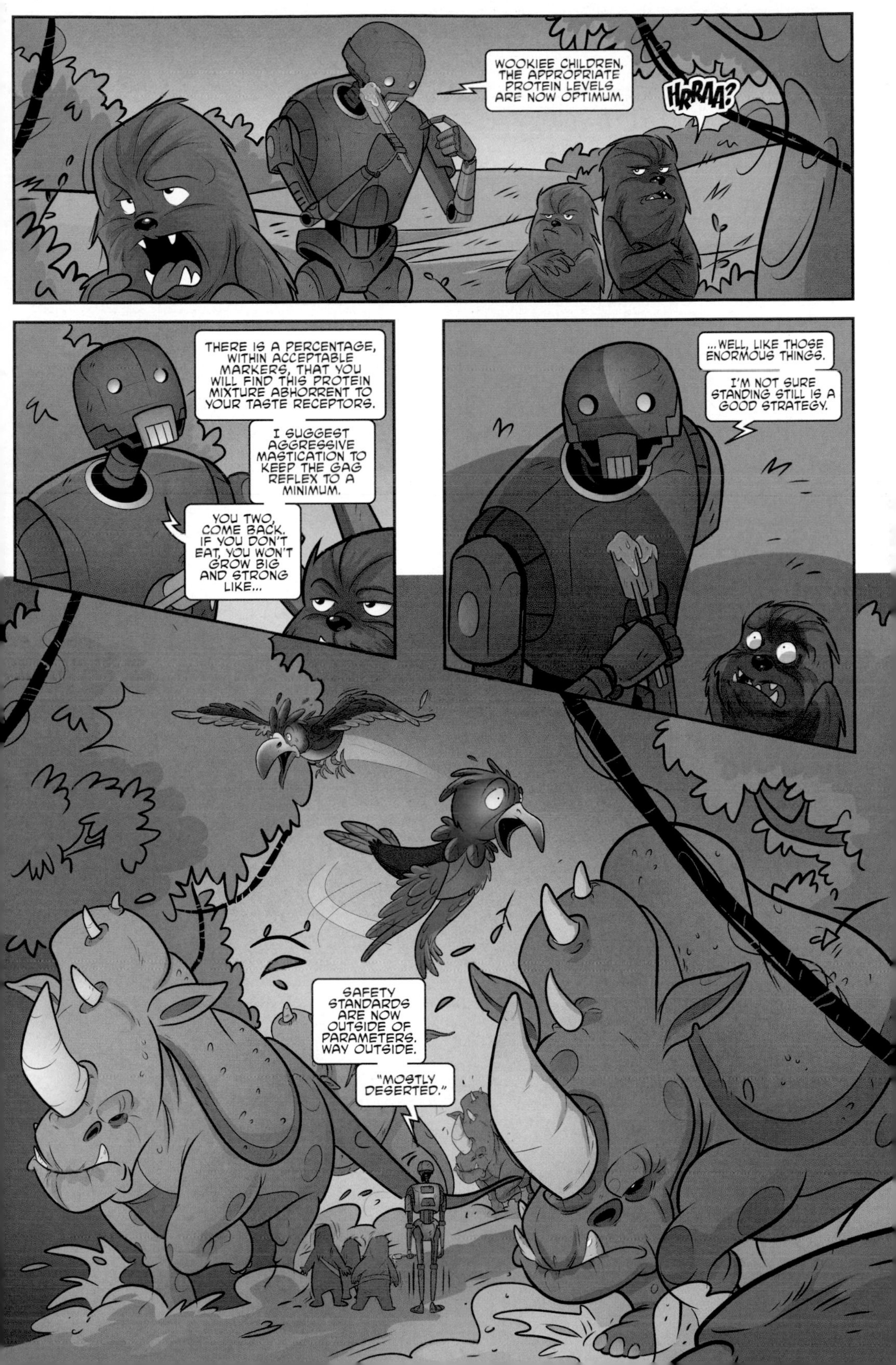
WOOKIEE CHILDREN, THE APPROPRIATE PROTEIN LEVELS ARE NOW OPTIMUM.
HRRAA?
THERE IS A PERCENTAGE, WITHIN ACCEPTABLE MARKERS, THAT YOU WILL FIND THIS PROTEIN MIXTURE ABHORRENT TO YOUR TASTE RECEPTORS.
I SUGGEST AGGRESSIVE MASTICATION TO KEEP THE GAG REFLEX TO A MINIMUM.
YOU TWO, COME BACK. IF YOU DON'T EAT, YOU WON'T GROW BIG AND STRONG LIKE...
...WELL, LIKE THOSE ENORMOUS THINGS.
I'M NOT SURE STANDING STILL IS A GOOD STRATEGY.
SAFETY STANDARDS ARE NOW OUTSIDE OF PARAMETERS. WAY OUTSIDE.
"MOSTLY DESERTED."

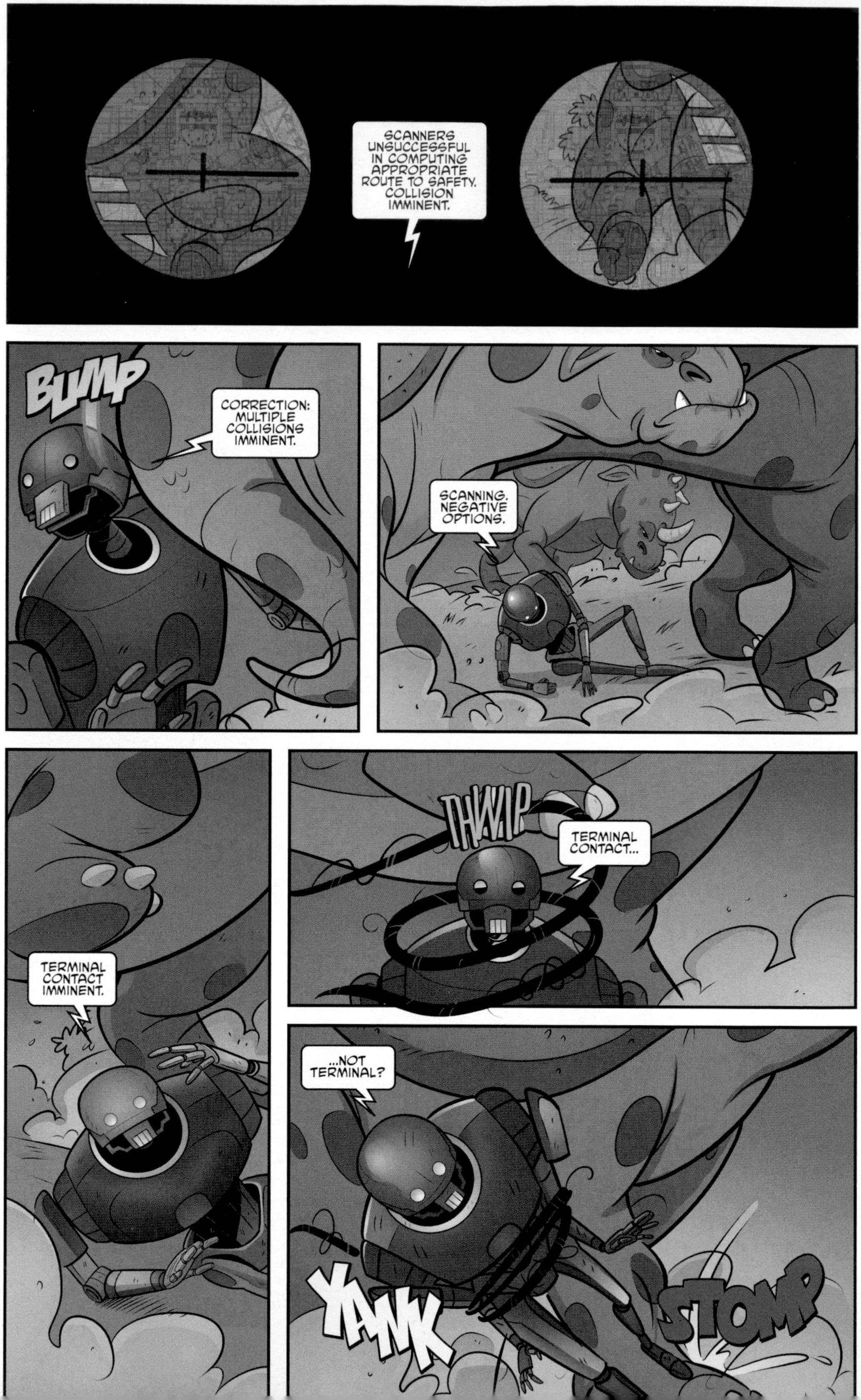
SCANNERS UNSUCCESSFUL IN COMPUTING APPROPRIATE ROUTE TO SAFETY. COLLISION IMMINENT.
BUMP
CORRECTION: MULTIPLE COLLISIONS IMMINENT.
SCANNING. NEGATIVE OPTIONS.
TERMINAL CONTACT IMMINENT.
THWIP
TERMINAL CONTACT...
...NOT TERMINAL?
YANK
STOMP

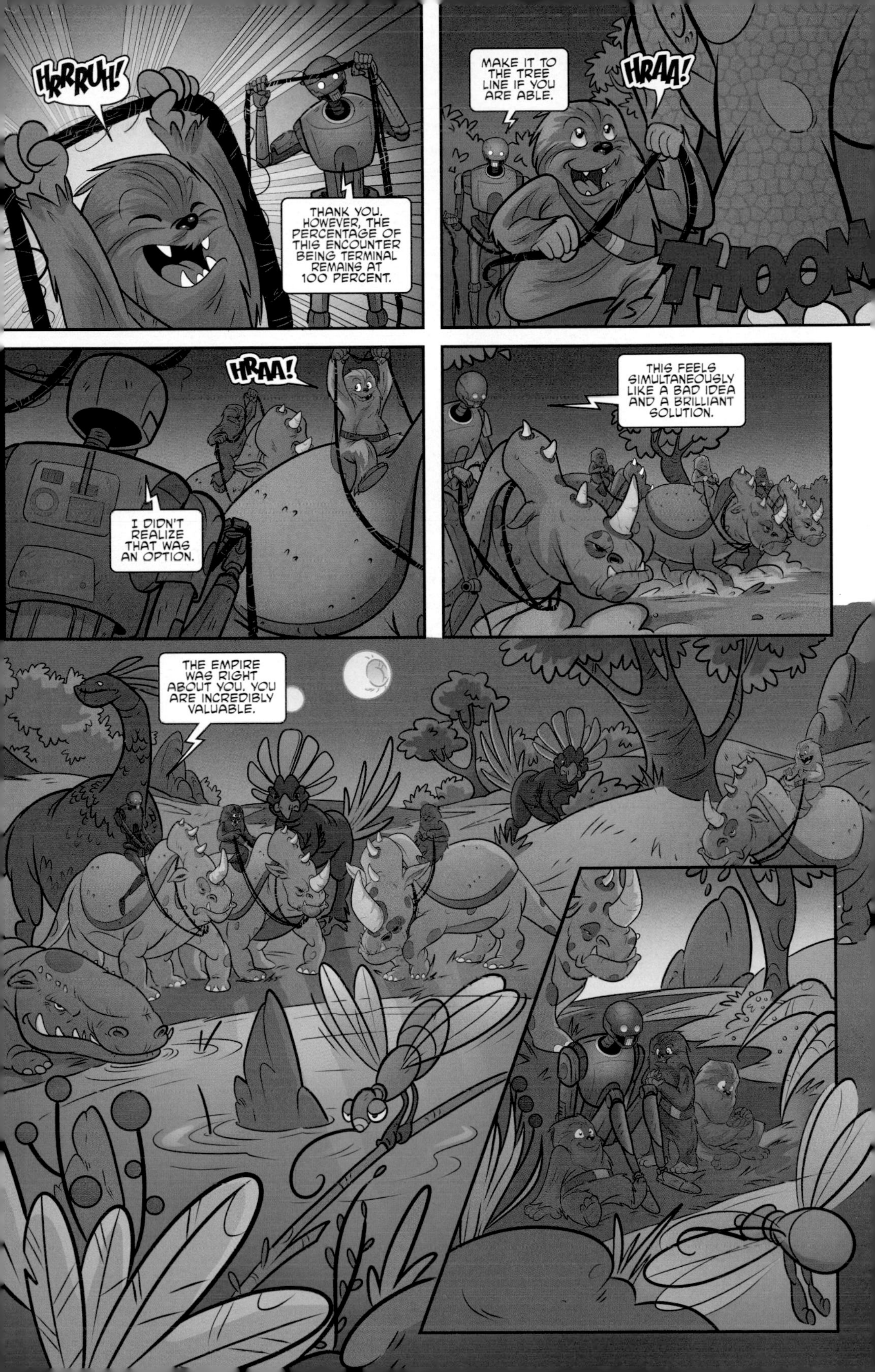
HRRRUH!
THANK YOU. HOWEVER, THE PERCENTAGE OF THIS ENCOUNTER BEING TERMINAL REMAINS AT 100 PERCENT.
MAKE IT TO THE TREE LINE IF YOU ARE ABLE.
HRAA!
THOOM
HRAA!
I DIDN'T REALIZE THAT WAS AN OPTION.
THIS FEELS SIMULTANEOUSLY LIKE A BAD IDEA AND A BRILLIANT SOLUTION.
THE EMPIRE WAS RIGHT ABOUT YOU. YOU ARE INCREDIBLY VALUABLE.

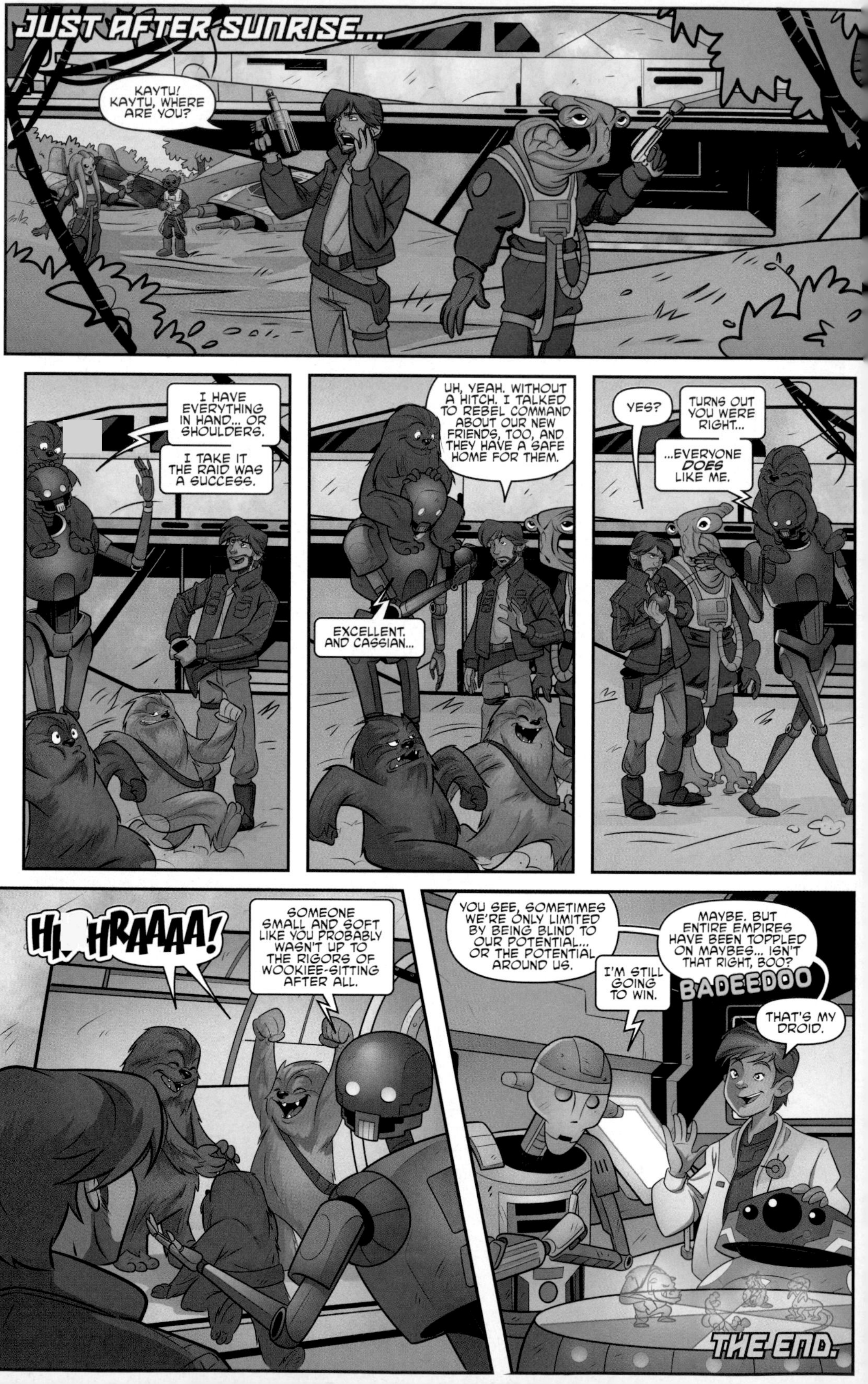
JUST AFTER SUNRISE...
KAYTU! KAYTU, WHERE ARE YOU?
I HAVE EVERYTHING IN HAND... OR SHOULDERS.
I TAKE IT THE RAID WAS A SUCCESS.
UH, YEAH. WITHOUT A HITCH. I TALKED TO REBEL COMMAND ABOUT OUR NEW FRIENDS, TOO, AND THEY HAVE A SAFE HOME FOR THEM.
EXCELLENT. AND CASSIAN...
YES?
TURNS OUT YOU WERE RIGHT...
...EVERYONE DOES LIKE ME.
HI… HRAAAA!
SOMEONE SMALL AND SOFT LIKE YOU PROBABLY WASN'T UP TO THE RIGORS OF WOOKIEE-SITTING AFTER ALL.
YOU SEE, SOMETIMES WE'RE ONLY LIMITED BY BEING BLIND TO OUR POTENTIAL... OR THE POTENTIAL AROUND US.
I'M STILL GOING TO WIN.
MAYBE. BUT ENTIRE EMPIRES HAVE BEEN TOPPLED ON MAYBES... ISN'T THAT RIGHT, BOO?
BADEEDOO
THAT'S MY DROID.
THE END.

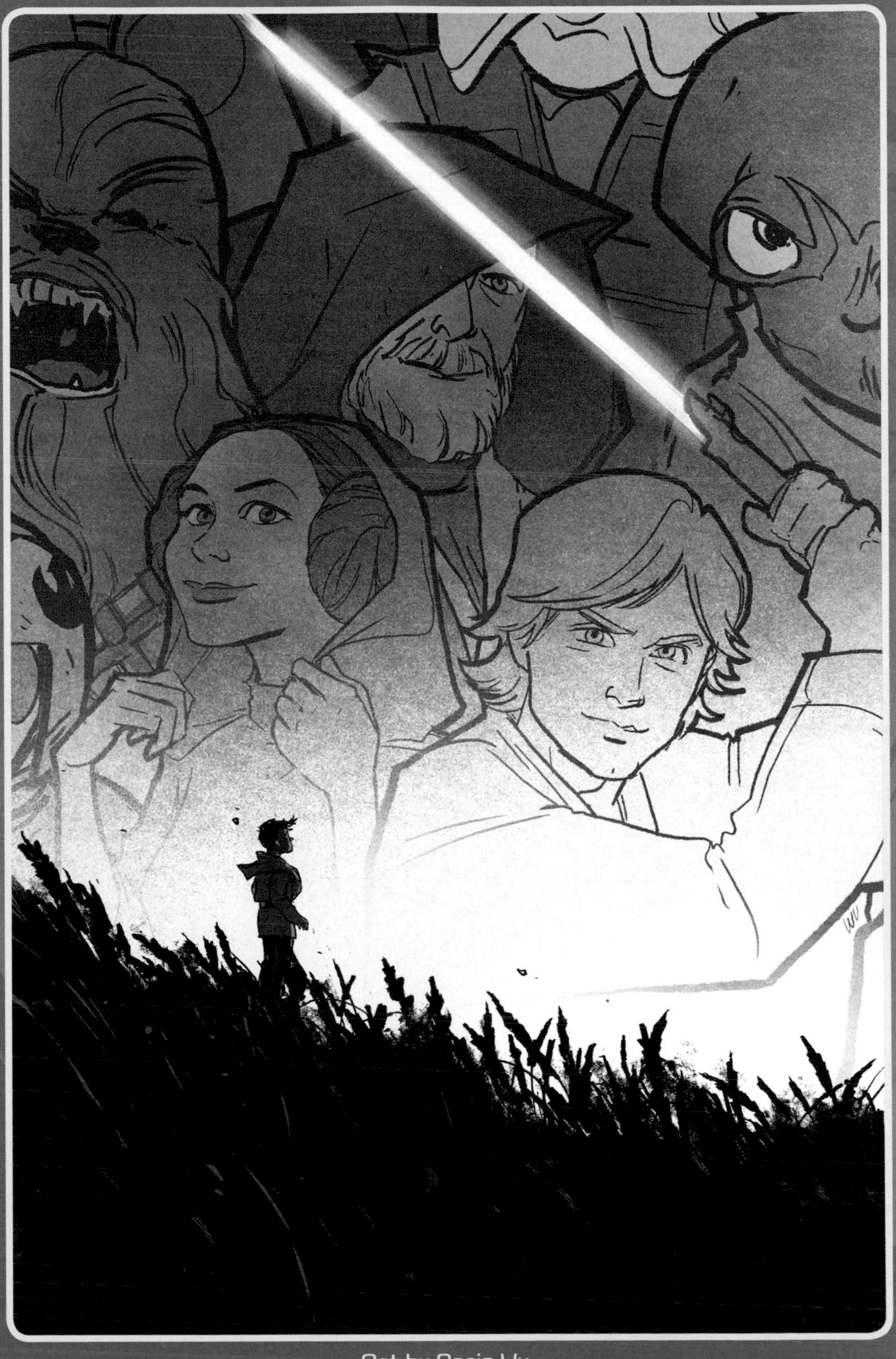
WU

Art by Annie Wu

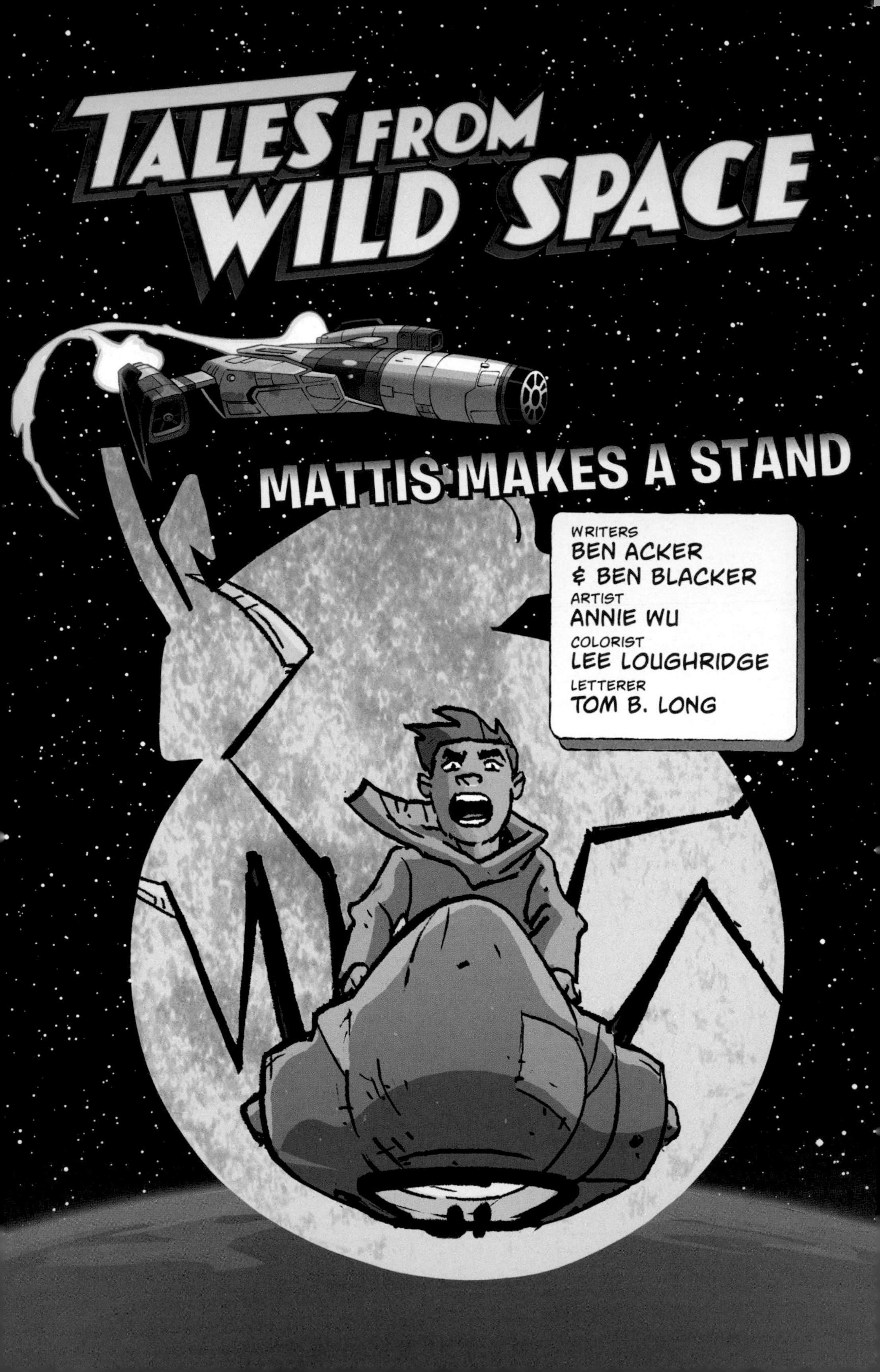
TALES FROM WILD SPACE
MATTIS MAKES A STAND
WRITERS
BEN ACKER
& BEN BLACKER
ARTIST
ANNIE WU
COLORIST
LEE LOUGHRIDGE
LETTERER
TOM B. LONG

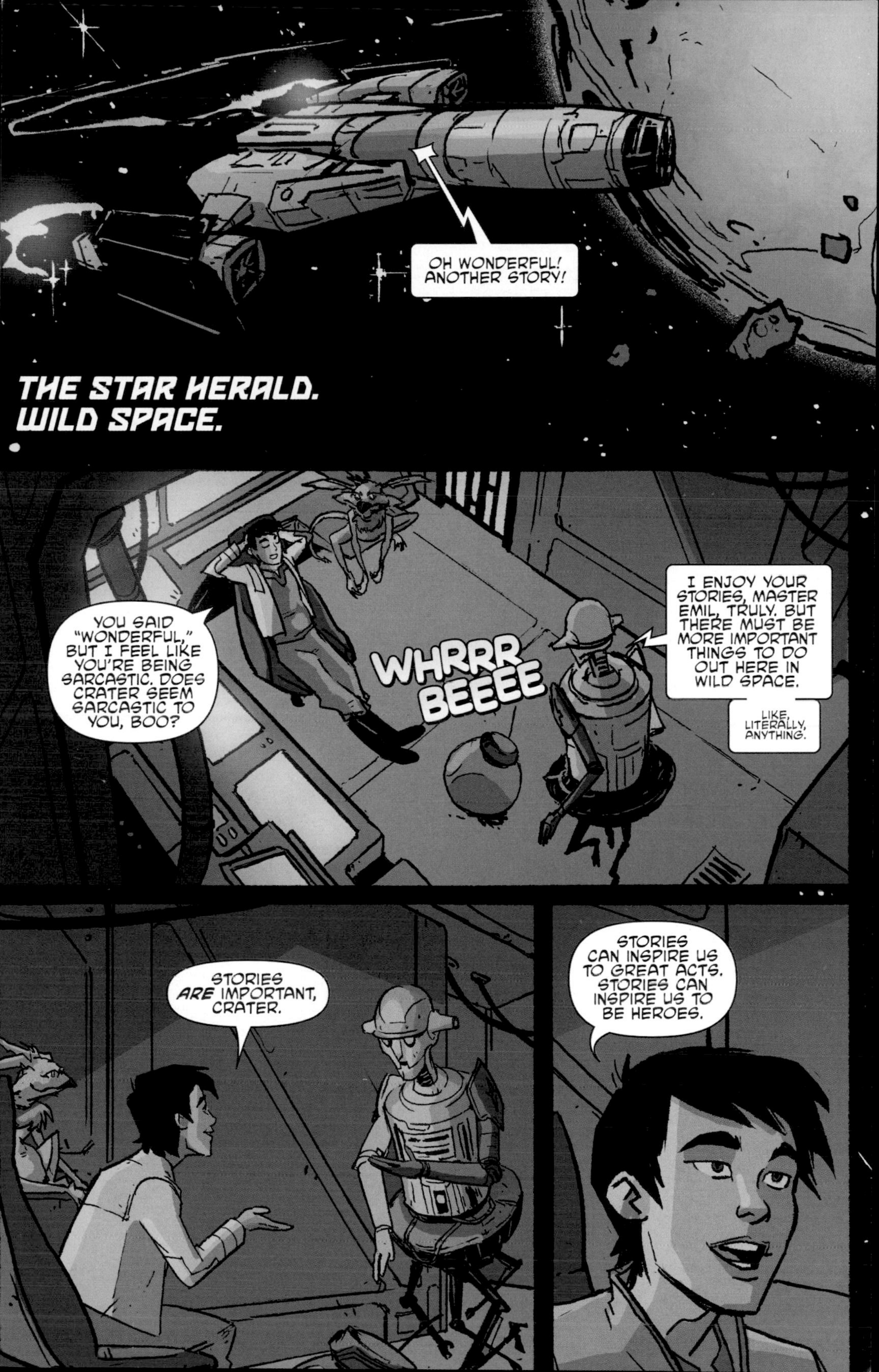
OH WONDERFUL! ANOTHER STORY!
THE STAR HERALD. WILD SPACE.
YOU SAID "WONDERFUL," BUT I FEEL LIKE YOU'RE BEING SARCASTIC. DOES CRATER SEEM SARCASTIC TO YOU, BOO?
WHRRR BEEEE
I ENJOY YOUR STORIES, MASTER EMIL, TRULY. BUT THERE MUST BE MORE IMPORTANT THINGS TO DO OUT HERE IN WILD SPACE.
LIKE, LITERALLY, ANYTHING.
STORIES *ARE* IMPORTANT, CRATER.
STORIES CAN INSPIRE US TO GREAT ACTS. STORIES CAN INSPIRE US TO BE HEROES.

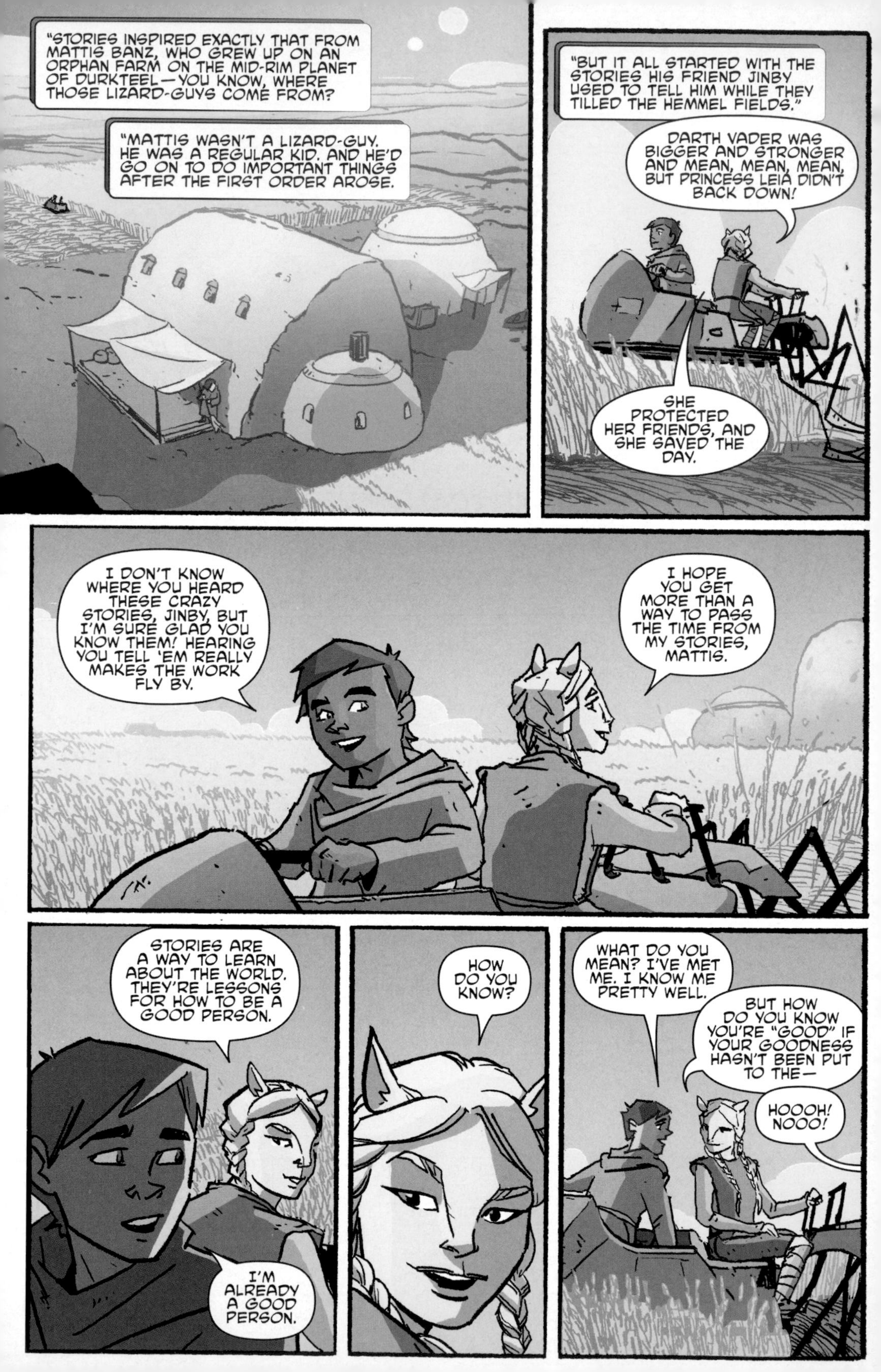
"STORIES INSPIRED EXACTLY THAT FROM MATTIS BANZ, WHO GREW UP ON AN ORPHAN FARM ON THE MID-RIM PLANET OF DURKTEEL—YOU KNOW, WHERE THOSE LIZARD-GUYS COME FROM?
"MATTIS WASN'T A LIZARD-GUY. HE WAS A REGULAR KID. AND HE'D GO ON TO DO IMPORTANT THINGS AFTER THE FIRST ORDER AROSE.
"BUT IT ALL STARTED WITH THE STORIES HIS FRIEND JINBY USED TO TELL HIM WHILE THEY TILLED THE HEMMEL FIELDS."
DARTH VADER WAS BIGGER AND STRONGER AND MEAN, MEAN, MEAN, BUT PRINCESS LEIA DIDN'T BACK DOWN!
SHE PROTECTED HER FRIENDS, AND SHE SAVED THE DAY.
I DON'T KNOW WHERE YOU HEARD THESE CRAZY STORIES, JINBY, BUT I'M SURE GLAD YOU KNOW THEM! HEARING YOU TELL 'EM REALLY MAKES THE WORK FLY BY.
I HOPE YOU GET MORE THAN A WAY TO PASS THE TIME FROM MY STORIES, MATTIS.
STORIES ARE A WAY TO LEARN ABOUT THE WORLD. THEY'RE LESSONS FOR HOW TO BE A GOOD PERSON.
I'M ALREADY A GOOD PERSON.
HOW DO YOU KNOW?
WHAT DO YOU MEAN? I'VE MET ME. I KNOW ME PRETTY WELL.
BUT HOW DO YOU KNOW YOU'RE "GOOD" IF YOUR GOODNESS HASN'T BEEN PUT TO THE—
HOOOH! NOOO!

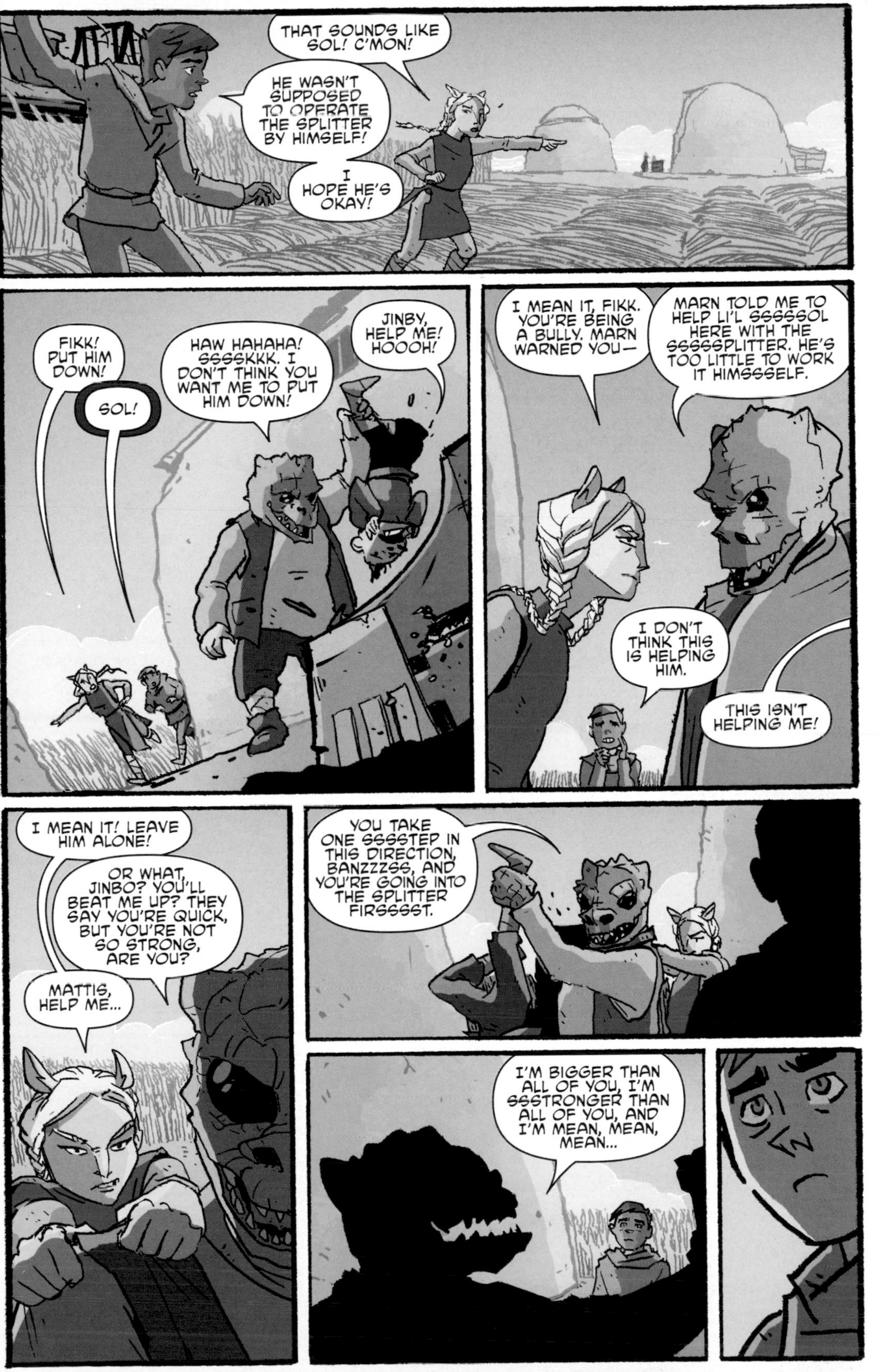
THAT SOUNDS LIKE SOL! C'MON!
HE WASN'T SUPPOSED TO OPERATE THE SPLITTER BY HIMSELF!
I HOPE HE'S OKAY!
FIKK! PUT HIM DOWN!
SOL!
HAW HAHAHA! SSSSKKK. I DON'T THINK YOU WANT ME TO PUT HIM DOWN!
JINBY, HELP ME! HOOOH!
I MEAN IT, FIKK. YOU'RE BEING A BULLY. MARN WARNED YOU—
MARN TOLD ME TO HELP LI'L SSSSSOL HERE WITH THE SSSSSPLITTER. HE'S TOO LITTLE TO WORK IT HIMSSSELF.
I DON'T THINK THIS IS HELPING HIM.
THIS ISN'T HELPING ME!
I MEAN IT! LEAVE HIM ALONE!
OR WHAT, JINBO? YOU'LL BEAT ME UP? THEY SAY YOU'RE QUICK, BUT YOU'RE NOT SO STRONG, ARE YOU?
MATTIS, HELP ME...
YOU TAKE ONE SSSSTEP IN THIS DIRECTION, BANZZZSS, AND YOU'RE GOING INTO THE SPLITTER FIRSSSST.
I'M BIGGER THAN ALL OF YOU, I'M SSSTRONGER THAN ALL OF YOU, AND I'M MEAN, MEAN, MEAN...

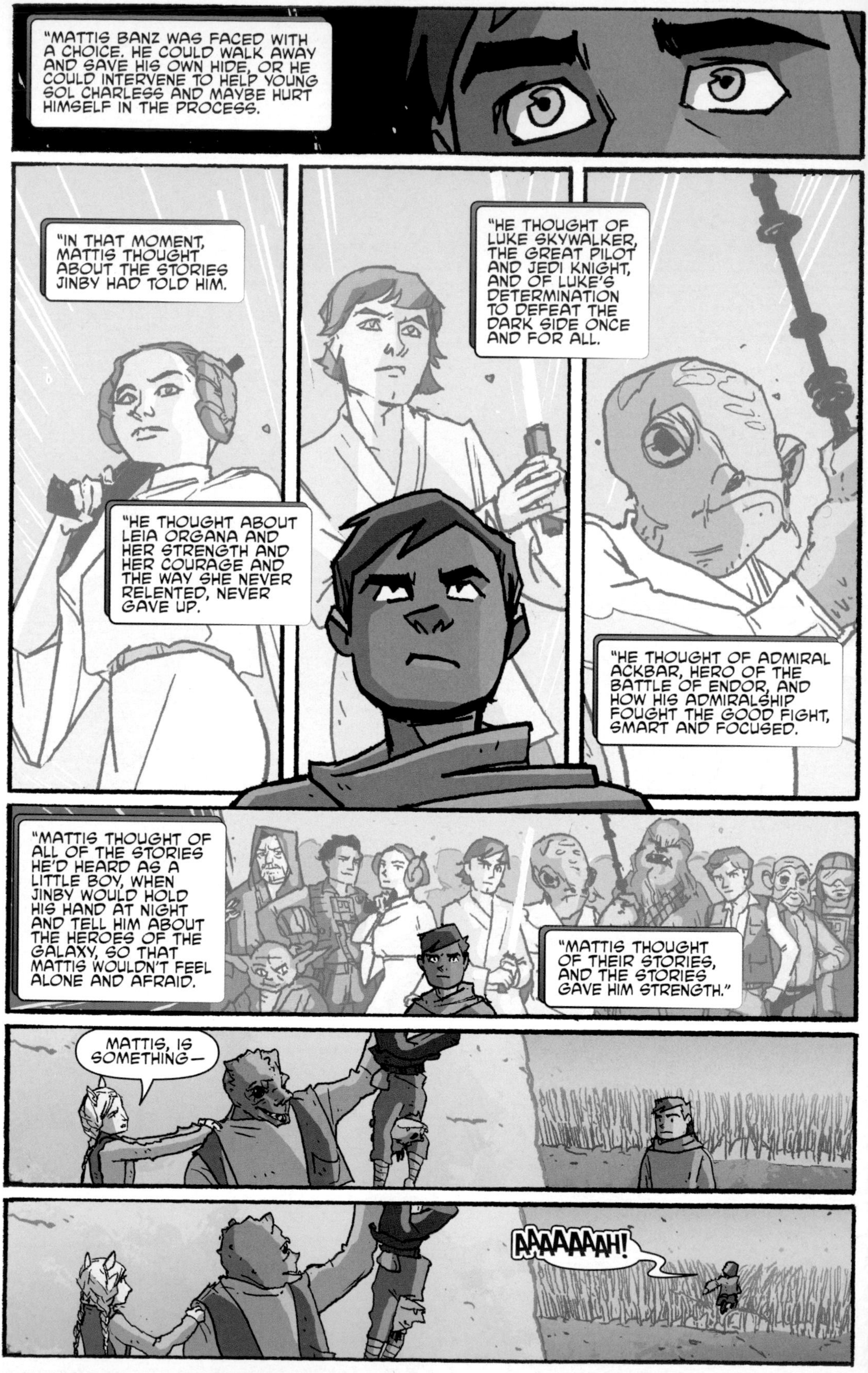
"MATTIS BANZ WAS FACED WITH A CHOICE. HE COULD WALK AWAY AND SAVE HIS OWN HIDE, OR HE COULD INTERVENE TO HELP YOUNG SOL CHARLESS AND MAYBE HURT HIMSELF IN THE PROCESS.
"IN THAT MOMENT, MATTIS THOUGHT ABOUT THE STORIES JINBY HAD TOLD HIM.
"HE THOUGHT ABOUT LEIA ORGANA AND HER STRENGTH AND HER COURAGE AND THE WAY SHE NEVER RELENTED, NEVER GAVE UP.
"HE THOUGHT OF LUKE SKYWALKER, THE GREAT PILOT AND JEDI KNIGHT, AND OF LUKE'S DETERMINATION TO DEFEAT THE DARK SIDE ONCE AND FOR ALL.
"HE THOUGHT OF ADMIRAL ACKBAR, HERO OF THE BATTLE OF ENDOR, AND HOW HIS ADMIRALSHIP FOUGHT THE GOOD FIGHT, SMART AND FOCUSED.
"MATTIS THOUGHT OF ALL OF THE STORIES HE'D HEARD AS A LITTLE BOY, WHEN JINBY WOULD HOLD HIS HAND AT NIGHT AND TELL HIM ABOUT THE HEROES OF THE GALAXY, SO THAT MATTIS WOULDN'T FEEL ALONE AND AFRAID.
"MATTIS THOUGHT OF THEIR STORIES, AND THE STORIES GAVE HIM STRENGTH."
MATTIS, IS SOMETHING—
AAAAAAAH!

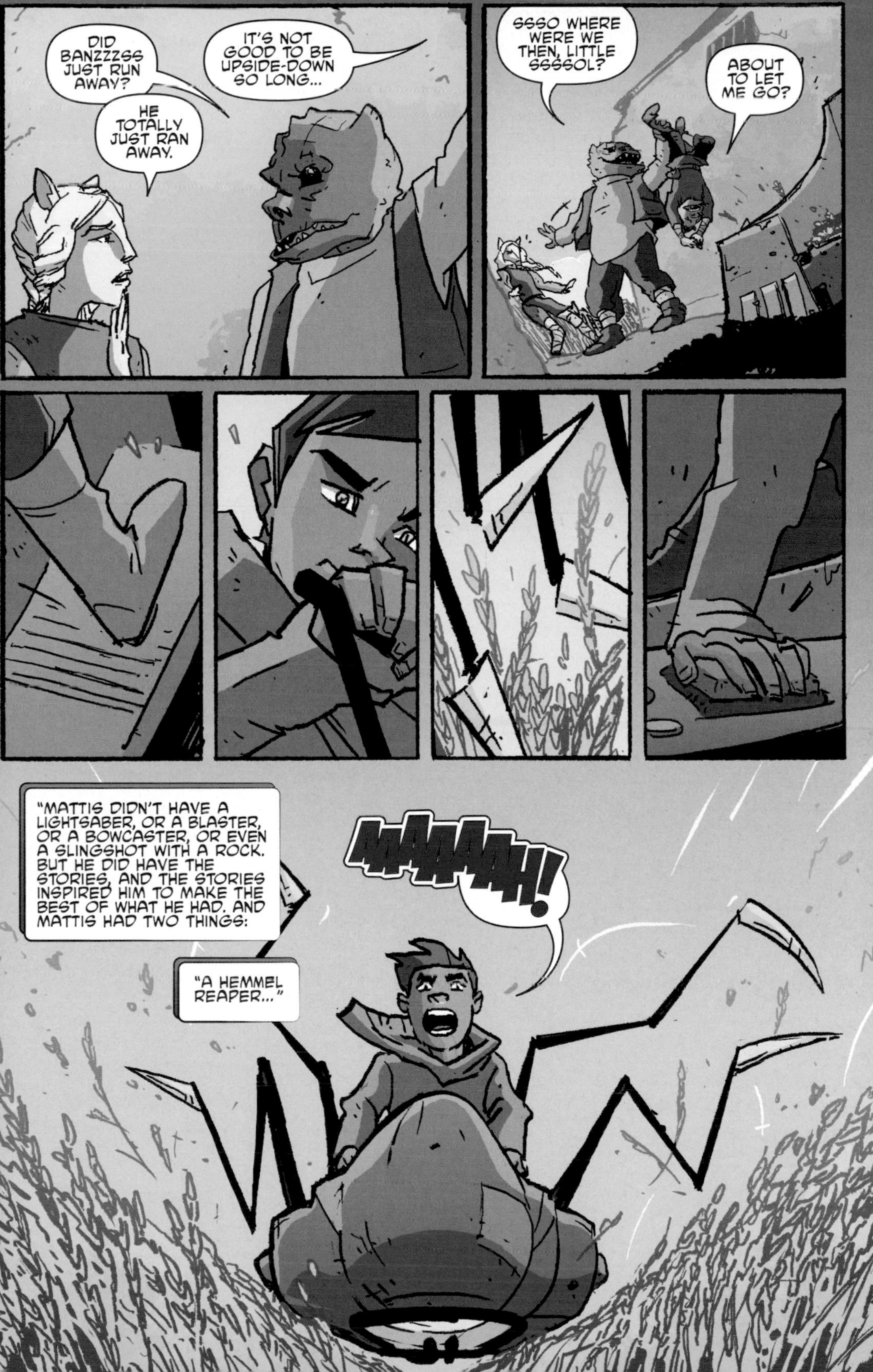
DID BANZZZSS JUST RUN AWAY?
IT'S NOT GOOD TO BE UPSIDE-DOWN SO LONG...
HE TOTALLY JUST RAN AWAY.
SSSO WHERE WERE WE THEN, LITTLE SSSSOL?
ABOUT TO LET ME GO?
"MATTIS DIDN'T HAVE A LIGHTSABER, OR A BLASTER, OR A BOWCASTER, OR EVEN A SLINGSHOT WITH A ROCK. BUT HE DID HAVE THE STORIES, AND THE STORIES INSPIRED HIM TO MAKE THE BEST OF WHAT HE HAD. AND MATTIS HAD TWO THINGS:
AAAAAAAH!
"A HEMMEL REAPER..."

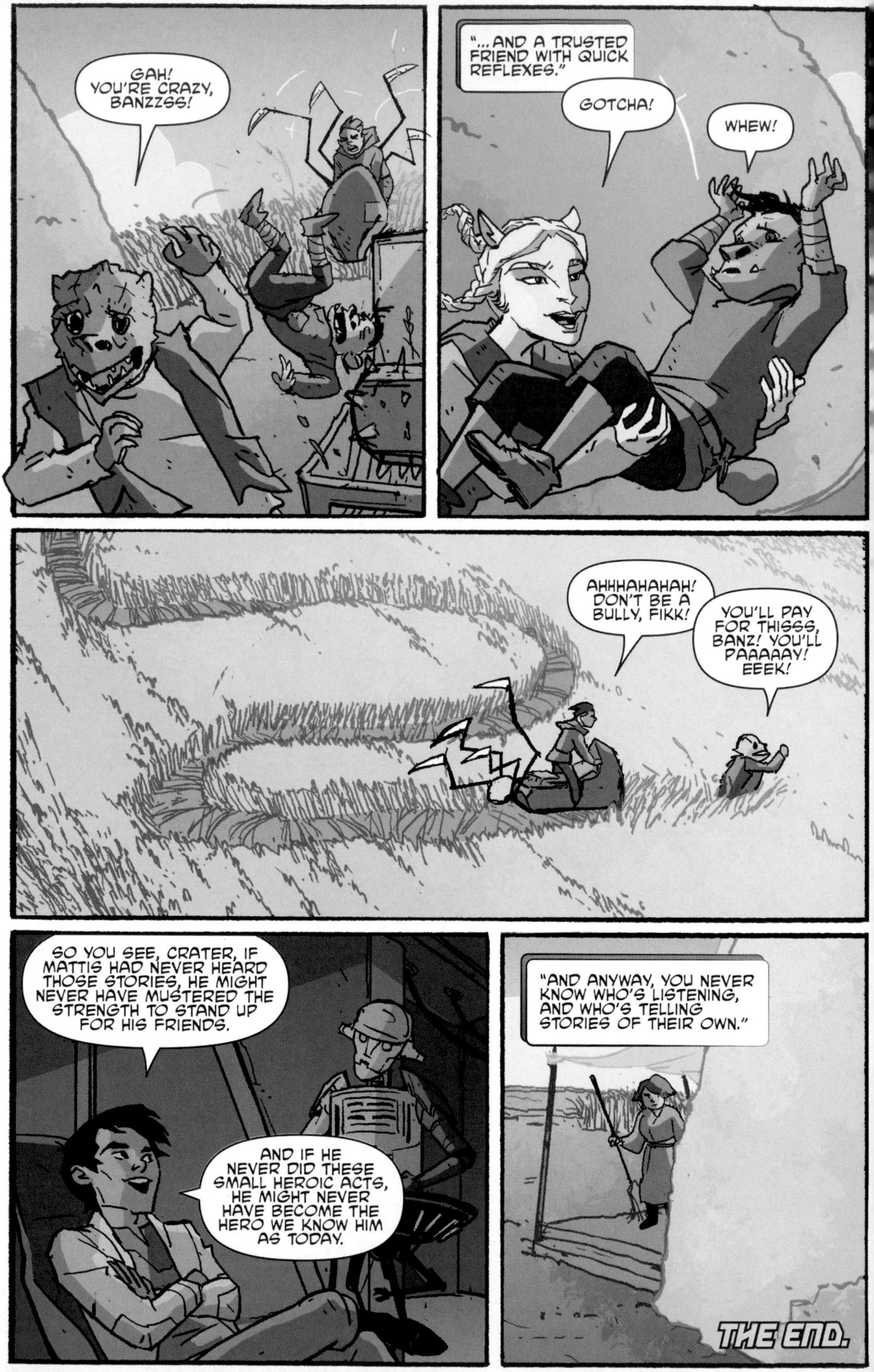
GAH! YOU'RE CRAZY, BANZZSS!
"...AND A TRUSTED FRIEND WITH QUICK REFLEXES."
GOTCHA!
WHEW!
AHHHAHAHAH! DON'T BE A BULLY, FIKK!
YOU'LL PAY FOR THISSS, BANZ! YOU'LL PAAAAAAY! EEEK!
SO YOU SEE, CRATER, IF MATTIS HAD NEVER HEARD THOSE STORIES, HE MIGHT NEVER HAVE MUSTERED THE STRENGTH TO STAND UP FOR HIS FRIENDS.
AND IF HE NEVER DID THESE SMALL HEROIC ACTS, HE MIGHT NEVER HAVE BECOME THE HERO WE KNOW HIM AS TODAY.
"AND ANYWAY, YOU NEVER KNOW WHO'S LISTENING, AND WHO'S TELLING STORIES OF THEIR OWN."
THE END.

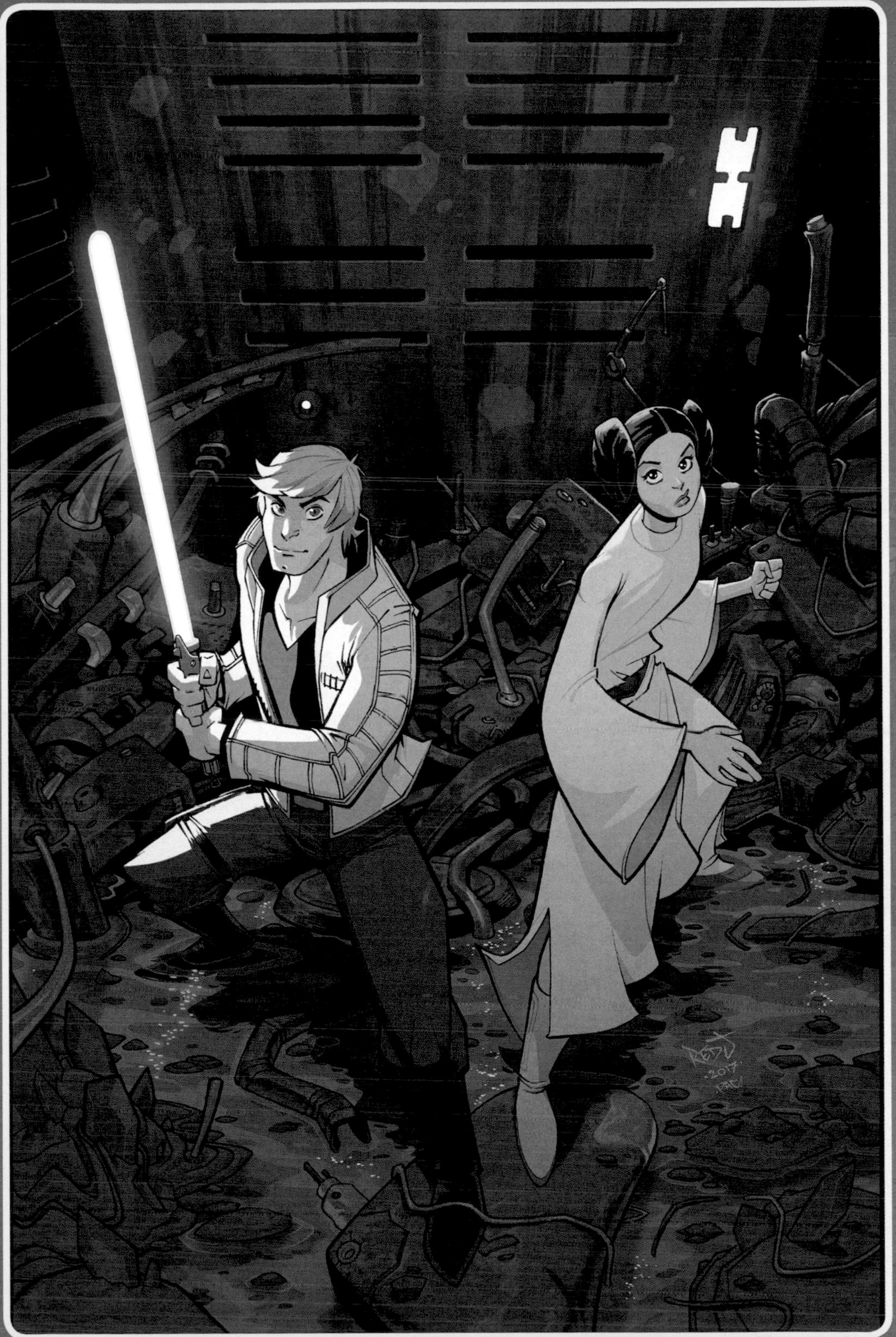

Art by Jon Sommariva

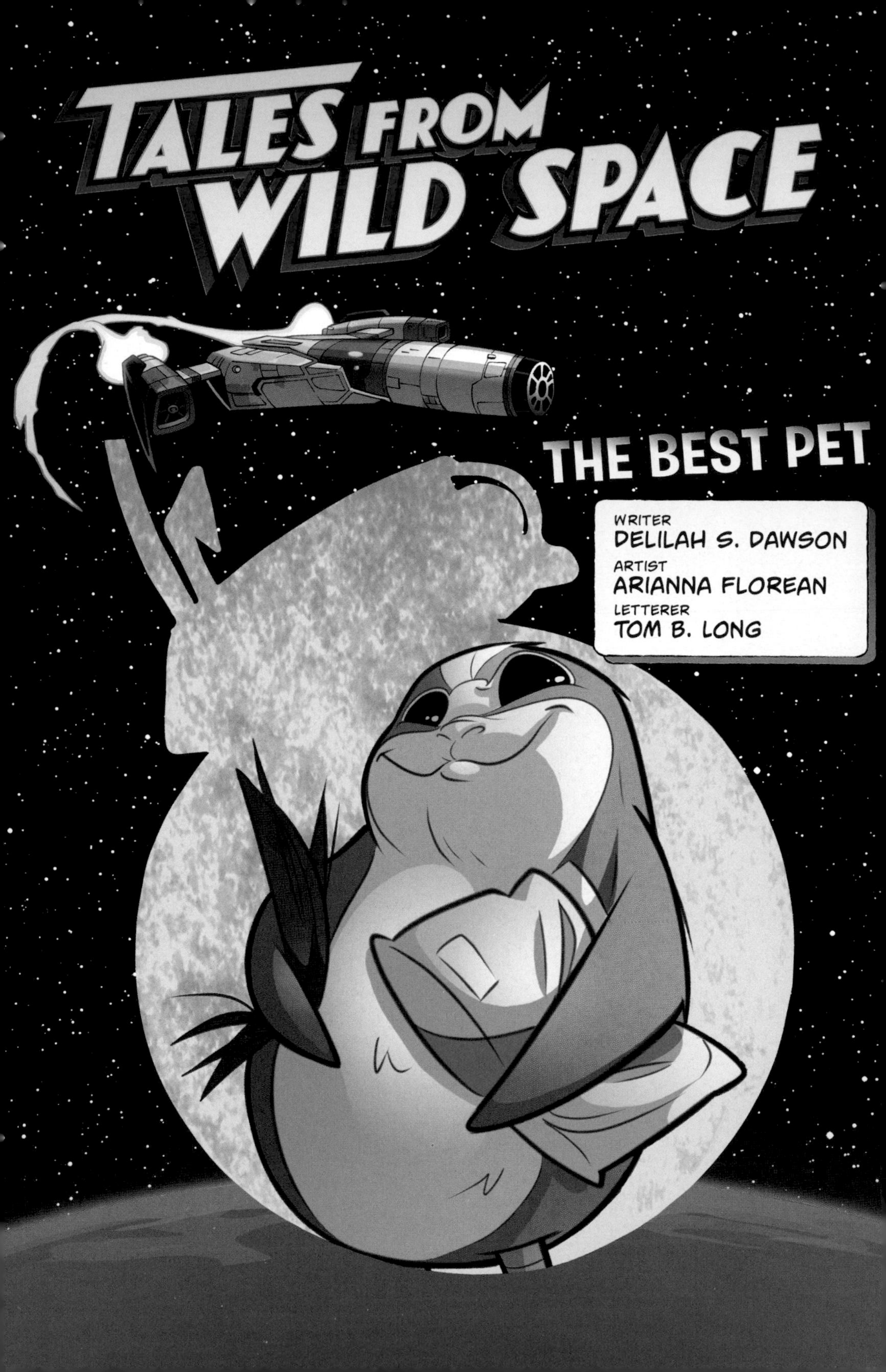
TALES FROM WILD SPACE
THE BEST PET
WRITER
DELILAH S. DAWSON
ARTIST
ARIANNA FLOREAN
LETTERER
TOM B. LONG

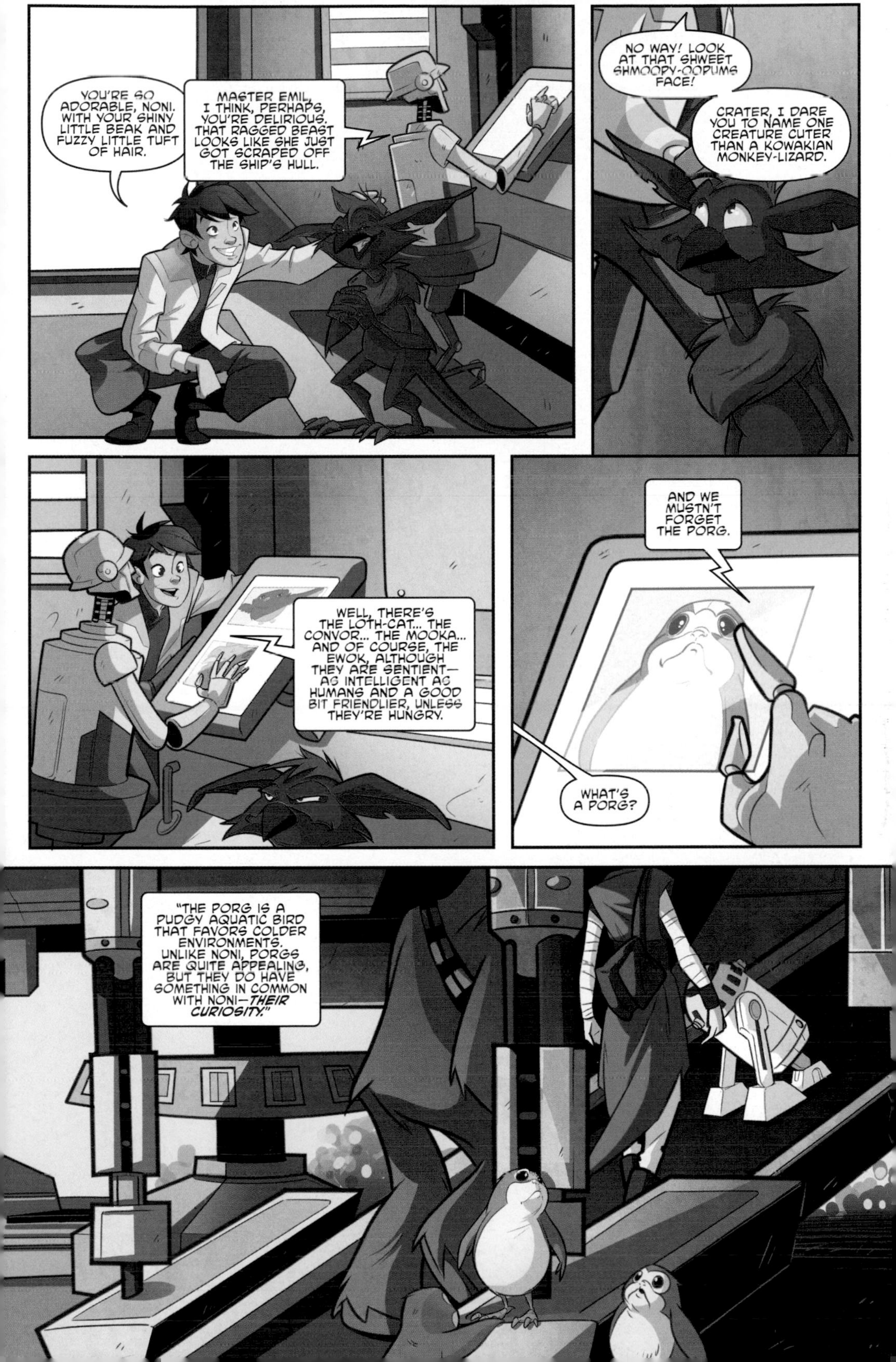
YOU'RE SO ADORABLE, NONI. WITH YOUR SHINY LITTLE BEAK AND FUZZY LITTLE TUFT OF HAIR.
MASTER EMIL, I THINK, PERHAPS, YOU'RE DELIRIOUS. THAT RAGGED BEAST LOOKS LIKE SHE JUST GOT SCRAPED OFF THE SHIP'S HULL.
NO WAY! LOOK AT THAT SHWEET SHMOOPY-OOPUMS FACE!
CRATER, I DARE YOU TO NAME ONE CREATURE CUTER THAN A KOWAKIAN MONKEY-LIZARD.
WELL, THERE'S THE LOTH-CAT... THE CONVOR... THE MOOKA... AND OF COURSE, THE EWOK, ALTHOUGH THEY ARE SENTIENT—AS INTELLIGENT AS HUMANS AND A GOOD BIT FRIENDLIER, UNLESS THEY'RE HUNGRY.
AND WE MUSTN'T FORGET THE PORG.
WHAT'S A PORG?
"THE PORG IS A PUDGY AQUATIC BIRD THAT FAVORS COLDER ENVIRONMENTS. UNLIKE NONI, PORGS ARE QUITE APPEALING, BUT THEY DO HAVE SOMETHING IN COMMON WITH NONI—*THEIR CURIOSITY.*"

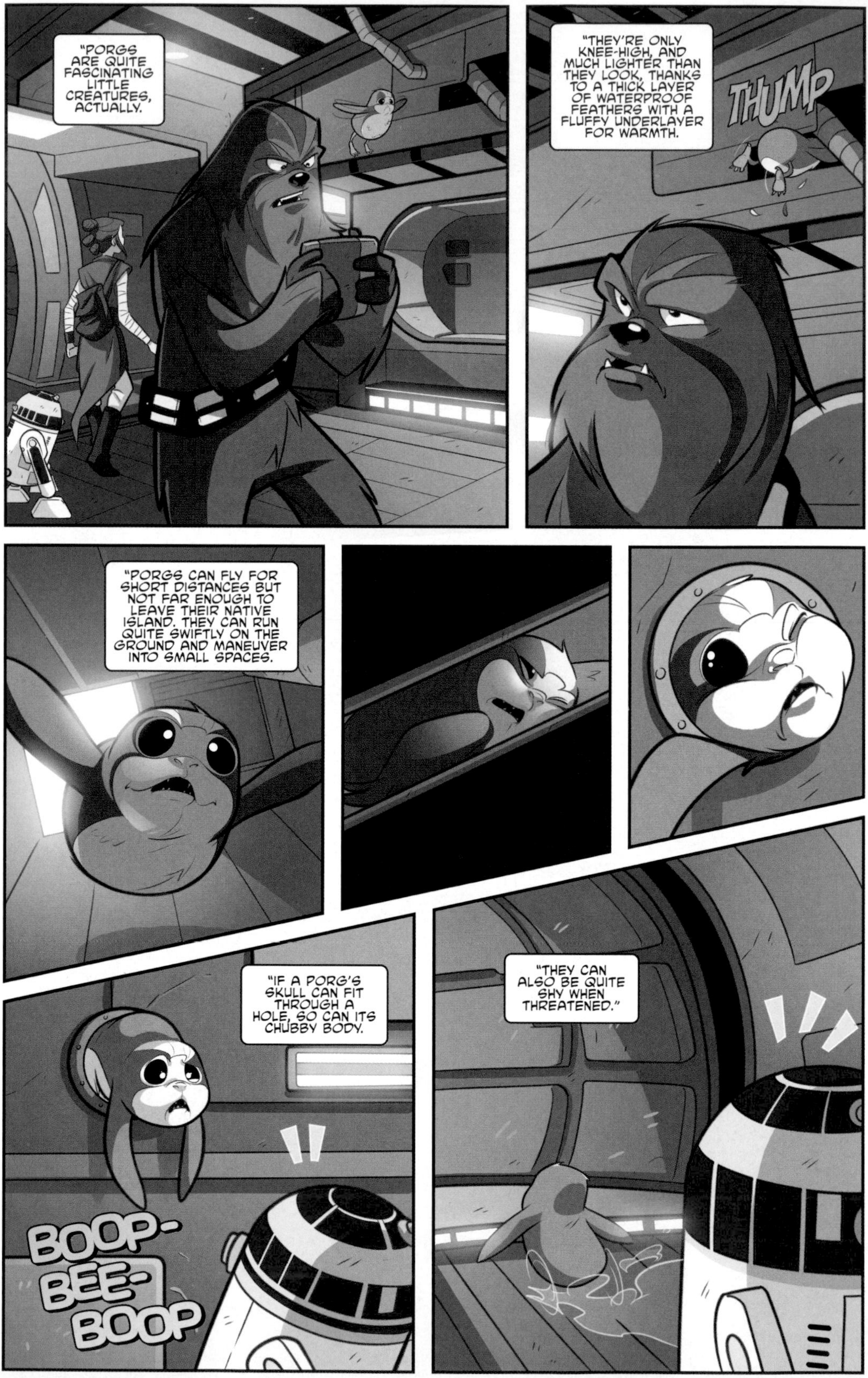

"PORGS ARE QUITE FASCINATING LITTLE CREATURES, ACTUALLY.
"THEY'RE ONLY KNEE-HIGH, AND MUCH LIGHTER THAN THEY LOOK, THANKS TO A THICK LAYER OF WATERPROOF FEATHERS WITH A FLUFFY UNDERLAYER FOR WARMTH.
THUMP
"PORGS CAN FLY FOR SHORT DISTANCES BUT NOT FAR ENOUGH TO LEAVE THEIR NATIVE ISLAND. THEY CAN RUN QUITE SWIFTLY ON THE GROUND AND MANEUVER INTO SMALL SPACES.
"IF A PORG'S SKULL CAN FIT THROUGH A HOLE, SO CAN ITS CHUBBY BODY.
BOOP-BEE-BOOP
"THEY CAN ALSO BE QUITE SHY WHEN THREATENED."

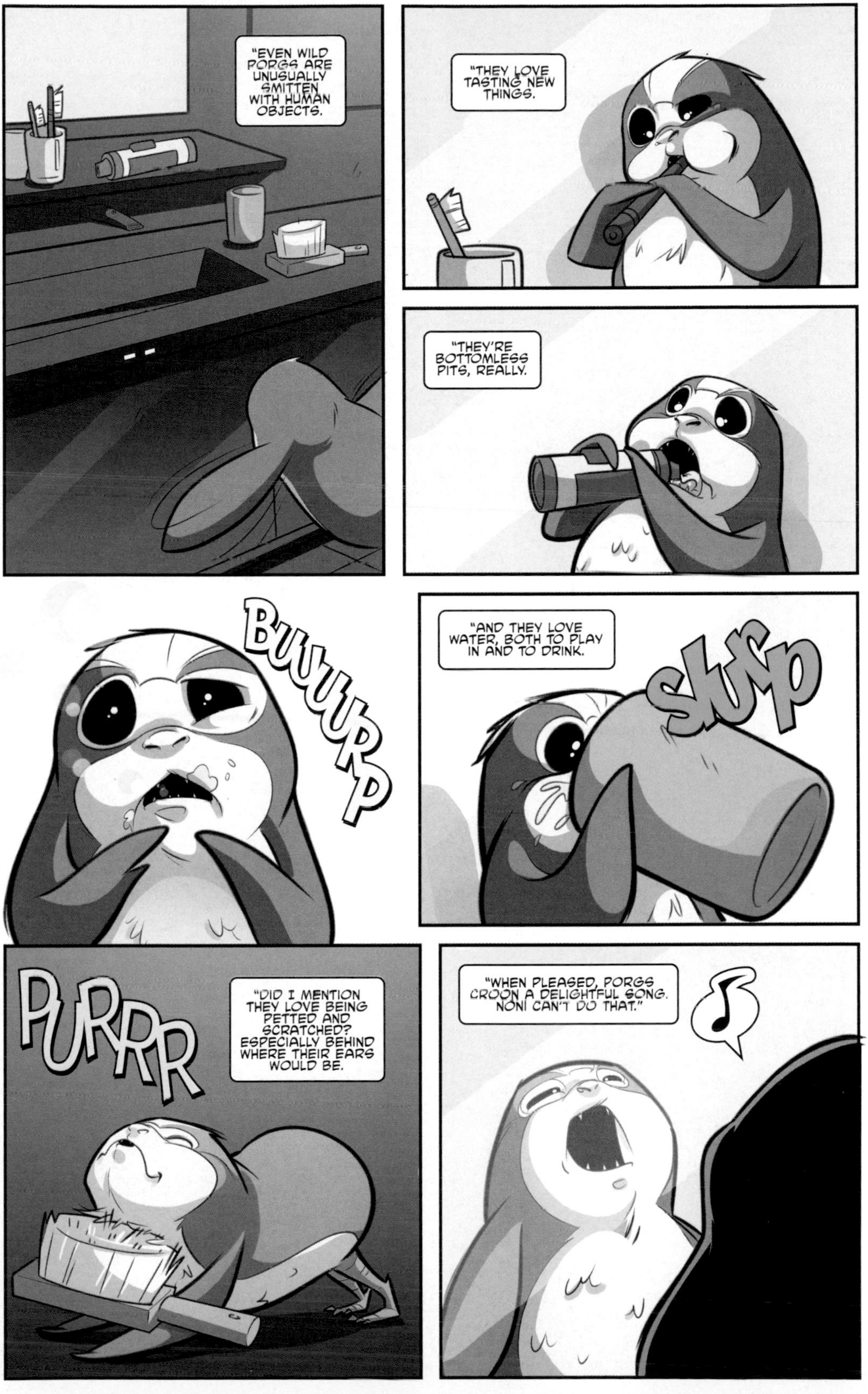
"EVEN WILD PORGS ARE UNUSUALLY SMITTEN WITH HUMAN OBJECTS.
"THEY LOVE TASTING NEW THINGS.
"THEY'RE BOTTOMLESS PITS, REALLY.
BUUURP
"AND THEY LOVE WATER, BOTH TO PLAY IN AND TO DRINK.
SLURP
PURRR
"DID I MENTION THEY LOVE BEING PETTED AND SCRATCHED? ESPECIALLY BEHIND WHERE THEIR EARS WOULD BE.
"WHEN PLEASED, PORGS CROON A DELIGHTFUL SONG. NONI CAN'T DO THAT."

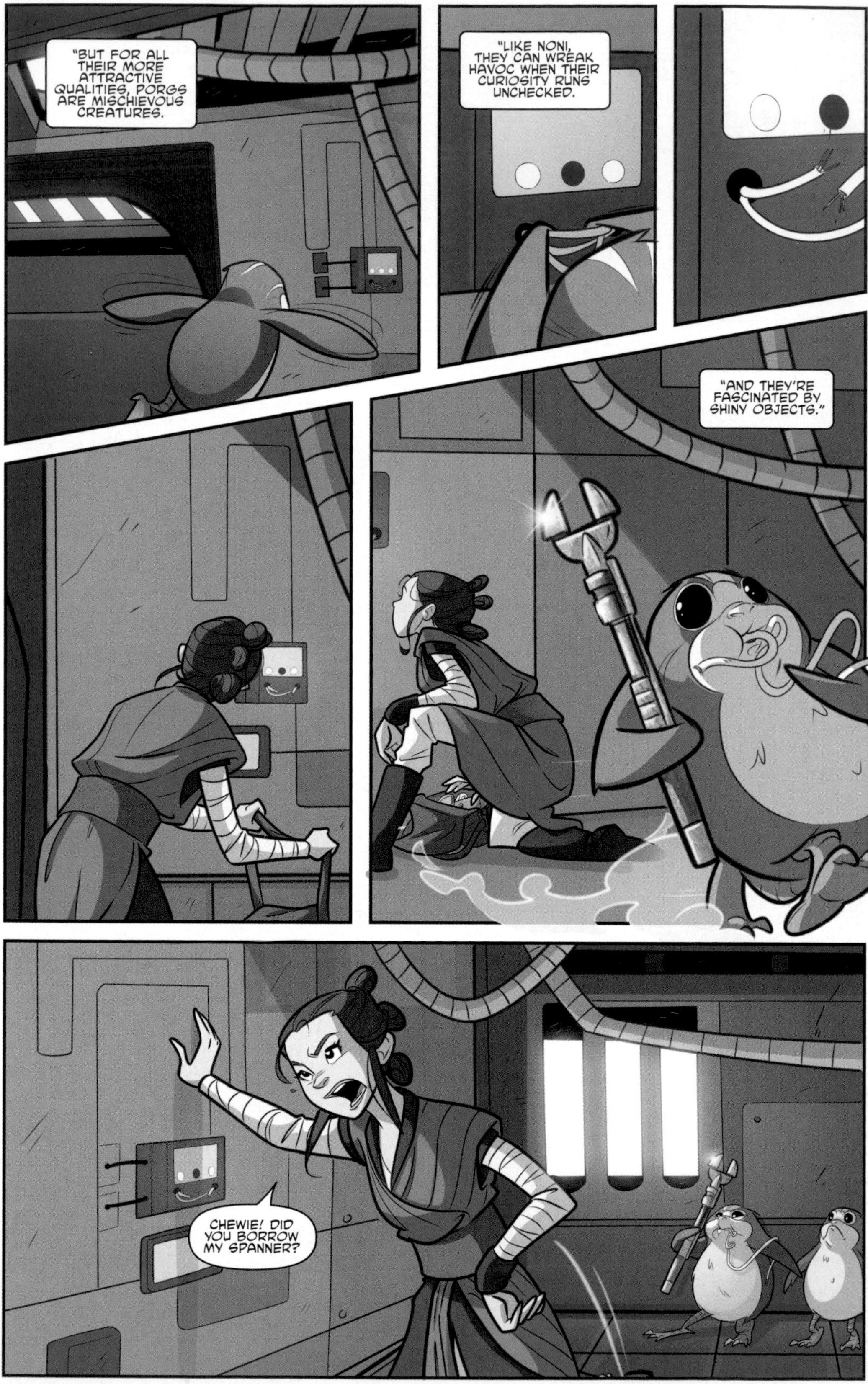
"BUT FOR ALL THEIR MORE ATTRACTIVE QUALITIES, PORGS ARE MISCHIEVOUS CREATURES.
"LIKE NONI, THEY CAN WREAK HAVOC WHEN THEIR CURIOSITY RUNS UNCHECKED.
"AND THEY'RE FASCINATED BY SHINY OBJECTS."
CHEWIE! DID YOU BORROW MY SPANNER?

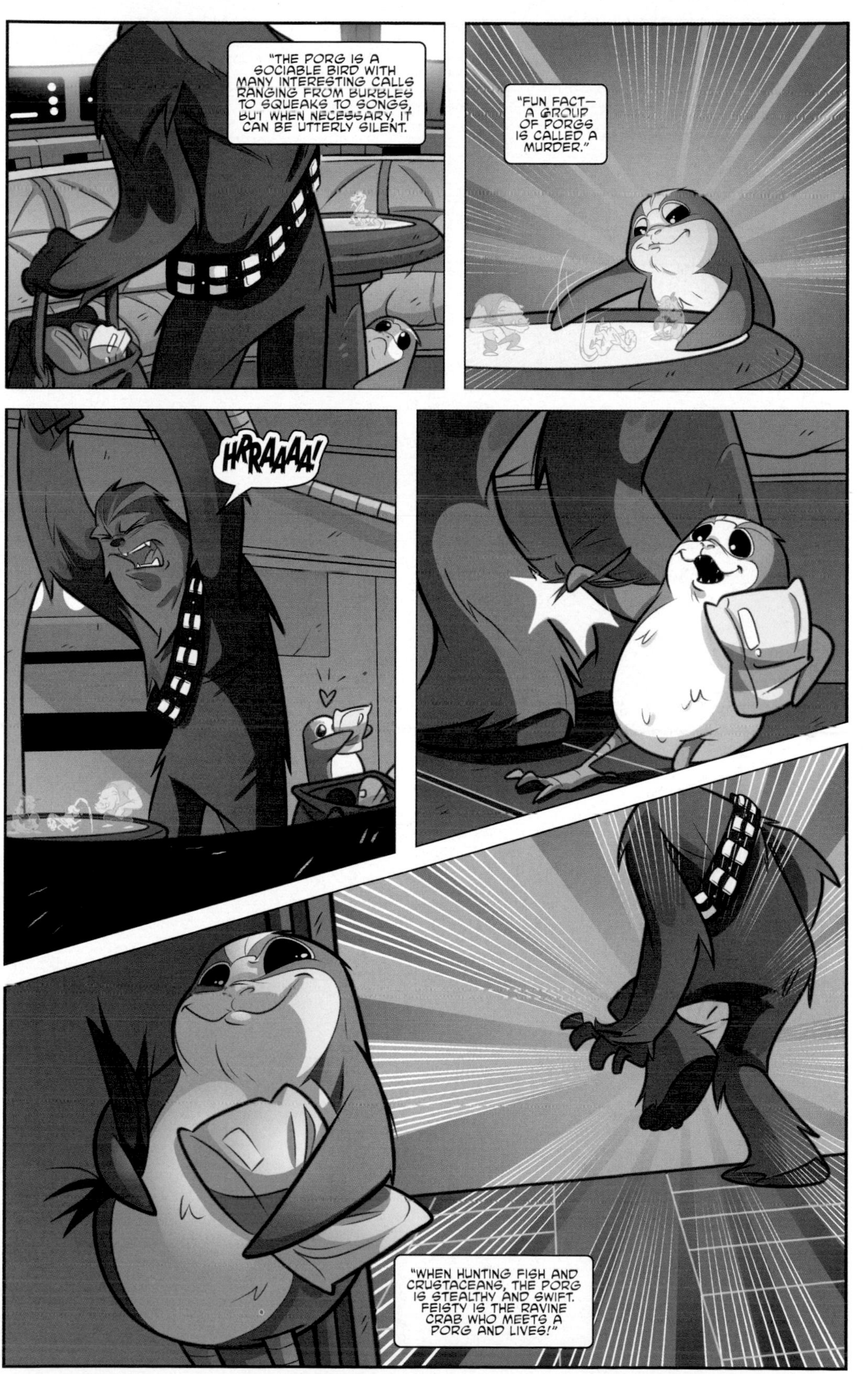
"THE PORG IS A SOCIABLE BIRD WITH MANY INTERESTING CALLS RANGING FROM BURBLES TO SQUEAKS TO SONGS, BUT WHEN NECESSARY, IT CAN BE UTTERLY SILENT.
"FUN FACT— A GROUP OF PORGS IS CALLED A MURDER."
HRRAAAA!
"WHEN HUNTING FISH AND CRUSTACEANS, THE PORG IS STEALTHY AND SWIFT. FEISTY IS THE RAVINE CRAB WHO MEETS A PORG AND LIVES!"

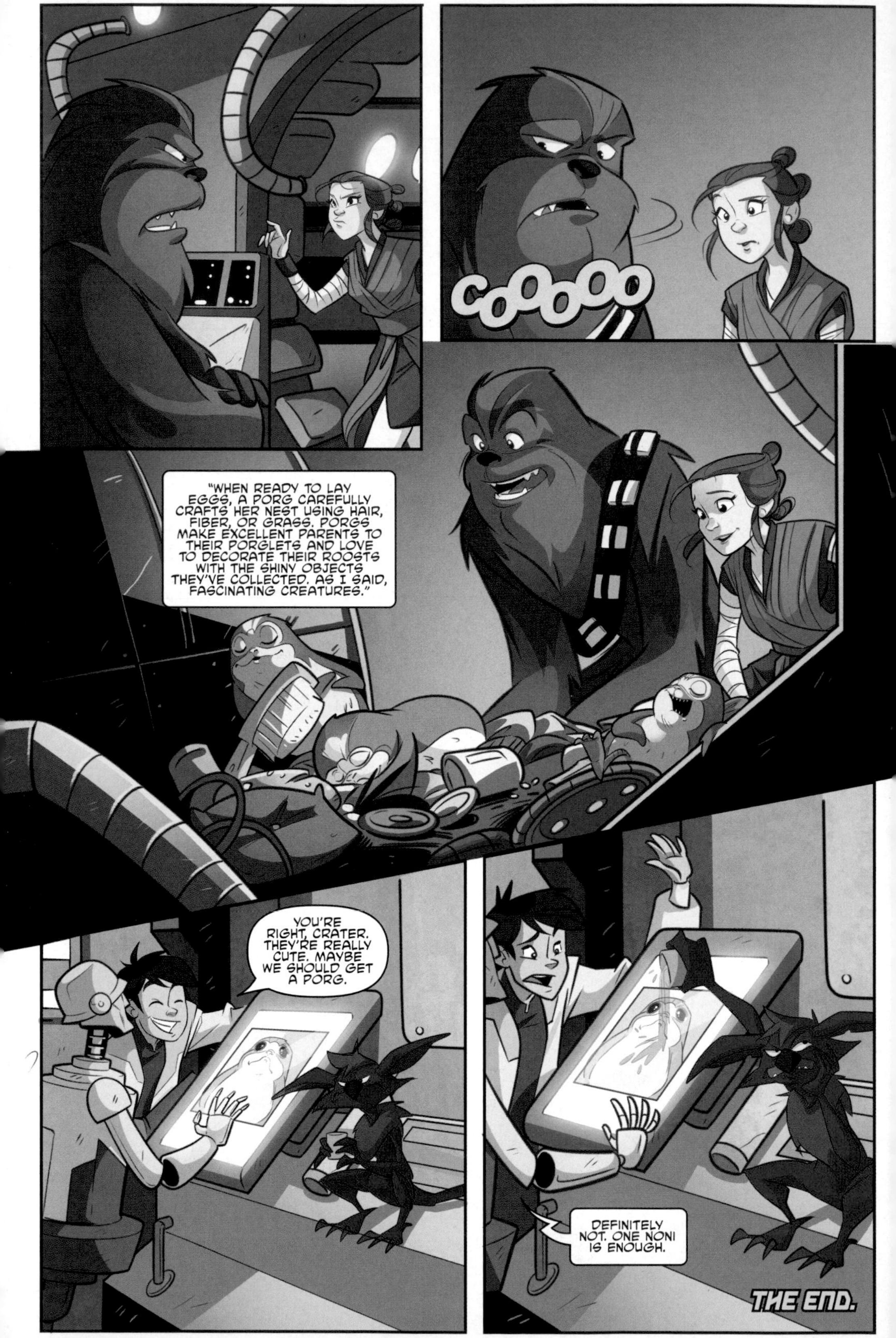
COOOOO
"WHEN READY TO LAY EGGS, A PORG CAREFULLY CRAFTS HER NEST USING HAIR, FIBER, OR GRASS. PORGS MAKE EXCELLENT PARENTS TO THEIR PORGLETS AND LOVE TO DECORATE THEIR ROOSTS WITH THE SHINY OBJECTS THEY'VE COLLECTED. AS I SAID, FASCINATING CREATURES."
YOU'RE RIGHT, CRATER. THEY'RE REALLY CUTE. MAYBE WE SHOULD GET A PORG.
DEFINITELY NOT. ONE NONI IS ENOUGH.
THE END.

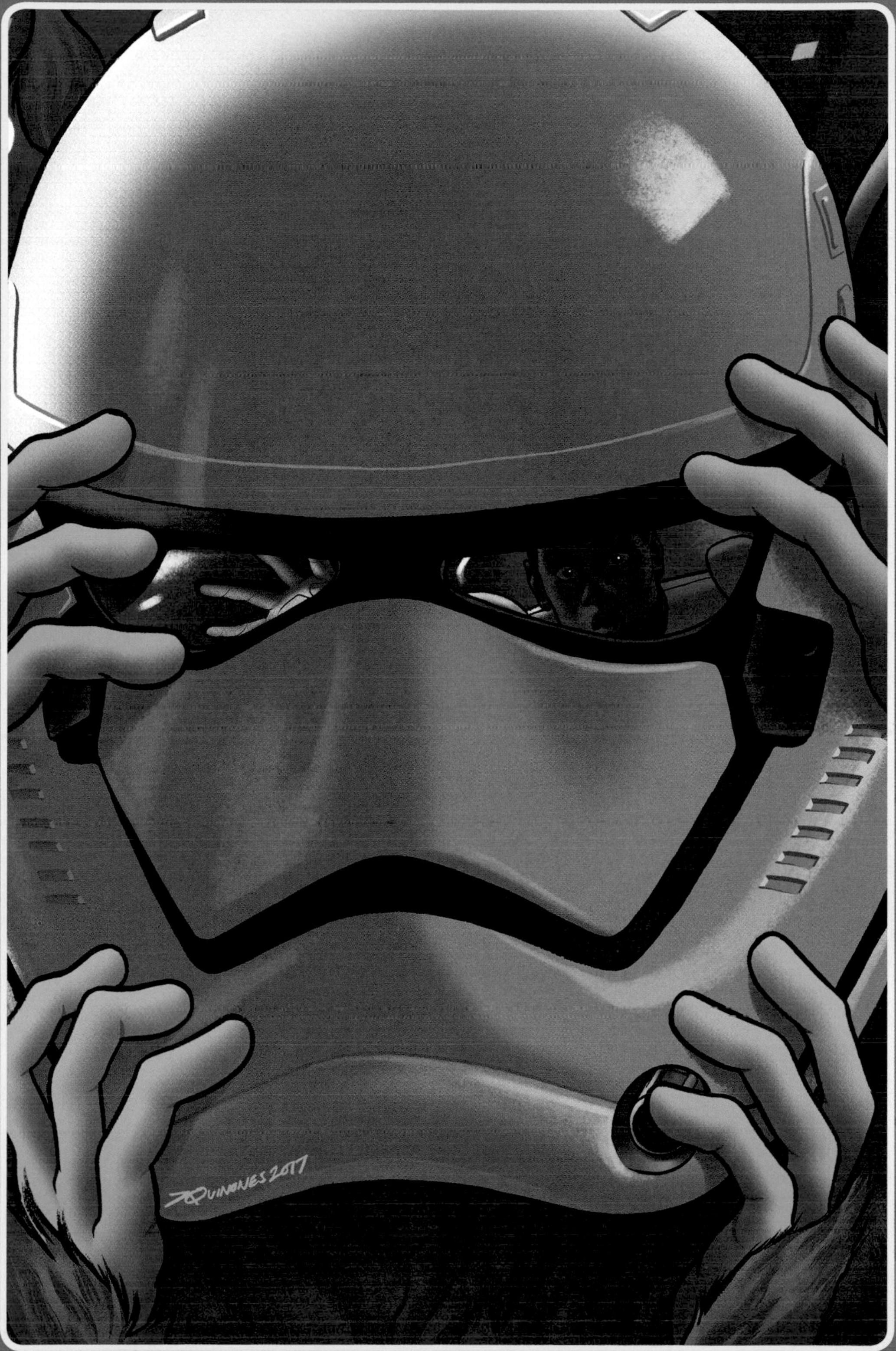
JQUINONES 2017

Art by Joe Quinones

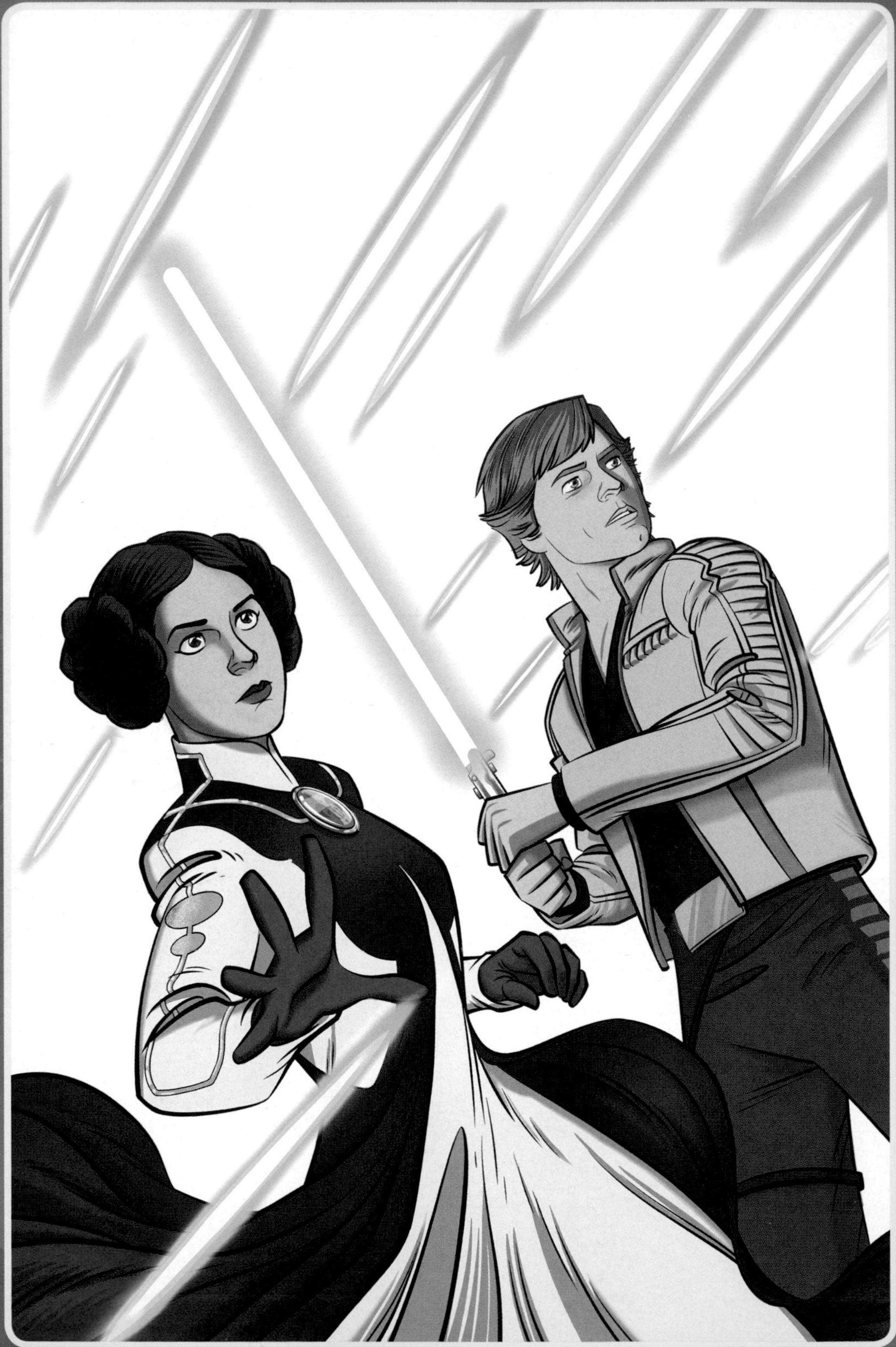

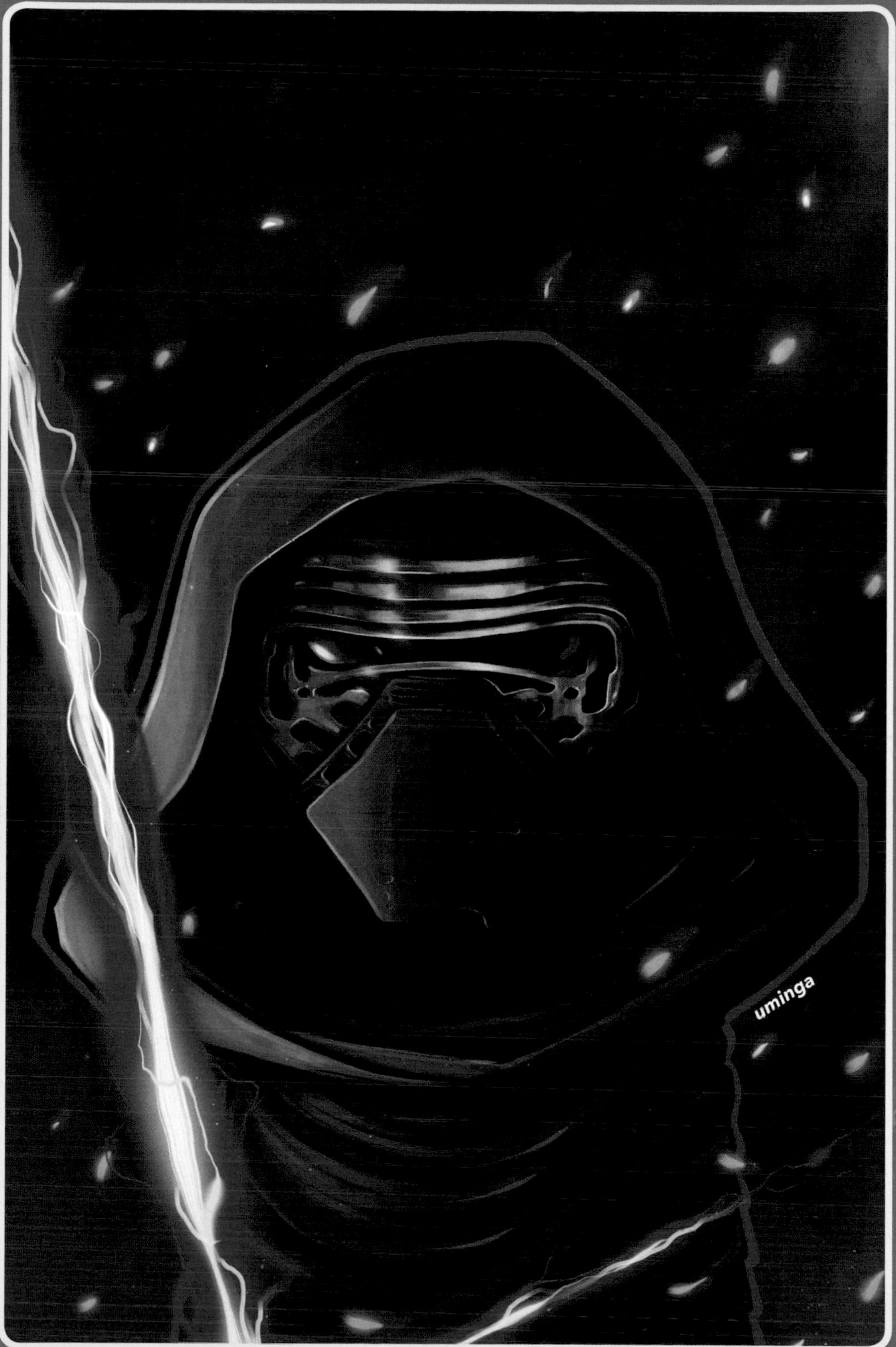
uminga

Art by Christopher Uminga

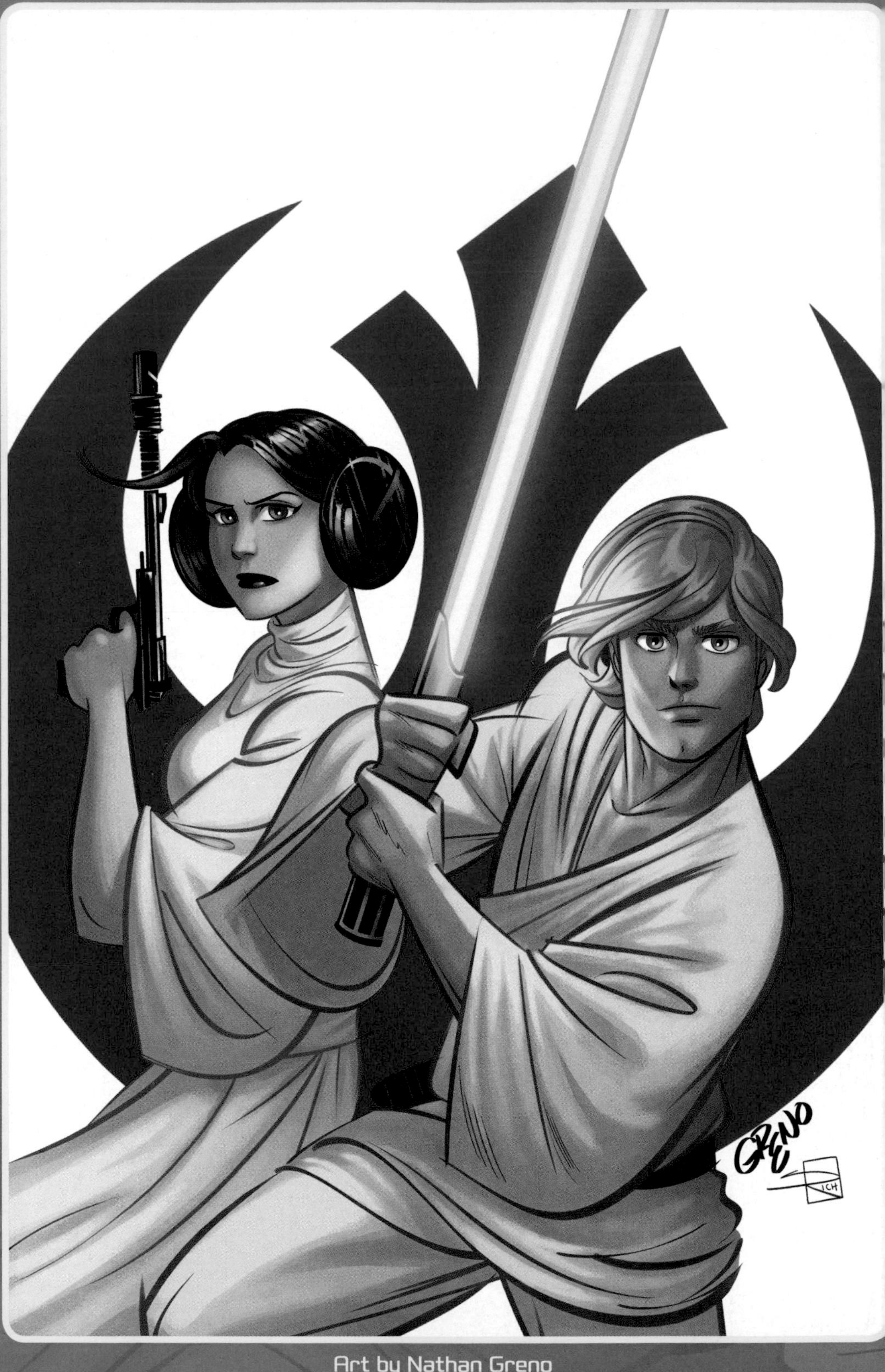
GRENO

Art by Nathan Greno

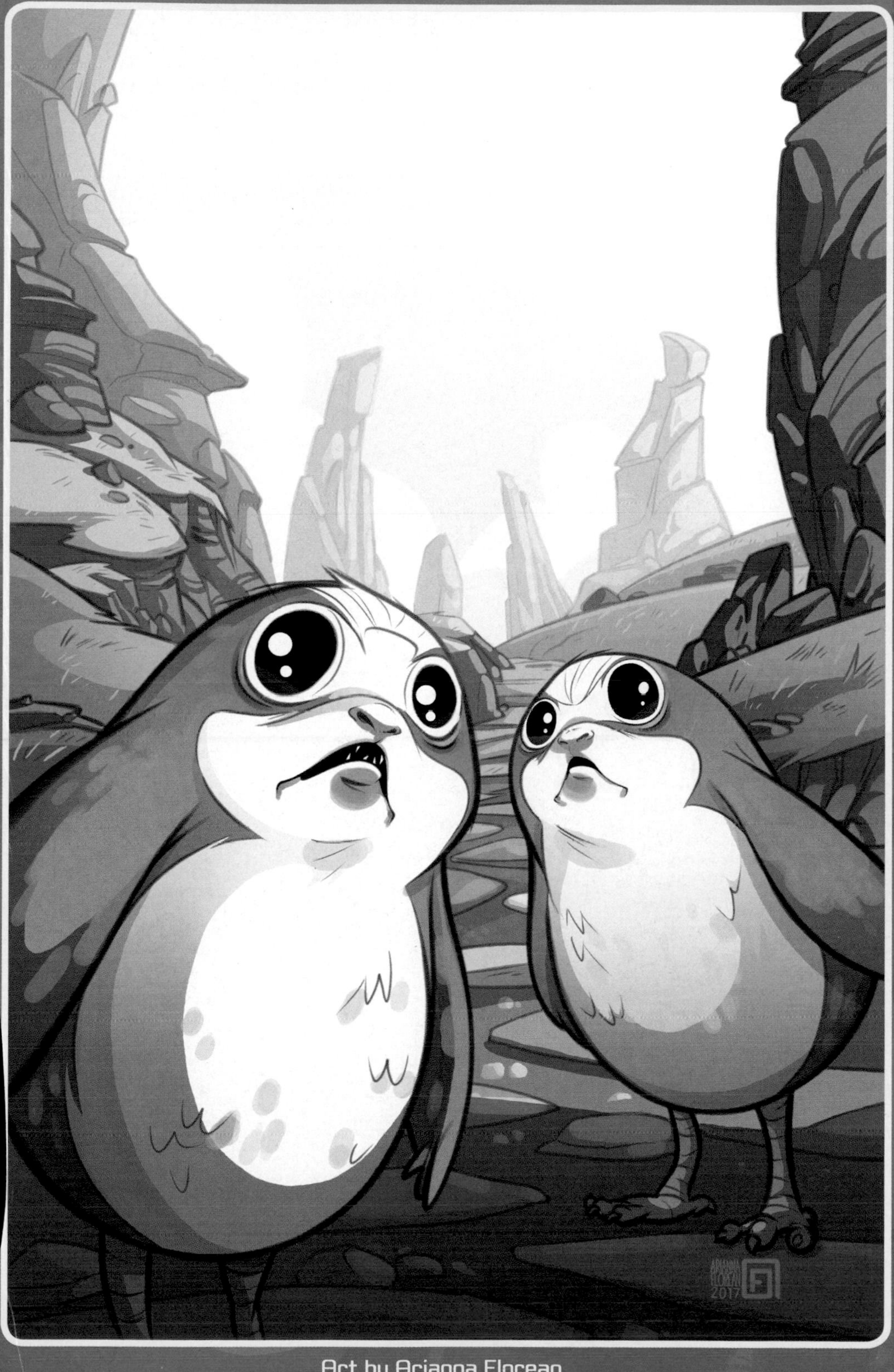

Art by Arianna Florean